To John

Gl
Apples

Ian D. Hall

Copyright © Ian D. Hall

First published in the UK

Published by Beaten Track Publishing
www.beatentrackpublishing.com

With the greatest
of Plunkin

Ian Hall

Beaten Track
www.beatentrackpublishing.com

Ghost Apples

First published 2020 by Beaten Track Publishing
Copyright © 2020 Ian D. Hall

All rights reserved.

The moral right of the author has been asserted.

Paperback ISBN: 978 1 78645 482 9
eBook ISBN: 978 1 78645 483 6

Beaten Track Publishing,
Burscough, Lancashire.
www.beatentrackpublishing.com

Dedicated to Tony Hards, an uncle, a friend,
and the one who set me on the path.

Ghost
Apples

Chapter One

TOM HAD FALLEN out with his father once again. It was a weekly ritual to which he had become accustomed; perhaps in some small way even enjoyed. By the end of a tough week of square bashing the latest recruits into shape, dressing them down on the parade ground, his top lip still vibrating long after the order for right wheel and left turn had been routinely—he would say wilfully—ignored, Tom's father would bring it home to what remained of the family and start on them, barking orders, making demands, and they would swiftly comply, no questions asked.

Tom's mother had lasted longer in the parade ground of the civilian than either could have imagined, both father and son distraught in their own particular way that she had died suddenly one autumn evening whilst taking the family dogs out for a walk, the mist crouching low upon the river that ran through the fields and woods at the back of their home on the very outskirts of the town, a natural border which provided a sense of safety from the demands of the city, of being kept away from the rigours of life in the army camp.

Cathy Solden's heart had given out, quickly, painlessly—so said the official documents, which had described the autopsy in a cold but meticulous manner—a procedure of which Tom's father would surely have approved, had the two ever spoken about it. Instead, it was left hanging as a permanent thread, which the fifteen-year-old boy had begun too habitually pull on, grasping at the only memory the two men shared that didn't have at its base the spectre of discipline.

1

Tom drew a futile drag on his rolled-up cigarette and took stock off his now familiar surroundings. When his father's patience had been tested to the limit, when the rigours of Her Majesty's Army had played its part on his health and mental frailties, Tom would escape to the painted-once-yearly shed, which stood proud against the onslaught of summer heat and winter woes, and succumb to his own form of relief: the pain medication had gone some way towards wiping clean the image of his mother's face with the water of his mind.

Over the last three years, Tom had turned the shed into a second bedroom. He had moved out the machinery, the power tools, the saw, the hammers and various sizes of nails and bolts; the grass trimmer had been placed under the stairs and only came out when William Solden barked his August orders to tidy the garden. The shed was a small island of defiance, an area of non-cooperation in a world of rigid format and dug-deep emotions. Here, Tom was king: the posters on the wall served to remind him of the outside world, the bands whose music he enjoyed, the female pin-ups of cinema he would never meet but to whom he had taken on the role of leading man in every story his imagination conjured as the weekend passed in a cloud of smoke and long, lost hours.

It started to rain, the gentle sound of Oxfordshire drizzle splattering against the one window to reality that the shed provided, facing the back door of the house, where his father was no doubt wrapped up in some new scheme to get Tom to buckle down in preparation for when he turned sixteen and was sent away to join the army whether he liked it or not.

Another drag. Finally, the meagre amount of local brew hit Tom's system. Supine on the camp bed, he watched the rain explode against the pane of glass. Like the black-and-white aerial pictures he had once seen in a World War Two book, the spatter of dots appeared haphazard at first, but soon, a detailed image of destruction emerged, the increasingly rapid explosions, a chain reaction of everything in the blast radius: gas stations sent fire into the sky, searing the clouds hanging innocently over the scene; people ran in terror as the fire consumed house after house, street after street.

Tom's gaze drifted to one of the posters—larger than the rest and bought from a record shop in Oxford rather than hastily torn from a magazine—and the scowling, earnest faces of the khaki-painted soldier and the red-robed creature he assumed was the artist's version of Death as they discussed the card held up for the onlooker to see.

"Not joining the army," Tom muttered, a sincere rehearsal of the laying-down of the law he would, come his sixteenth birthday, deliver in person to his father, and for which he suffer the consequences, most likely being told to leave the house. That was all right; he wasn't really invested in it anymore since his mother died.

The urge to drown out the world with music that nobody else could hear was one his father's generation didn't understand, but to the alienated boys and girls in this small town, it had become a place of safety. He groped the stone floor for his Walkman and then for a tape, any tape, that would take him further from this place. His fingers grazed the plastic edge of a case but succeeded only in knocking it out of reach. He redoubled his efforts and grasped the cassette firmly, a small victory dance playing out in his mind. When the rain comes and you have no place in the world, every little victory counts.

He hadn't noticed the daylight outside diminish—the effects of the joint and his complete obliviousness to the world beyond the rain-shaped scorch marks on the shed's solitary window. With a flick of a switch, the bulb above flared like a calling card to the heavens, to which he was not immune, hurting his eyes and making him squint.

This was not new: all bright light hurt his eyes and had done so for several years. A doctor told him there was nothing to worry about, while his father told him to get a grip and stop making excuses, be a man. For Tom, it was little more than the inconvenience of having to wear sunglasses when he was lying down listening to music. Sliding them into place, he studied the tape he had salvaged from the floor and gave it a nod of approval—a classic of Americana, loaned to him by Keith Screpple, an army brat like himself, who along with his family, had been shipped back home to New Jersey after he got in trouble with the town's police for setting off a quantity of high-grade fireworks in one of the main drains that took the overflow of rain down to the river.

These days, any album Tom picked up spoke to him in ways that none of his peers could understand. The girls, for the most part, were divided in their opinions of the aesthetics of Culture Club, Wham! or any other act that came their way, titillating their growing curiosity of sex and evoking shrieks of laughter, chatter and gossip about boys—behaviour oddly out of step with the demands of the era to look cool, to dress smart and be seen. There were a couple of exceptions. Lorna, who was into rock music, didn't really give a damn about the clique and was like himself—an outcast in the eyes of the Dangerously Groovy. Lorna would come around sometimes, but only when Tom's father wasn't there to kill the vibe. It was thanks to Lorna that Tom had his limited stash of dope.

Then there was Heather, a girl for whom he would have given up every leading role to be her supporting co-star, but who saw him as a mess, an out-of-control creature she only gave the time of day as he was less dangerous than the preening, domineering lads in their school year—boys on parade all jostling for her attention. They stood no chance. Tom's cassette tapes came from Heather, bought from the stores by her dad, a regular guy who steered clear of William Solden, afraid he, too, would end up a casualty in the army man's private war.

How much grass did he have left? Enough for one more smoke?

A noise from outside the shed, slithery, the sound of wet leather being thrown in a raging fire.

The noise had been loud enough to overpower the music on his Walkman, and he took off his earphones, imagination running riot. He looked out of the window, but a mist had enveloped the shed, shrouding the darkness of the approaching night.

Tom was not given to being alarmed by the sudden and unexplained. Many years of coming to understand his father had taken their toll on his stoic psyche, but something inside him took notice of the sense of unease, the possible distress. Burglars perhaps? It wasn't unknown, although they tended to keep away from this side of town as a rule. Too many police officers lived in these streets and closes, which backed onto the fields. Perhaps it was foxes sniffing around the leftovers that inevitably found their way to the ground once the neighbour's cat had ripped open a bin bag.

Another sound. The mist tapped against the glass, pushed by the wind that stirred in apprehension.

Tom rose and walked stealthily to the side of the window and peeked out, not wishing to confront head-on whatever was out there. The lock on the door rattled. Maybe his dad had finally had enough of his son's weekend retreat into stoner life and had come to drag him back into the house to deliver his ultimatum. Stand up straight, turn left, wheel right, stand at ease, stand to attention and repeat forever.

Straining his neck to take in the window's narrow field of vision, he saw a light, a dark glow, grubby, insistent, not enough to hurt his eyes but enough to squint as if he were concentrating on a mock exam in school. Inside the light, he saw the silhouette of a man dressed in a suit and top hat, a walking cane in his left hand—not for aiding in the act of walking it seemed. Tom squinted harder, the man's face coming into focus, followed by a wave of revulsion at the sickly yellow hue of his skin and black eyes that stared towards the house and threatened to pull

3

Tom into their darkness. Breaking away, he looked towards the wide-open back door. His father must have fallen asleep without locking up.

Tom turned his attention back to the yellow-faced man, noticing now that the colour was in streaks, as if the creature had undergone treatment for jaundice that had somehow made it worse. His hands, large and ungainly, reached out, fingers knotted, riddled with bumps. His fingernails, though tinged with the same yellow as his features, were transparent, long and pointed, almost flimsy.

The man walked towards the house, the mist following him as if by command, then suddenly looked back at the shed, and Tom experienced the same kind of apprehension he'd felt when one of the dogs had come back from their walk alone, brown lead trailing in the mud.

Tom started banging his hand against the window. He was afraid. The figure grinned and placed one knotted, bony finger over its cracked mouth, quietly shushing Tom's shouts of alarm.

The shed was locked, the key still in the hole, as it made it harder for his father to burst in and witness his son's fall from potential soldier to the unwashed layabout. But it was of no consequence; the figure had turned away, back towards the house.

The mist closed up tight around the dark light, reminding Tom of a coal miner's torch when the air was thick with gases and impending disaster. Tom scrabbled to unlock the door. He may have spent the day goading his father about his mother's death and the US airbase up the road, the nuclear weapons the Americans had buried under the soil ready to unleash their terrible fallout and plague across civilisation, but he cared for his dad, albeit in the small chunks between being constantly drilled about his future.

The man entered the house, and a few seconds later, Tom heard a scream that turned him cold. He let go of the key and let his arm fall to his side, defeated, unsure what to do. A minute

4

later, the man walked out of the house and strode towards the shed, momentarily out of sight before appearing at the window. He looked directly into Tom's eyes and held up a key. It was the key to the shed. The figure smiled and bowed down. Tom edged closer, watching the figure put the key on the grass, out of reach, and then slowly raise itself up to its full height. It pressed its face against the glass pane, and Tom sprang back, the hairs on his arms, which had only started showing the previous summer, standing to attention, his heart pounding a double-quick march. The figure repeated the gesture of silence, the finger raised slowly and with solemnity to the grinning mouth.

Then the mist cleared and the figure was gone, vanished into the darkness as if a figment of Tom's imagination, a nightmare brought on by the weed. Even as he was convincing himself that was what had happened, he heard the distant sound of sirens blaring, waking up the night and bringing reality crashing down upon his life. He staggered backwards, topping onto his makeshift bed, and screamed for help.

Chapter Two

MOST PEOPLE IN the town only heard about the bombing raid over North Africa later in the day, but Cheryl Frampton had watched in youthful wonder, a mixture of bravado and fear for the unknown reprisal that might visited upon the area she lived in. The papers tomorrow would be full of jingoism, rabid hostility and perhaps in some quarters a measure of caution and dismay that the Americans sought to strike and use the English countryside as the base from which war could be launched. However, for now, the press was its usual mix of titillation, football, gossip and the occasional note of sincerity.

Cheryl gripped her overladen orange newspaper-round bag as she counted the planes taking off in the distance. The death of Simone de Beauvoir hadn't hit the British press to any great extent; the fallout of the allegations of Kurt Waldheim's Nazi past was rumbling on; the speculation of the Trans World Airlines flight bombing a few days before was levelling out; Chernobyl was but a place so distant in the mind that it would not register upon the young girl's imagination until a week after the explosion. Still, she counted the airplanes out and watched them fly overhead.

With the planes speeding their way to Libya airspace, Cheryl resumed her morning paper round. Not much further to go; enough time to stop and throw some stones into the river that ran through the woods; enough time to dream of hot, buttered crumpets for breakfast and to think of a way to avoid the selection of the school sports day teams later in the week. Five more houses: the groundkeeper's cottage guarding the entrance to the old estate which bore the name of the town would be the first of them, and it would see her paper bag almost take on the vacuum of space, as the vast majority of the daily papers would be dropped off there. Collectively, they weighed a tonne, but it was worth it. The Christmas tip that came Cheryl's way had kept her afloat for the last three years, had kept her from asking money she knew her mother didn't have, not since her dad had skipped town in search of adventure when she was nine.

Cheryl's mother had been against her taking up such a job. "Not for girls," she kept muttering; not the early mornings, not with the route being so far from home. Cheryl had played for time, grinding down her mother's fears with subtlety and care, even asking her to come with her for the first two weeks. Soon after, her mother relented when she worked out for herself that it meant the limited amount of money coming into the house would be eased, and her daughter was being responsible for her own actions; the extra five pounds a week towards the housekeeping was also a factor.

Cheryl had worked hard, the morning route and the local paper run in the evenings after school, the odd additional route here and there when it was snowing and other delivery boys and girls could not be bothered to leave the comfort of their beds, or when the day was too nice and too hot to be lumping around a bag stuffed full of newspapers over a three-mile route. And then, of course, were the little extras: the advertising sheets of paper, the allure of country living promised by attaching a conservatory to the house, the local shops that lined the town's small high street spreading their wares across flimsy sheets of paper—special offers and money-off vouchers. Every one of those which Cheryl delivered meant more money and was a step closer to the future she wanted, now only a few thousand deliveries away.

Cheryl had few friends. It didn't matter to her really. Analytical at a young age, she seemed to alienate people quite quickly, her manner off-putting to those in her age group, who could not handle the intensity of her beliefs, of not choosing to go to Oxford on a Saturday with the other girls and watch the boys play on the video games at the arcade, laughing and giggling, making hopeless advances and attempts at small talk, which always led to the boy to assume the girl in question liked them. None of that appealed to Cheryl; she wanted out of the town at the first opportunity, to see the world, so she skipped any social activity that was proposed, avoided contact with her peers and just walked the route and put the money away.

As she came upon the shortcut she always took through the woods, cutting a good fifteen minutes off her round, she thought she heard a sound, a deep snorting, and sensed something animalistic, restless and buoyed up by the airplanes that had disturbed its sleep and turned its head to thoughts of food.

Cheryl gave it little heed. Soon forgotten, it was a moment, like so many others, that in her plans meant nothing. She wandered on, not noticing the mist that started to rise up around her feet, the small tendrils of vapour clawing at her jeans, then the tights, and nibbling down on her ankles.

The river, more like a wide rushing brook as far as Cheryl was concerned, had been a source of entertainment for children and adults alike for centuries. The wooden bridge that spanned the water was often neglected in favour of the rush of water further upstream, which gushed from a height of six feet and was often greeted with squeals of delight or good-natured curses issued in exasperation when someone pushed their friend into the deeper water, soaking them to the bone. Ever logical, Cheryl didn't wade through the water, especially when she was carrying her papers. One misstep on a slippery wet stone would send her over, and her papers would be carried downstream, the news melding together in a ball of ink and type, photographs of the guilty obscured by the unrelenting torrent.

Cheryl crossed the bridge, an old tale of trolls floating up from childhood fears quickly suppressed. She stopped halfway and admired the blossoms on the trees; April was her favourite time of year, showing its youthful valour once more, its resilience to renew in the face of winter's forceful, fierce tirade. Picking up a small broken twig from the wooden planks beneath her feet, she made a wish, dropped it over one side of the bridge, then walked to the other and watched the twig float serenely onwards. Her wish was always the same; part of her understood that it might never come true.

That sound again. Close, heavy, and for the first time, she noticed the mist which dragged at her heels as traversed the woods. Her mother had once told her of a series of phone calls she had taken during the night, the heavy breathing coming down the complexity of wires, the unknown and unseen unsettling her, making her anxious, ultimately terrifying her when the person on the line finally spoke her name. Not long after that, her mother unplugged the telephone and advised the phone company that she no longer wanted to have one in the house.

The mist crept forward, slithering to the edge of the bridge, where it sank to the water's edge and rose up like a wall, leaving only the bridge clear, the early morning sun beating down with spring elegance upon the stretch of wood upon which Cheryl was standing, her eyes on stalks as the mist turned yellow and the chill of the air made her shiver.

She watched the gloom surround her, the mist glistening and pulsating with life. She was unsure whether the sound of heavy breathing was hers or came from inside the mist itself. The air seemed to vibrate, to quiver as if agitated by its inability to push aside the yellowing mist that encompassed all aspects of the bridge besides the space above Cheryl's head.

For a brief moment, she thought she heard a voice ask for permission to approach, the spoken fumble of a teenage boy asking for a dance and already prepared for the inevitable pain of rejection. She dismissed the thought immediately. *Not logical, there's nothing there, just a freak weather episode, just my mind telling me I've worked too hard and this is payback for the neglect of sleep.*

She fought hard, but her inner argument had no conviction, the matters of fact which had served her so well over the years, the consistent analytical thought that other girls shied away from, and which kept Cheryl alone, suddenly deserted her. Under the bridge, the troll lurked and ate the goats that dared to cross.

On the riverbank Cheryl had left behind, the mist parted slightly, a gap through which the trees revealed themselves again, sparkling with fruitful spring joy, and a moment of relief swept over her. Surely, this aberration of weather was coming to an end. But then the mist closed up again, the work of a skilled seamstress stitching together the tear in double quick time and with no sign of the mend, an invisible seam. In its place stood a tall figure, long fingers extending from large, grotesque hands which hung at the end of impossibly long arms. It raised one of its hands to its mouth and placed a finger over the grinning lips.

It was the act of being shushed that drove Cheryl to the brink, sullying the purity of logic that life was not a random progression to which others of her age were slaves. It was routine, predictable…and it all came tumbling down around her as she started to scream. She was still screaming later that evening when the search party, organised by the manor house's groundskeeper and her mother, found her close to the field which backed onto Tom Solden's house. Whatever had transpired left both children in a state of nervous exhaustion, screaming their heads off in terror and talking incoherently of a manmade of mist.

Chapter Three

THERE WAS VERY little incentive to being the editor of the town's newspaper. It certainly didn't come with the prestige Sam McCarthy thought she deserved—the kind of prestige that was available if she were to jump ship and take one of the offers that came her way whenever she was in touch with the newspaper's owner. Those offers wouldn't be around forever; sooner or later, the paper would shut down, leaving this backwater's only means of keeping up with local events to the girls' Saturday afternoon tearoom gossip. In truth, most of the gossip was centred on the local 'tycoon', who owned two farms and made a habit of driving his new car down the high street with the windows down for everyone to marvel at the way he wore his driving gloves.

Posh, arrogant idiot. One day, I'll start a petition to have the main road turned into a pedestrian area 'for the benefit of the local people' so I don't have to see his smug, round face passing my office window every couple of hours.

Sam sat back in her chair. Time dragged towards the end of the day, so close to being able to leave and get back to being on-call at home. She was never truly off the job, though, equally, she never had to wish for a dull moment because it was all dull. Any stories of monumental interest were covered by the tabloids and the broadsheets—

Air attack on Libya, a tactical blunder or retaliation for Berlin discotheque bombing?

While it had been made clear to Sam in a terse interview with some low-ranking official that the main bulk of the aircraft had

11

been sent from RAF Lakenheath, it was well known the support had come from just a few miles away, that the town had its own angle on the story, yet she could not see it go to print.

The boss had warned her off. The scene she wanted to create was too explosive, volatile, he said. She would get her turn, but for now, she had to step away from the story, act like it had never happened.

The Death of the Investigative Journalist. She had long thought it would be a good title for a play, and she would have written it herself, but whilst she was good—excellent, in fact—at coming up with a headline that could stir the heart or confuse the conscience and, ultimately sell copy by the thousand, actually sitting down and creating a work of fiction... Well, she would have to leave that to Simon Kinsey, general nuisance and her roving reporter— her *only* reporter, thanks to cutbacks and the trimming of the fat of the land. They shared some duties, and quite often a desk, once even a fumble after hours in the darkness of the office, from which neither of them ever fully recovered, Kinsey because he had been in love with Sam since he started on the paper straight from school, and Sam because the memory appalled her, for it had lost her the respect of someone she truly loved.

She had felt dirty for weeks afterwards and had considered resigning. Since then, she had worked diligently to keep her name at the forefront of the owner's mind, and despite constant speculation of a takeover and all resources being sent to Oxford or, worse still, London, she had kept the paper on its feet and interesting—no small feat when nothing ever happened in this town.

The clock on the wall opposite the desk clicked on slowly. The pub down the street would soon be heaving, and Rebecca would be left on her own, sitting amongst the frenzy of older men traversing from pub to pub, playing darts and talking endless garbage. Would she forgive yet another late night? Would she stay and nurse yet another gin and tonic? Or would she go home, turn on the stereo and delve back into the mother-daughter dynamic that had seen its best days destroyed by blame and fear.

A police car went past, its siren pulling Sam out of her melancholy blues, then another—an unheard-of situation in the town. Not even Oxford United beating Aston Villa in the Cup Semi-final to set up a match against Queen's Park Rangers in a few days' time had warranted two police cars. Sam knew little about sport, local or national. She didn't care for any of it, especially not football. However, she knew the value of good local connections, and whilst Kinsey had been at the match to interview several players, it was Sam who pieced the story together into an account of the event which drew interest from several of her peers and glowing praise from the owner. Kinsey could do all the donkey work he wanted; she wanted out, to get deep and dirty, where the true base of journalism was...

Or perhaps she should just write that play.

Out of bored curiosity, Sam reached for the telephone, stretching across the desk and around the half-drunk coffee Kinsey had left by his typewriter, refusing as he did to move with the times and write his articles on a computer, which was good news for Sam: the office couldn't stand the expense of two new machines.

Before she could pick up the receiver, let alone dial out, the phone rang, causing her to jerk in surprise and inevitably catch Kinsey's coffee with her elbow. The cup wobbled dangerously and then righted itself, mocking her with the deeply ingrained stains like tide lines marking the passage of Kinsey's days. She had given him that mug—a 'welcome' present, back when there had been two other journalists, a secretary and a receptionist. Her team.

She picked up the phone, already sensing who it was.

"Hey, boss!" Kinsey shouted down the line. "Glad I caught you before you went to the pub." He gave a short but humourless laugh.

"Get to the point, Simon," Sam snipped coarsely, though she usually tempered her impatience with her colleague because it wasn't his fault. He was on edge these days, when he used to be so damned cheerful it irritated her. Sometimes she wished he could experience something truly awful just to bring him back down to a place where she could at least look him in the eye and not be constantly reminded of the reason Rebecca's father had left the family home.

"Did you hear me? I said you need to get up to Sterhan Close as soon as you can. Two kids have been found a couple of hundred yards apart in suspicious circumstances."

"Dead?"

"Both still alive, but one of them was locked in a shed and his father killed as he slept in the house. I'm going back there now—I had to run around the streets to try and find a phone box. You know what the vandalism is like on these estates."

If there was one thing Sam did admire about Kinsey, it was his dedication to the job, never wanting to let a dog lie still. He had uncovered many good local stories in his time and had pursued each one with the kind of rabid intensity she could respect. He'd also turned down the offer of a more celebrated job in London, but for very different reasons. He was a local boy—born at home, attended the local school—and knew everyone by name and profession. He would be lost in the capital.

In her haste to leave so she could collect her daughter from the pub and drop her off at home before seeing for herself the Big Story—the one which didn't involve airplanes and the damage wrought on foreign soil—Sam knocked over the eternally stained cup and watched as it tumbled off the desk and hit the ground, handle first, with a sickening crack. She looked down at the shattered remains and wondered for the third time that day whether life as a playwright would be more agreeable.

Chapter Four

SIMON KINSEY HAD been speaking to the police with the earnestness and professionalism Sam McCarthy had instilled in him on the day he first sat at the desk as a fresh-from-school trainee. She hadn't expected him to see the year out—sixteen years of age, very little going for him academically—except that his easy-going nature somehow endeared him to almost everyone he met, including his maths and science teachers. Those subjects had confused him, but put him in front of a typewriter and he could blow the socks of anyone. His English was excellent, his local knowledge was astonishing, and he'd brought that easy-going nature to the job. It had played a part in keeping the newspaper afloat, indeed, in turning its fortunes around so completely that it made a profit, but that didn't stop the cutbacks; the owner, Kinsey suspected, wanted to offload the company and take both he and McCarthy to London, but Kinsey would not leave. He was a Perchester man through and through.

One of the few people Kinsey could not connect with was standing a few feet away, his manner that of the self-righteous and self-absorbed, ideas not just above his station but on a completely different platform nobody else was allowed to access. Between Mr. Marbon and the local vicar, Kinsey could never decide whom he detested more, but on today's performance, Marbon was hands down the most unpleasant and obnoxious, even when he had done something good, as he had today, in leading the team of police through the thick woods that surrounded the manor house. He still cultivated an air of talentless superiority, and that had not changed in the years that Kinsey had known him.

Forced by convention—if he wanted to get the story right—Kinsey endured Marbon's time in the sun. The man had tales about everyone he had ever met, and if you distanced yourself from him and saw through the lies, he made your life intolerable. Kinsey watched for the telltale signs: in spite of being in the company of the landowner and his wife for most of the day, he believed Marbon had something to do with the girl's disappearance; it was all too clean, clinical.

Facts were facts, though. Marbon was clean, and that seemed to fuel his bragging to the police. "I know every square inch of this wood—it was the same as when I was a cab driver up north. I made it my business to know all the shortcuts, the ways to get the people home the quickest—"

No, I never once looked at their faces, I never had time, I kept my eyes on the road...

Kinsey smiled at his own silent interruption and wrote down the groundkeeper's words in shorthand. Kinsey felt a tap on his shoulder and turned to see McCarthy standing beside him. There was no talk, just the conscious due care of colleagues, of the editor and her one-night stand basking in the glow of Marbon's momentary self-importance.

Finally, the police constable and Sergeant Wilcox thanked Mr. Marbon for his time and told him there might be further questions—would he be available? Of course he would; it was his civic duty, after all.

Kinsey had questions, but none that were relevant to explaining what had happened to the two teenagers found less than a couple of hundred yards apart screaming for their lives and talking nonsense of a manmade of mist.

"So, Mr. Marbon, what do you have to say of the accusations of embezzlement that forced you to leave Ireland back in 1974, the rumours that you were a gun runner for the IRA, the young woman found dead in Dublin from a drug overdose only an hour after you had been talking to her at the Bonnycliffe Hotel?" So many questions, not enough evidence...*yet*.

Sam McCarthy noticed the fixated look that Kinsey was giving Mr. Marbon and decided to intervene.

"*I* will interview Marbon. I want you to talk to the neighbour who found the boy. Find out how far away was the key, if he could have put it there himself, whether he's to blame for the girl going missing, did they know each other—they had to be in the same year at the school. Both have the same figure in their story, but I gather young Tom Solden is a bit of pot-head—it shouldn't be hard to connect a few dots there."

Kinsey took the hint: *get out of here and find a lead that the police don't have, don't antagonise Marbon.* He smiled at her, but it was one that didn't show his usual persona. There was so much hate in him for Marbon. McCarthy had never asked him why; she knew too much of the journalist as it was.

Kinsey strode off, hoping Marbon would see it as confidence. He heard McCarthy greet the man, ask if he had time for a few words for the paper, and the unquestionable joviality of one who had scored the biggest day of his life. Of course the hero of the hour was *honoured* to speak to her! Thankfully, Kinsey was out of earshot quickly and immersed in his own task.

Nothing like this had happened in the town before. Sure, there had been children going missing for years, most of whom were found and had just run away. The closest cinema was in Oxford and a train journey away in Banbury, there was a drama group, but with so few places. Why would they want to stay in a town geared up for the middle-aged, the middle class and the beige, who saw the annual snooker tournament at the Elysium Club as the highlight of the year and the Christmas social at the Golf Club as a rite and a ritual?

For the youth of the town, there was nothing. It was no wonder there was epidemic of drugs making its way into the pockets of the young. The easily bored made for good customers.

That, of course, fitted Tom Solden, but as far as Kinsey could ascertain, Tom was only into dope. He had seen the young lad around the town, not to talk to on a regular basis; the dominance of his now-dead father was enough to keep him under the radar, but people remarked that he was polite, always willing to help out a neighbour if they asked him, which was how he managed to afford his drug of choice, but he was also into music—Kinsey wondered how a fifteen-year-old could afford to buy all those tapes and still have enough to score from a dealer.

The girl was a different matter. Cheryl Frampton had no known friends but was also diligent. She worked hard, her schoolwork was impeccable, and she was driven, not into the drug scene but by her desire to leave the town for good. The only connections Kinsey could see between her and the boy was that they were the same age, attended the same school, and that Cheryl had been found close to the place where Tom's mother had been found dead a couple of years beforehand.

Kinsey had known Tom's mother in school. She'd married young—a soldier from out of town—and had a child early. Mental fatigue and depression had set in, but she mustered on, protecting her child from her overbearing, career-minded husband, who was a good man but a tyrant towards their son, constantly telling him he wasn't good enough for the forces, his hair was too long—the usual stuff. Too much discipline under the guise of care, abuse under the cover of concern.

Kinsey watched all but two of the police cars drive away and relaxed, his natural smile returning to his face, his demeanour unfolding. Blow Marbon. *Let him have his day and relish the sunshine on his face.* One day, Kinsey was sure, he would expose Marbon. If he was wrong, so be it. At least he would see the insidious creep languish in hot water for a while.

As Kinsey had expected, the account from the neighbour who had found Tom Solden locked in the shed proved that the boy could not have, at least directly, contributed to the Cheryl Frampton's disappearance. The lady may have been touching eighty, but she was sharp—a retired teacher from London, too savvy for her own good, eyes like machines. She showed Kinsey where she had found the key, placed on the grass some ten feet from the shed door.

"Could someone have locked him in after the young girl was found?" Kinsey asked with what he hoped wasn't too suspicious a manner.

The retired teacher tutted in exasperation, no doubt the same sound she had made for forty years whenever one of her pupils had asked a stupid question. "Young man, Tom Solden was a good lad. Yes, he liked to get stoned, but we all did that in the sixties. He only ever had one visitor to the house, and she didn't stay long. Too scared of his father. I watched him from my bedroom window. He went into the shed not long after seven. Nobody came to the house. Nobody came around the back—you saw the gate to the alleyway was locked—only a couple of us have keys, and here is mine."

She proceeded to take a bunch of keys out of her coat pocket. The huge selection baffled Kinsey, at which she gleamed and explained, "I am in charge of the village hall in Lower Sitton, on the committee of the parish church on the high street, and I look after the vicar's house when he is away with his wife and daughter. I may be old, but I keep busy."

Kinsey broadened his grin. The old woman had pulled him back into reality without making him feel small.

"Did you see any fog rolling in from the fields or woods, out towards the manor house?"

The old woman's piercing green eyes looked into his, chilling his soul a little. "Mr. Kinsey, I was awake early. I heard the thunder of the planes taking off from the airbase. I watched the poor young boy go meekly into his shed. I counted off the hours. I heard the planes come back from their mission. I heard screaming coming from my next-door neighbour's garden, and I rang the police station. I found the key in broad daylight. I'm talking to you now, and I see you are tired, lonely and angry. More than that, you are afraid. If I see all that, had there been any fog or mist, then undoubtedly I would have seen that as well."

Kinsey conceded and upon reflection thought he might have preferred to have gone a few rounds with Marbon. The former teacher may have looked frail, but she was as tough as they came.

It was with inward relief he heard McCarthy shout his name from the other side of the alley's gate. The old woman gripped his hand. "Listen to the boy. Just because I didn't see anything, it doesn't mean it didn't happen." Her tone softened, and her grip relaxed. The brightness in her eyes, though, remained intense as she showed him back to the alleyway.

Kinsey took one more glance at the fence that separated the fields and the backs of the houses. Beyond it, the darkness of the evening closed in for the day.

Chapter Five

AN OFFICE IS a cold, sterile place during the night. The light emitted from the overhead bulbs gives off a feeling of retribution for crimes committed of which no one knows, but you keep working. You keep typing in the hope that you get to close the door behind you and become once more the jailor rather than the inmate, before dawn shows her face.

Kinsey hated working at night, closed away, huddled over his typewriter and waiting for his tired brain to come up with an interesting line that might captivate the reader, make them think, keep them entertained, give them a reason to see the world for what it was. The packet of biscuits by his side and endless stream of tea did little to alleviate his frustrated silence when sitting opposite a woman who tolerated your every breath with unresolved fury.

Was this what he'd wanted all those years ago, when he stepped through the door and the jangle of a newly installed bell had announced the arrival of an unprepared stranger in the realm of disenfranchised, egotistical, self-proclaimed saviours of local news? Of course it was, and aside from the casual eye-rolls that came his way from those who had known him since he was a boy and were perplexed by how he had come so far without formal training, he was happy with his lot.

Perhaps it was time he asked if he could have a go at writing the story on McCarthy's machine.

There was working at night in an office, and there was working in the field—opening night of a new club in Oxford, a cinema show or a gig, the young bands on their way to the 'big time', filling the town's only pub with their noise and hopeful dreams, sweat-drenched air ripening in the nose while pool balls rattled at the other end of the bar. Or the final desperate acts of recognised penance—an old man with a guitar and a handful of seasoned songs marking time, the insensible noise of a fruit machine adding colour and vibe to his words and forgotten dreams, the curse of another day lost and a fiver down the drain both swallowed by the slot of indifference...

That side of the job was the perk, and Kinsey didn't need to move away to know where he wanted to be. He liked travelling out to Oxford for the football and looked forward to the League Cup Final weekend down at Wembley—who wouldn't anticipate a great day out when visiting such a monument for the first time? But in his heart, even in the false light provided above his head, he knew *this* was the point; this was what he had strived for since leaving school armed only with O' Levels in English, Drama and History.

Over the top of his typewriter, he watched McCarthy steam through her editorial, her mind an oiled automaton, a well-versed system, but there was little flair to her words. Precise, thought out quickly, no room for imagination, she would never have made a playwright. Not for her, the crushing damnation of the beautiful ending where the hero finds their true love after conquering unimaginable fears. McCarthy was an android who blinked and asked the right questions, a robot with a pair of legs to die for, who was still the best and worst thing that had happened to Kinsey since he split up with Elaine Caxton in fourth year after her father was caught selling false identification to the teenagers on the American airbase housing estate for fifty pounds a go.

Kinsey looked down at what he had thus far written and wondered if he should add the neighbour's name. It always played well with the community; it was reason sales of the paper had kept him in a job here rather than having to prostitute himself to the London papers or magazines. Add a name, provide context, send them a copy, gratis, for their contribution, and almost every time, they'd buy another dozen copies for their family and friends in other towns. Kinsey had even found a way to make extra money by on occasion offering framed copies as souvenirs. He was careful not to advertise his services to the wider community, but it was another couple of quid in his pocket, and he always made sure it was a perfect fit.

To hell with it. He had asked the old lady for the quote, what would it matter?

> *I found the boy screaming, his hand bloodied from trying to rip open the door, deep scratches along his arms. The poor love was incoherent, consumed by distress at what he saw. I just don't know how he will cope on his own, now that he is an orphan...*

Kinsey liked that final line. It evoked readers' sympathy. Nobody, unless you were a monster, wanted to see children without their parents. That small sentence conveyed the reality of the situation—never mind the figure shrouded in mist; this was about a boy whose father had been murdered by an unknown assailant, an opportunistic burglar, perhaps only Dad had got in the way...

No, that isn't right. Kinsey reached absent-mindedly for another biscuit. *The boy's dad was asleep, sparked out in front of the TV, still in his uniform and no doubt dreaming of the moment the bombs rained down on Libya.* Kinsey amended the words and pulled the sheet off the typewriter, a couple of crumbs falling unnoticed into the wells between the letters.

The rest of the paper had been put to bed over the weekend: the usual assortment of advertising space and wanted ads, a follow-up piece on the strange smell in the wind on the Hollow's Estate, a feature on the local football team caught in the shadow of Oxford United's trip to Wembley, a restaurant review—Kinsey, happy to

23

dine on chips and curry sauce from the Chinese hidden away up an alleyway off the high street, always left those to the boss—and an excruciatingly brief summary of the events thousands of miles away in another country on another continent, where people died at the hands of pilots from a base just down the road.

But there, in full black and white, accompanied by an old school photo of the two children, was the story Kinsey and McCarthy had been chasing all their lives—a front page that would sell, keep the owner happy for months and stay the hand of execution that hovered above their heads week after week.

Did they need to show a photograph, no matter how grainy, of Marbon attempting to look solemn in the role of the hero but coming off as the smug bastard that he was? Of course! Only Kinsey could see the self-assured superiority radiating from the man's face; others who didn't know the manor house's employee would see the concerned father of a misplaced child.

But it wasn't Kinsey's call. McCarthy had final say on content. The machine speaks, and all must obey. Kinsey stood and stretched. He felt knotted, conflicted about the day. There was no way the kids had seen what they claimed. It had to be a bad batch of weed. Yet Cheryl Frampton was not that type of a girl. *Perhaps we don't know everything—we have no idea what goes in a teenager's mind—*

His thoughts were interrupted by McCarthy letting out a huge sigh, a customary signal to others that she was finished, tired or in need of a drink, occasionally all three.

The clock on the wall mockingly showed Kinsey it was almost two in the morning. It was with a tinge of regret that he realised McCarthy still had to go home and face her daughter's wrath, injured by her mother's 'feeble excuse' for not being home and being normal like other mums. Kinsey, not devoid of sympathy and even acknowledging his own small role in the family's destruction, hoped for McCarthy's sake that Rebecca would be asleep when her mother pulled up outside the house in her Escort.

"I'll send all this across in the morning with the layout," McCarthy said, and then, seeing the clock, added, "Thanks for staying late, big story, it will be worth it on Thursday when we see the results."

It was the first time she'd spoken to him all night, but Kinsey took the thanks. He'd have killed for a lift home. The local cab firm would have all but shut down for the night, and he didn't trust the singular driver who habitually loitered by the market square, looking as if he enjoyed his flask a bit too much. Kinsey would rather walk home than find out if he was right.

McCarthy locked the paperwork away and put on her coat, smiling at Kinsey, but it was one of those *please let's just get out of here without you asking me to take you home* smiles. Kinsey turned off the kettle at the socket and pocketed the remaining biscuits. There was nothing in the fridge at home, and the Chinese would be closed by now. The alarm was set, the light switched off, its usual fizz of fading translucence a sign that in the end it wasn't just McCarthy and Kinsey who were becoming obsolete; the nature of their profession was on the way out too. The door was locked, and there was nothing to do but say good night. It remained unsaid until McCarthy opened her car door and looked back at Kinsey in the yellowing light that hung above them.

"Do you believe the kids? Their story, I mean."

Kinsey shook his head. "Bad weed. At least it's not heroin. I've seen what the effects of that can do."

McCarthy nodded her head and got into her car. She stayed where she was for a minute and then wound down the window, the squeaking noise of glass against rubber amusing Kinsey for a second. "It is a shame, though. I would've loved to be covering the bombing of Libya tonight. Imagine the scene at tabloids and broadsheets—what beautiful mayhem." Without waiting for a reply, McCarthy wound up her window and drove off home to make peace with her daughter, or perhaps creep into the house and quietly drain a bottle of red before falling restlessly to sleep on the sofa.

Kinsey watched her drive away into the night and wondered if tomorrow would be a better day. Pulling up his coat's lapels to cover his neck against the chill of the night's air, he set off for home, keeping an eye out for the welcome sight of a light on in the pub along the way. He could do with the after-hours talk to take his mind off the story, though it more often than not came down to chewing over ideas for attracting more customers. 'Keep the Yanks out of town' was one that was always rebuffed, given their money on a Saturday and Sunday night made up for the lack of clientele during the week.

Alas, there would be no after-hours chatter tonight. The town was silent; the driver of the only night taxi was snoozing behind the wheel, happy in his world of whisky-induced slumber; how Kinsey envied him.

As Kinsey walked onwards, pondering morosely over the cold, lonely space that would greet him, he didn't notice the layer of mist hanging around the gates to the park, nor the yellow tinge that seemed to froth and fry as it seeped out into the street.

Beyond the gates, obscured by the shadows of the night, a figure watched with fascination as Kinsey passed by. The figure started to follow, not too close, just enough distance that Kinsey would not hear or feel anything suspicious. The figure should not have worried; Kinsey was lost in his own thoughts, his mind caught in a fog of his own.

Chapter Six

KINSEY HEARD THE doorbell ring and decided to ignore it. It had been a difficult night—one that had not seen him drop into any semblance of sleep till almost five. The doorbell rang again, followed by a heavy thumping on the oak panelling. He was tempted to shout obscenities out of the window, but the thought of his neighbour calling round to admonish him for his lack of Christian behaviour made him bite his tongue. Mrs. Delamare was a woman he dared not cross. He opened one eye and squinted at the clock: half past six. He'd been asleep for less than two hours—what arsehole would commit such torture?

The banging on the door repeated more urgently, more forcefully. Cursing the morning, Kinsey pulled himself out of the bed and walked gingerly to the open window, looking down. Below him was Sam, an angry, agitated Sam, who looked like she'd tear down the door if he didn't acknowledge her. Imagining Beatrice Delamare jotting down the time of his latest infringement, he called out as quietly as he could and made a mental note to play some Iron Maiden later. If she was going to complain to the residents' committee anyway, he may as well make the most of it.

**

"What the hell, Sam? It's half six in the morning."

McCarthy looked up to where the disembodied voice came from and snarled inwardly. "I've been trying to call you since six. Don't you answer your phone?"

"I pull the plug at night. I don't like being dragged from my sleep—especially when I have been up half the night writing about a murder and children covering their tracks."

McCarthy reined in her anger. Kinsey had a point, and it wasn't his fault she'd received a call from the police—she wondered if she could get away with pulling the plug too; the world surely wouldn't end if she did.

Kinsey was on the verge of closing the window. The mood he was in, he might not even appear at the office today, and Sam couldn't afford for that to happen. Choosing her words carefully, she said, "There's another child gone missing over at Lynnsford, along where the river goes past the windmills. Some school trip from Liverpool down here to study the effects of intense farming."

Kinsey may have been exhausted, but he perked up at Sam's words. He disappeared from the window, reappeared a moment later, whistled to gain Sam's attention, then threw a bunch of keys down carefully so they didn't disappear into the undergrowth that was doing its best impression of a front garden.

"Let yourself in and put the kettle on. I'll get dressed."

Sam hadn't been in Kinsey's house for quite some time, and the thought of entering now triggered memories and the resonance of shame at being caught by her ex-husband as she committed an act of impulse and desire. Hesitating, she let herself in to what had been the Kinsey family home before his siblings flew the next and his parents downsized. The somewhat distasteful décor of classic film posters instead of works of art always bothered the snob in Sam McCarthy—King Kong on top of the Empire State Building swatting at aeroplanes, Gene Hackman as Popeye Doyle looking pensive, the shark one that everybody raved about when McCarthy was a much younger woman, and there, at the bottom of the stairs to greet the overnight visitor as they emerged from another drunken night, Janet Leigh caught in the shower by an elderly woman wielding a knife, her blood-curdling cry echoing down the years into the minds of the susceptible. It was all too much for Sam. *What's the problem with a copy of a Renoir or a Matisse instead of all this gore and pulp fiction nonsense?*

Choosing to ignore the posters, she hurried through to the kitchen, where there was only one framed poster to deal with. She was surprised to see it had changed since she'd last been there: instead of a promotional picture from *Alien*, in its place were the recognisable figures of Grace Kelly and Cary Grant in a still from *To Catch A Thief.*

Maybe he's developed some taste, after all.

Sam filled the kettle and switched it on. Finding no milk in the fridge, she searched the cupboards. No tea, no coffee...

Sod this. We'll just have to get something on the way. The roadside café on the Wealdstone Road would be open by now.

Kinsey came rushing down the stairs, his appearance altered from the man she had woken in a blaze of door-knocking and bell-pushing.

"Where's the tea?"

He needs a wife, or at least a proper girlfriend to knock some of that male arrogance out of him and kick him to shape. "You're out of milk and tea. Come on. I'm buying."

If Kinsey hadn't been awake when they left the house, he certainly was by the time they reached the café. Sam kept the windows open, filling the car with the cruelly cool Oxford air. With a cup of tea inside him, he was soon bursting with thoughts about the story that was developing.

Lynnsford was on the edge of the large expanse of woods that dominated this part of Oxfordshire. While not big enough to be given the grand title of 'forest', but woods encapsulated several villages surrounding the town of Perchester. Running through the woods was the river itself, a crawling beauty, its natural grace concealing the snare of the whitewater beast that had taken the soul of eight-year-old Sally Witherton when she'd ventured in for a paddle on a family picnic in 1956.

As the pair approached the area in which police officers were already gathered, they went over the facts again. The party consisted of eight sixth-form pupils from a school in Liverpool. Their geography teacher had brought them down to his sister's farm to study the effects on the surroundings caused by intense farming practices on one of her fields, and to look at ways it could be avoided in the future. The farm was also the site of three examples of nineteenth-century windmills, a local point of interest which used to draw many an artist to the area to capture the scene forever. As teenagers do, by the end of the third evening, they'd become restless: this trip, the teacher had reiterated, was not an opportunity to shirk school for a day but genuinely for study and work. He'd hoped some of his students would be inspired to go off to agricultural college, though he appreciated some just wanted to get out of Liverpool for the week.

The police officer standing at the entrance to the farm waved them both through. Their relationship with the local police was tight, built on trust and good management and handy when they wanted to get background information on a suspect or a lead.

Sam brought the car to a halt, squeezing down on the brakes a little too hard on the gravel and seeing dust spin up into the air. She apologised with good humour, and Kinsey raised his eyebrows.

"You are a little late, Samantha," the officer closest to them said as he brushed his jacket down for effect. "They found the lad, and he's in a bad way. They took him out to Wendlefields Hospital. His teacher's going to be in serious trouble when the school finds out."

Kinsey chimed in before Samantha could—another habit of his she found increasingly frustrating. "Where was he found, Bill?"

"On the Brightwell path by the river, about a mile into the woods. You know where that gypsy camp was found about five years ago, just by there."

30

Sam and Kinsey nodded knowingly. A travelling group of around thirty people had been found living in the woods during the summer of 1981. They had cut down some of the trees and pulled up the remains of a small outbuilding that had been gutted by fire the previous year. Sam was sure they weren't doing any real harm, but public opinion in the town and outlying villages was one of contempt, and the letters and phone calls she and Kinsey had taken during that summer had kept them busy—had kept her from her home and family. As the battle lines were drawn, with protestors on both sides of the debate digging themselves in, and the good and meaningful seeking ways to protect the small group, the number of hours both journalists spent in each other's company had started to interfere with their judgement.

***

Kinsey looked out of the corner of his eye at McCarthy. Was she also was thinking of that moment which had messed up their working relationship? He wondered for the first time that morning, if she had spent the night talking to Rebecca—had she got any sleep before she was awoken by the rolling news? He felt a pang of shame, brutal and unpleasant. To dispel the feeling that was beginning to knot in his stomach, he dug out his phone and searched for Wendlefields, confirming it was the private psychiatric hospital on the road to Oxford.

The police officer, glancing at Kinsey's screen, said, "I don't know if you're aware, but they took those other two kids there. The ones we found last night. The main hospital couldn't hold them—they were really freaking out—so they transferred them just before midnight."

This time, Kinsey felt McCarthy look at him. Much to his relief, he saw her mouth was open in shock. What the police officer had told them was news to her too.

"No, we didn't know that," she said quietly, almost inaudibly.

Kinsey's mind was racing. Sure, both teenagers were beside themselves when they were found, but they'd recovered enough to give their full names and addresses before the ambulance transported them. They'd seemed coherent, and they certainly seemed to understand where they were. Was it just a precaution? How serious was their condition now?

"And this new lad," McCarthy said, "he's been taken there as well, you say? Same condition?"

The police officer nodded. "He was found screaming, thrashing at anyone who came near him." He consulted his notebook before continuing, "One of his classmates told us he was gone for only an hour, but he'd seemed agitated before he left. His girlfriend broke up with him, the classmate reckons—she was concerned he was going to do something silly. She told the teacher an exaggerated story, and he pressed the panic button. None of them were aware of the goings-on of yesterday. They'd all been too wrapped up in the tasks set out for them by the farm owner."

"Any knowledge or suspicion of drugs?"

"Not that any of the group was aware of. If anything, it seems the lad was very anti—kept himself fit, wanted to become a farmer. Not much call for that up in Liverpool, I suspect."

"Can you take me down to the place where the lad was found, Bill?" Kinsey asked.

With a further nod of compliance from the officer, McCarthy said, "I'll go talk to the teacher and the boy's sister. Meet you back here in an hour?"

"Sure," Kinsey agreed, and without another word passing between them, the two turned their backs on each other and went off in opposite directions.

***

McCarthy looked back once, wondering if Kinsey was all right. He seemed odd, not in his usual good humour. She'd known him a long time, and even when he was brooding over a piece, he rarely gave her cause for concern. He irritated her, certainly. Just looking at him reminded her of what she'd done and what she'd lost, but she still she felt a duty of care towards him. She was worried he was drinking too much, and about the lack of food in his fridge. The kitchen looked a mess, and although she didn't like to say, despite the shower, there was a lingering, almost insistent smell emanating from him.

Her thoughts were still on Kinsey when she found the teacher and his sister knee-deep in conversation at the farmhouse table, their body language that of conspiring assassins contemplating the downfall of a king.

"Hello...Mr. Whittle, is it? I'm Sam McCarthy. I work for the town newspaper. I wonder if you could tell me what happened here?"

***

As he saw her approach, Paul Whittle stood up a little too quickly, his hand outstretched, his grimace of responsibility masking what he knew. He needed to cover his tracks quickly. The boy was alive, but there would be questions asked, and his actions would be called into question.

Chapter Seven

As KINSEY WAS being led to the spot where they had found the latest child screaming manic protests of having seen a figure in the mist, Fiona Frampton was sitting by the bedside of her sleeping, heavily sedated daughter. Fiona closed her eyes and tried to recall if there had ever been a time when she was as worried about her child as she was in that moment. Cheryl had always been an independent girl, refusing to tag along with others, declining party invitations, avoiding girlish heartbreak by rebuffing the attentions of any boy who so much as looked at her, and denying herself a childhood, her mind firmly set on the next deposit in the bank and the news that consumed her daily life.

What the police had omitted to tell Kinsey was that not long after Cheryl had been found and taken to the John Radcliffe Hospital, the vision of the man in the mist had returned. Fiona could only watch on as Cheryl fought off the imaginary creature, her eyes blank, her features almost unrecognisable as a snarling feral beast replaced her reluctantly beautiful child.

Now Cheryl slept, her hands and feet restrained, a thick, brown belt across her waist; to her side, a machine monitored every vital function, her mind a quagmire that needed to be securely observed, censored, saved.

Fiona released her daughter's hand. The tight grip she had lovingly employed had numbed her fingers, and whilst she would have held on forever without protest, she needed a glass of water, a cup of tea or stronger to keep her alert yet calm. Despite the early April morning rising over the county, the close-fitting blinds pulled across the barred, secure windows of the facility were designed to block even the strongest rays of sunshine, and Fiona felt as trapped as her daughter would feel when she awoke and tried to move.

When she awoke—such a thing to consider. Not for the first time during the hours since Cheryl had been found babbling incoherently and screaming to keep the man in the mist away, Fiona wondered who her daughter would be after her ordeal. This trauma would surely change her, even if Cheryl didn't know it herself. Fiona also wondered if she should call her ex-husband. In his time, Ken had been a good father, but if she called him, it would dredge up the past, confirming his daughter had been going out alone at all hours to earn money—money he was supposed to provide. Inevitably, the conversation would turn to Danny, and while Fiona felt no ill will towards Ken, she could have quite cheerfully slapped Danny to hell and back.

Cuddly, reliable Ken. There was a time when he'd been all Fiona had ever wanted. He was dependable, hard-working, a good friend and close confidante, and had been since they were at school together. Then he'd had an accident at work, and all that closeness, all that faithfulness, slowly ebbed away.

Fiona wandered from the private room out into the hall, her eyes, raw from tears that had run dry several hours ago, searching for the doctor who had accompanied them in the ambulance to Oxford where they could provide Cheryl with urgent specialist care, the doctor had told her kindly, touching her shoulder in a soothing gesture. All Fiona had thought about was how she was going to pay for such care. The private facility was hidden away beyond a barrier of meadow and trees, far back from the main road between the town and Wendlefields. She had walked across that very meadow the day Danny had told her he was taking Ken away from her, to get him some real help.

"I cannot do it here, Fiona love," he had drawled in his North Yorkshire accent. "Ken's body is broken, and yes, it will heal, but I cannot make him better with you and Cheryl fussing over him. He needs time—for his mind to remember who he was. You see that, don't you? The damage to his body, to the skull—that will improve by itself, but he needs a different scene if his mind is ever to recover. I have a little place by the sea in Whitby. He will be fine there. He will be a new man." Then like the kind doctor in the ambulance, Danny had touched her shoulder with the comfort of a liar. This was the man who would steal her husband.

Oh, they had all talked, the few friends she'd had, before they too had slowly drifted away. She'd endured the gossip, the strange looks in the supermarket queue, the chatter that suddenly died down when she entered a room. Ken's insurance had meant she could keep herself locked in the house, and Ken, bless him, had insisted she should have every penny, despite Danny's reproach and so-called concerns for his *friend's* state of mind, but it had barely covered the bills, and it couldn't make up for being left to raise Cheryl on her own.

Then today—was it today? The last twenty-four hours had been a nightmare blur of time—another man had touched her shoulder and promised all would be well, that her daughter would be safe, that she would recover because the staff at Wendlefields were the best in the country.

There were a couple of nurses at the desk murmuring as they went over a patient's charts—Cheryl's? Or the boy who had been brought in soon after her? He was a strapping lad, full of rage, strong, athletic, handsome…Fiona felt of flush of feminine guilt, for the boy had reminded her of Ken back in the schooldays. As they had tried to sedate the boy, he had thrashed out, breaking a glass pane with one swift kick, knocking over a desk with the next, and punching a nurse in the jaw—she'd lost a tooth in the process. When they finally subdued him, he had fallen to the floor, and a second needle went into his neck.

A caretaker had come and brushed up the glass, the desk righted, and the nurse led away to be treated. But nothing was ever completely neat and tidy, as Danny had proved when he denied Fiona access. She'd only wanted to see what progress her husband was making. There were always small spots that remained unseen and were missed in the clean-up. In the corner, as white as the skirting board that joined floor to wall, lay the nurse's tooth, forgotten for now, a memory of the morning that would sit in quiet contemplation, waiting to be found.

Fiona approached the two nurses at the desk, smiling weakly, almost ashamed to ask. "Is there somewhere I can get a cup of tea at all, or some water?"

One of the nurses looked up horrified by her own neglect. "I am so sorry, Mrs…erm, Frampton. It has been a rather tense morning for us. We don't normally have people in with our patients. I honestly forgot you were there."

Fiona continued smiling, the kind of smile that others assumed was out of understanding. She was polite and appreciated the vocation that all nurses displayed, but underneath the façade of meek capitulation, she was still a mother who was frightened for her daughter. She wanted to rage, to tear down walls, to fight like she had never fought before, not even when Danny had taken her Ken away. She wanted scream and shake the world apart so that people knew she was there, that something unspeakable had almost succeeded in scaring the life out of her daughter.

But Fiona was not that kind of woman, so she swallowed down any burning resentment and allowed one of the nurses to gently lead her by the arm into the clean, bleach-smelling room that served as a communal rest area for the staff. Fiona wanted to weep, not at the gesture but at the thought of being so compliant. Danny had said she could not have coped with looking after *Kenneth*, and she would have liked the chance to prove him wrong, but deep down, she wondered—would she cope if Cheryl took a turn for the worse? She feared the answer would be no.

The nurse brought over a cup of tea and sat beside her, placing her hand on Fiona's and telling her the team would do all they could for Cheryl, that she was in the best possible place for the care she needed.

Fiona found herself asking, though she already knew the answer, "Is the boy here—the one found locked in his shed?"

The nurse shook her head. "I can't talk about specific patients, but..." She lowered her voice to a level which Fiona strained to hear. "There are three kids about the same age as your daughter, all having seen the same thing—the same man."

There was an edge of contempt to the nurse's voice that left Fiona unsure on how to respond. She smiled again, watery, apologetic, and then, like so often in the past, excused herself from the situation with a soft thank-you and went back outside to the hallway. Passing the desk, she glanced over an open newspaper left there—a raid over Tripoli, people dead, planes which had taken off from the airbase up the road, all in another country. So much death; so much terror.

A memory surfaced: a day out in the Midlands back in 1974. She and Ken had taken a train to Birmingham for a few hours' shopping, just the two of them—a chance to do something without a child in tow, Cheryl safely at home with her grandmother, playing with toys, not a care in the world. Since the union meeting in which the workforce was told half of them would be let go at the end of September, Ken had been working six days a week, fourteen hours a day—long shifts with little reward, barely keeping their heads above water. They had both giggled like children, real laughter perhaps for the first time since Cheryl had been born, all the way from the train station—at the time, it marked the town's boundary but now cut a swathe through the centre of it—to Birmingham.

The cold day had warmed up by the time they arrived in the city centre. Fiona preferred Birmingham to London; it was less packed, more open, less confusing. Everybody was gearing up for Christmas after a year of strife. The country was in freefall, and Ken had been distant, he said because of the pressure of work, but for a few hours, Fiona had him by her side and only pleasant decisions to make of what to get their daughter for Christmas.

They'd had dinner, bought presents, laughed too much and shown their love to each other. A couple shyly embraced as darkness bled its way into the air above and office workers poured out onto the city streets. Fiona suggested a couple of drinks before the last train home—anything to keep the day going, to keep Ken in a good mood.

Time, though, ticks away even the most jovial of moods. It eats into the happiness and lets the core of sadness show through, a once-snug worm shrouded in the blood of a bite taken from the apple. Fiona recalled later that she thought she'd seen the woman who left a briefcase by the rear entrance of the Mulberry Bush. She could have given evidence to the police, but Ken had told her not to, to play dumb and not get drawn in. They were lucky to be alive. They'd left twenty minutes before the bomb ripped through the foundations of the pub underneath the Rotunda. Why had they left? They'd been so happy, revelling in their first proper day together with none of Ken's grumpy sulking. He'd been lucky. He'd kept his job, but he was expected to work harder, provide more, be more cunning in how the business went forward. He was exhausted, and his mood had reflected it.

In the years since that night, Fiona had let it fade into memory and permitted her former husband's point of view become her own, so that now, in her mind, she had been the reluctant one; what had happened was not her business, but it had still happened. She remembered the screams, the horrible, piercing, damning screams of the injured, the pleas of the dying, the quiet condemnation of the dead. Standing outside, she had been trying to make her husband laugh again, the bag of toys in her hand, when the blast had knocked her to the ground. In the silence that followed, her ears ringing, her vision impaired by dust and smoke, it took her a while to discover Ken had been thrown through the air and landed a few feet away. Then came the screaming, so much screaming—*who was screaming?*

Commotion around her, the memory segued into the now as the nurse who had made her tea and held her hand rushed past, almost knocking Fiona over, the cup not being so lucky as it slipped from her grip and shattered on the floor.

The screaming grew louder, peppered with the sort of language she had only heard her father use when he was drunk, which, before he died, was almost every day. Fear stabbed her chest again—was that Cheryl? Was her baby in pain? The sound developed into something feral, aggressive, a fox chewing at its leg to free itself from the farmer's trap. Fiona put her hands up to her ears and ran back to the private room, nonplussed yet relieved by the sight of her sweet, often weird, determined daughter, quiet and unmoving.

The screaming went on. Two more nurses and a doctor ran past the room, and Fiona followed gingerly, every step a reminder of those she had taken outside the Mulberry Bush, towards people stumbling in blind confusion, the scene of carnage seared into her memory. This time, there was no smoke, no fire, no glass on the floor, no panic in her mind, just concern. Another doctor ran from the opposite end of the corridor, his white coat flapping around a frame no longer suited to such a task.

Fiona felt Ken's hand on her shoulder, pulling her back from the scene, the wailing of police cars and ambulances, the terrified gossip of onlookers and the silence of the injured. *We cannot help them, Fi.* His words, cracked, the strain he was under finally shattering, had been the turning point, the moment he had left her. Or had he been thinking of leaving her before that day? Had he wanted to see her happy one last time before telling her it was over?

A rush of images bombarded her. Her throat dried, her vision blurred, not through smoke or the after-effects of the bomb that was followed shortly after by another on New Street, but by tears constant inadequacy, of a life spoon-fed by a lie.

She reached the room within which the screaming was now acute, stabbing at the ears and splitting the air in half. She didn't recognise the boy before her, had never seen him before. One of the nurses was trying to keep hold of him, pinning down his arm while a doctor attempted to stick a needle in him. The boy bucked as if possessed, the sudden motion of his body snapping the restraint that held his left leg, freeing him to kick out at the kind nurse, sending her flying across the room with a crunch of bone as her shoulder connected with brick and mortar.

Fiona pressed her hands hard against her skull, drowning out the sound, but she kept her eyes open. A doctor with a yellow, ethereal face looked down at the boy yet made no attempt to help his colleagues. Then, with a final choking sound, the screaming stopped, and the boy whispered his last into the air, spraying blood over the needle-wielding doctor's white coat. All the while, the yellow-faced doctor watched on, and then almost as if an afterthought, he looked directly at Fiona, probing deep into her mind. Placing a bony finger to his smile-stretched, thin, cruel lips, signalling for her silence.

She never saw the nurse being helped up from the floor, didn't hear the doctor pronounce the boy dead. She simply fell to the ground, blessed relief sweeping over her.

Chapter Eight

HOW MUCH FURTHER, Bill?"

PC Bill Taylor stopped walking and looked back at Kinsey, whose face was drawn and tired.

"Not enough sleep again last night, mate? I told you all that drinking after hours and the constant running around would eventually catch up with you."

Bill leaned back against a tree and laughed as Kinsey struggled to catch up. Bill's brother Desmond had been in the Kinsey's year at school, but Bill hadn't known the local journalist until they were introduced one evening at the police station.

"If you want local knowledge, Bill, you can't go wrong with getting to know my old pal Simon. He'll always be able to point out to you the whys and wherefores of this old town." Desmond respected Simon Kinsey, and even though he had moved away for a new life in Cornwall, he never failed to remind Bill of the kindness of the man who had saved him from being beaten up in school on his first day.

They would never be the type of friends that Desmond believed they were, but Bill knew, despite the ten-year age gap, he could trust the journalist's discretion when push came to shove. He had helped the police with their investigations and arrests on many occasions, even keeping some of his colleagues in beer when money was short.

Kinsey finally caught up and put his arm out against the tree. "Cheeky bugger. If your brother was here now, he'd make your life a misery for mocking the afflicted. I will have you know that McCarthy and I were busy finishing the story of the two kids well after midnight, and what were you doing? Snoring on the sofa, listening to those worn-out reggae albums your brother left you? Getting to second base with Shirley from the hockey club?"

Bill raised an eyebrow in mock contempt, but there was something in Kinsey's tone. The smile was there, plastered all over the man's face, but his words, the way he delivered them, were like barbs of wire scraping at Bill's ears. Kinsey may have been amiable, a good man to be around, and Bill had seen him drunk—had helped him chase the final drop of whisky from a bottle of twenty-year-old malt—but this was something he hadn't seen before. The man was in pain. Bill let it go and pointed down towards the river.

"Down there. See where the grass has been pulled out at the root? That's where we found the boy."

He slapped Kinsey on the back and carefully slid down the small embankment. Kinsey followed, a grimace on his face that he didn't let his old friend's kid brother see.

***

Buck up, Kinsey. Nobody needs to see how shit you're feeling.

Kinsey mustered up the strength from somewhere to slide down the embankment and join Bill Taylor. In front of them was the patch of ground on which the lad from Liverpool had been found, foaming at the mouth in incoherent, vile words and shrieking that there was a man in the woods coming after him. Of course, a search had found nothing, but after the events of the day before, nobody was taking chances.

There was not a single blade of grass left in the immediate area, a perfect circle torn out, shredded apart and scattered to the April winds.

"What does that look like to you, Bill?"

The policeman pondered for a moment before replying dryly, "Someone making a point about the way the woods are kept, or someone who just doesn't like grass."

Kinsey frowned. There was something in the circular pattern, an image that sprang to mind of safety. He got down on his knees and looked closer at the patch of bare ground left by the frightened, terrified boy. There were scuff marks and grooved-out indentations as if the boy had been constantly turning in circles, whirling around as if being attacked from all sides.

"This is a keep, a barrier he dug out to keep himself safe." Kinsey said under his breath, though still loud enough for Bill Taylor to hear.

Tutting aloud, the policeman heaved Kinsey up by his elbow. "What foolish notions are these going around your head? Look, I don't think you are well, mate. You look like shit—even worse than yesterday over at the Sterhan Close. What's going on?"

Kinsey shrugged off the helping hand. "Just a bad case of the vapours. Need a holiday—get out of the country for a week or two, sit on a beach and look off into the distance."

If Bill Taylor suspected anything major, he didn't show it. He laughed and smacked Kinsey on the back more forcefully this time. Kinsey winced and screwed his eyes up.

"You leave town? I'm amazed you even go to Oxford. Your idea of a break is a week propping up the bar in the Swan and Signet with a bag full of loose change for the juke box and challenging all-comers to a game of pool. Don't give me that holiday shit, Kinsey." Bill Taylor laughed once more, heartily and without malice, and Kinsey joined in, though Taylor's words had cut something deep within.

"How far are we from the traveller's camp site, Bill?"

"Just beyond that group of weeping willows along the bank—about a couple of hundred yards away."

"I want to take a look at something. Won't be long."

"Do you want me to come with you?

Kinsey noticed concern flash in the policeman's eyes. It was momentary, but it was there. What did Bill think he was going to do? Find a tree, lasso a rope to it and kick out at the April air?

He almost asked the question aloud but managed to keep it to himself. He didn't know what was wrong with him today. Sure, the pain was bad, but he wouldn't normally bite someone's head off for showing a measure of compassion or friendship.

"All good, mate," he said instead. "Look, you go on. I know you—your stomach will be grunting soon. Shirley doesn't feed you like your mum does, eh?" This time, Kinsey laughed for real, and Taylor joined in, his deep rumble filling the surroundings and causing a couple of birds in the reeds to startle and take flight.

"Good point! I'll walk on ahead—if I see your boss, shall I tell her that you won't be long?"

Tell her want you want. "Yep, that's cool. See you later—give Shirley a hug from me."

Kinsey didn't wait for a reply. He turned his back on the Jamaican-born policeman and walked off further into the woods, sticking close to the river line, treading firmly into the earth to make sure he didn't slip and fall. He walked for more than 200 yards, nearer 300, and thought he had missed the clearing completely. Furious with himself for letting pain dominate his thoughts, he readied to retrace his steps. Then, almost as if he had stumbled upon some ancient artefact left unguarded on a café table, he found the clearing, hidden by a circle of willow, rowan, ash and Midland thorn.

He scrambled through the abundance of angelica, St. John's wort and asphodel, taking care not to crush the flowers, and emerged in the middle of the clearing, within it several shallow ruts caused by caravan wheels. The ground was bare of grass for fifty yards in each direction, in its place the leaves of asphodel sparkling with the April morning dew. Over his head was clear sky, a central chute of air untouched by a single branch or stray protruding twig, and he heard birdsong—a warning: *here, strangers dwell.* A line from Tennyson crept into his mind and took root: *Others in Elysian valleys dwell, Resting weary limbs at last on beds of asphodel.*

For the first time since he was a boy, he wanted to lie down on the slumbering, quiet earth, be still and motionless. Lowering himself gently onto the flower heads, calm washed over him. *I could fall asleep here forever and know I would be safe*, he thought and recognised it was true. *Is that what brought those travellers here? Did they dig out the circle? But that was years ago—this would all have grown over again.*

Kinsey put his hand to his forehead. No pain; no headache. Whatever this place was, it had awoken something in him that he could not name. In the distance, a twig cracked, and the birds above him stopped their song. Leaning up on one elbow, Kinsey saw mist rising from the river and felt an instant chill flow through the circle. Standing from his bed of flowers, he watched the mist thicken and shift, moving in a swirl like the beginnings of a tornado. He stayed calm, reminding himself there was nothing to fear; deep in his gut he knew he was safe.

The swirl of mist grew in intensity and took on a sickly jaundiced tinge as if someone had thrown yellow dye over Turner's 'Chichester Canal'. The air began to smell different, and the tentacles of the mist probed for microscopic holes in the protective circle, injecting disease in minute quantities into his space. Kinsey was not sure if colour could feel emotion, but he was certain that the woods could: an evil had wandered into its domain, and it was reacting to it. In front of him, the mist cleared slightly, and a tall, pale-faced man appeared, his sunken eyes staring into Kinsey's. Long, sharp teeth bared, the man sniffed the air, recoiling at the aroma of asphodel. His body juddered and shimmered, phantom pain etched upon his sallow, gaunt features. Kinsey stood perfectly still, intuitively knowing he should not confront the man before him; the stranger could not get through the barrier provided by the trees and the flowers that formed the circle.

The figure, surely more creature than man, placed one of its long, bony hands on a nearby tree that was half in, half out of the circle. On the healthy bark, a bright, silver shadow started to appear, to grow and spread, crawling and penetrating deep into the tree itself, rotting it from the inside, but only to the point where it joined the circle. From Kinsey's side of the barrier, the tree still flourished, grandly majestic in its opulence, yet the longer the figure in the mist held onto the trunk beyond the circle, the more the bark withered away, crumbling into dust until all that was left was the perfectly preserved half, its newly revealed wood glistening.

In the distance, Kinsey heard the muffled sound of someone calling his name but didn't respond. He continued to watch the figure, its anger growing, its teeth bared back to the yellow-stained gums. Kinsey heard his name again, the mist making it hard to detect from which direction, but he recognised McCarthy's voice, her distinctive bellow when she was on the verge of losing her temper, and she sounded closer than before.

Still, Kinsey didn't reply. He wasn't sure he believed what he was seeing was real. The rationalist in him told him he was dreaming or hallucinating—had he absorbed some of the asphodel? It was known for its natural high, which was not unpleasant, but the after-effects could be deadly, but no. The balance of evidence told him this *was* real. What the kids had told the police was true: this being existed and could send a child's mind off-kilter, yet somehow had not infected Kinsey.

With another shout, McCarthy found her way through the trees into the clearing. The figure, upon hearing her voice, drew back, letting go of the tree. The mist folded in on itself, and the yellow tinge dissipated, fading into the background until there was nothing there, nothing but an ordinary woodland glade with untouched grass beneath Kinsey's feet. No flower heads, no rotted tree burned and scorched by a demon's hand; just McCarthy standing in front of him, talking softly, asking if he was all right.

Kinsey blinked and focused on her face, deeply etched lines betraying her...what? Hatred? No. Deeper than that. Concern. Alarm. Fear.

"I said, are you all right, Simon?"

Kinsey stared at her, bewildered. When was the last time she had called him by his first name? Long before they had slept together, perhaps when he was a kid, sixteen and fresh from school, eager to please, impatient to learn from her. Twenty years ago. He smiled at the thought and then recoiled as McCarthy slapped him, the collision of palm and cheek ringing through the air around them.

"Seriously, Kinsey, what the fuck is the matter with you? I was calling you for ages! I could see you standing here, staring into space, clear as bloody day. I don't like being ignored." She stepped back a pace and folded her arms tightly. If they'd been in the office, this would be the moment before doors slammed. McCarthy was a volcano ready to blow. Yet Kinsey felt calm, at peace. He wasn't scared. His headache had gone, and he didn't want to have an argument about his behaviour or be drawn into discussing why he would never intentionally ignore her. It all made little sense to him at that moment.

"Did you see the figure?" he asked. "The pale-faced man standing by that tree?"

"What man? There was only you standing here like a mannequin about to fall over."

"There was a man," Kinsey insisted. "He came out of the mist—surely you saw the mist?"

"Kinsey, look around you. It's a beautiful morning—well, for us it is, anyway. There was no mist, no man. Just you with a goofy expression on your face. Did you smoke a joint last night? Stop off at that friend of yours and pick up a tab? I've warned you before—not when we have a story to follow up."

She was still furious, and Kinsey couldn't understand why.

"No, look…" He put his hands out in front of him, palms towards her, and chose his next word carefully. "Samantha…I think I saw what the three kids saw, but it couldn't get to me. There seemed to be a barrier it couldn't get through. It tried to intimidate me by making that tree over there appear to rot. I promise you, I have not felt this good in a while. I'm wide awake and sober—I haven't taken anything other than a sleeping pill when I got home from the office last night."

***

McCarthy looked Kinsey in the eye. She thought she always knew when he was spinning her a yarn. He was damn good at his job, and while he could be a lousy human being, the one thing he didn't do was lie. Even when her ex-husband gave Kinsey the chance to offer a simple denial, he refused to take it. It hadn't been about ownership, a simple fumble in the cupboard during the dull hours; Kinsey genuinely cared for her, had done for years.

"We had sex," he said, "but I didn't do it to get one over on you, or to take her from you."

"If I didn't have so much to do today—if there wasn't a follow-up we needed to get down on paper immediately—I would cane your arse, Kinsey. There's something wrong, and you won't open up, but we need to go to the facility at Wendlefields. One of the boys has died, and it wasn't a nice, easy death, apparently."

***

If peace and understanding had become a part of Kinsey's recent mantra, then it was blown apart under the heavy fire of reality. It was bad enough that three kids had been exposed to who knew what, but to die so young—it broke Kinsey's heart, one up until that moment he'd forgotten he had.

Walking back through the woods and past the remaining police officer left on duty at the farm gate, Kinsey asked McCarthy again if she really hadn't seen the figure, the mist, the flowers, the half-rotted tree. As McCarthy drove them both away from the scene, she looked at Kinsey out of the corner of her eye and shook her head. "There was just you, silent and dumb." She smiled broadly. "Just the way I like you."

Chapter Nine

C YRIL MARBON DETESTED going into town at the best of times, but walking two miles there and two miles back early in the morning was something he could have done without. Yesterday, a hero, today, a dog's body once more, playing fetch and carry for his master. He grumbled as he walked, slipping back into his old language as he did so, one far removed from the cultivated country accent he had affected over the years; one that would have struck fear into people of a certain disposition and station in life.

He knew the woods like the back of his hand, every shortcut hidden by the overgrown grass. He could, if he'd wished, navigate from the gatehouse to river with his eyes closed, but he hardly ever closed his eyes. Too many ghosts waiting to catch him asleep. He powered on, his lengthy stride double that of the young girl he had found screaming yesterday morning. The police had played their part, but it was all down to him, *the hero*. Something to share with his old comrades—if ever he saw them again, not that it was ever likely. Several were in jail, old men before their time; others were dead; some had gone missing, last seen heading to the USA—Boston, New York, anywhere the home flag still meant something pure. The new kids running the show in their place had certainly stepped up the game, all too fast and furious for his liking. If he were in charge, if he'd still had the ear of the leader as he had back in '72, no one would have survived the Hyde Park bombing.

Marbon thought on this as he walked purposefully through the woods. It was a shame when civilians were hurt, but it always served a purpose. The pictures of now-dead kids, of smiling, loving grandparents torn to pieces made great headlines and sensational broadcasts. He had nothing personal against them; it was about bringing the targets home, making the British public aware it was all done in retaliation: an eye-for-eye for the devil you brought onto our shores. He swore under his breath as his foot snagged a branch.

"All legitimate," he mumbled. "All appropriate." Especially the one in Brighton. He had cheered that night, albeit tempered by discovering the intended target had survived, but still. That aside, it was a great day. He had been late taking the papers to the sitting room for his master. Thankfully, the old man had been late down too, celebrating his own deal with farmers in the area—animal feed at a more reasonable price, a substantial profit made all round.

Another branch poking out almost tripped Marbon this time.

"All valid targets. All valid targets." Marbon's accent grew more pronounced as he repeated the words of rhetoric. He regretted not being part of the group for a decade or more, so many wasted opportunities, but then he would have probably been caught by now and ended up rotting in a jail like so many others. All for the cause. He thought back to the hatred he'd felt when he switched on the news back in February '79. Some old friends had not gone home that night, Glasgow being their final call at the bar.

Deep in thought and showering himself in resentment, Marbon didn't notice the woods stir, the trees groan under the weight of their branches, bark cracking from the strain of the movement, wood splintering and the grumble of the earth shifting under its own volition. Wrapped up in his own world of hate and fear, Marbon didn't hear a thing.

"Why did that girl have to die? All I wanted was fun. Don't I deserve it? I had to let go of the responsibility of command at some point, to function as a human being. Sex is a human need—not my fault I picked up a junkie. Nasty creatures—I fought against that decadence. It's the only part of the deal the Americans hated."

They'd had such a good evening together. A disco, several drinks and then several more. She'd been fun, bright—just the girl he'd been looking for, one who might even be sympathetic to the cause. Then, as he checked them in to the Bonnycliffe Hotel, he noticed her drop something on the floor: a small, clear, plastic bag containing a substance Marbon knew only too well. He said nothing, just smiled as she headed to the door, looking over her shoulder to check he was following her.

"Damned junkies. It was her that drove me out of the group, not the money. I could explain that. Embezzlement my arse. That was mercy money for the families caught up in the awful vice that the Americans had brought to the table."

Still, he pounded on. A bright, clear morning always made him feel better.

She was found dead the next day, and Marbon became a wanted man, even though he insisted to anyone who'd listen that he was not to blame for her death.

"Ah but, you would say that, Cyril." He affected a high-pitched, mocking tone. "Of course you would. Not guilty—you weren't even in the room when she died—but the staff remember you, the middle-aged man fondling the bottom of the young teenage girl. Bit sick, don't you think? Do you not understand the pressure you have put on us? For God's sake, man, you were meant to be heading the campaign this winter. Now we might have to call off the Birmingham job! What were you thinking..."

A repeated chorus from the room, the sound of one man's voice echoing off the walls, condemning him to run out of town, no praise for his past efforts, just a warning scurrying around his ear. *Get out, get out, get out.*

Marbon brought an end to that train of thought. It never led anywhere productive. Already, the resentment was too much for him.

"Concentrate on yesterday. You were a hero again. You were a big noise, and didn't that piss off that bloody local reporter?"

If he hated anyone more than his old commander for the injustice he had caused, then Simon Kinsey came a close second. He had been a thorn in his side for years, always asking questions, scrutinising him, even one time in the pouring rain shoving a series of photographs under his nose, each attaching him to some atrocity or other. Marbon had had enough by that point. Quick to anger at the best of times, he lashed out at the journalist but, failing to connect with a punch, fell to his knees. Kinsey had stood over him, grinning as if he had beaten him, as if his demise in the rain was proof positive he had been there the night when Birmingham was bombed. But Marbon was a patient man. One day, he would have his revenge on Kinsey—on all that let him suffer.

Circling the river, he saw in the distance the fields that led to the estate in which Tom Solden and his father had lived. From there, it was only a short walk to the town, if you knew the right way.

So busy in thought was he, Marbon didn't notice he was being followed, nor that the air around him had become stale, musty, decaying as he breathed.

Chapter Ten

I F KINSEY AND McCarthy had hoped to keep the story to themselves for another twenty-four hours, then the scene that greeted them at Wendlefields soon dispelled that journalistic expectation.

Outside the building, a huge crowd had gathered, some national news reporters whom McCarthy and Kinsey recognised, some locals who had caught wind of the morning's events. Between them and the door stood a middle-aged man dressed in what had probably started out as a smart, well-tailored suit, now ripped at the shoulders, scuffed and torn for all to see on national television that very night, as to the right of the crowd, Kinsey spotted a BBC cameraman and a reporter talking over the crowd's angry, accusing roar.

"Shit!" McCarthy hissed.

While he didn't feel much like it, Kinsey grinned for appearances and muttered, "There goes our story, Sam." He turned towards her, allowing his face to register the displeasure they both felt.

The crowd became more vocal, more animated, and in the distance, Kinsey heard the sirens of two police cars. Catching one of the newspaper men by the arm, he smiled, letting his teeth to show. "Hey, pal, how long you all been here?"

The reporter looked at him, no recognition in his face, not even a glimmer of the usual joviality of the dailies when they smelled a good story.

"About twenty minutes. Got a call from the editor a couple of hours ago about a strange occurrence in the woods yesterday.

Luckily, I was in the area, getting ready to interview a couple of servicemen from up at the airbase." The man turned his attention from Kinsey for a brief second, shouted something that vaguely sounded like an insult to the man in the suit, then added, "Pleased, really. The story in Tripoli is just too far away, and this, well, this is on our doorstep, isn't it? Young kid dying, two others in seclusion—what do you think? Drugs, mass panic, kids looking for attention…" His voice petered out, as he turned his attention back to the mob demanding answers that nobody dared believe.

Kinsey stepped away from the crowd and pulled McCarthy with him. She gave him a hard stare but followed his gaze to the two police cars, which had come to a screeching halt yards from the rabble. Six officers spilled out and waded through the crowd until they were standing guard in front of the man in the tattered suit. Kinsey spotted Bill Taylor snarling with pleasure at three of the encroaching reporters. *Poor sod. Bet he hasn't even had a chance to call Shirley and tell her he wants an early night tonight.*

A voice boomed out from behind them all, and Kinsey could have danced a jig of delight had his headache not returned with a thumping start. The crowd parted and allowed Inspector Sears through, the sudden hush causing Kinsey to chuckle inwardly.

"Ladies and gentlemen of the press, and to all you others who have come down here today looking for answers, my name is Detective Inspector Laurence Sears. Some of you know me. Some of you I have had the pleasure to meet on various occasions. Some—" He looked in the direction of one or two of the newshounds from the more disreputable, sensationalist red-top newspapers. "—I'm surprised you can tear yourself away from the events unfolding in North Africa. Now, I must ask most of you to leave, or have you forgotten this is private property? At the moment, there is nothing to tell you, but know that in due course, the hospital will be releasing a statement."

"What danger are our kids in?"

"Is there a pervert on the loose here?"

Several other people chimed in with questions of their own, and for a brief second, the melee threatened to break out again, but Inspector Sears was a no-nonsense kind of officer, twelve years in the armed forces, fast-tracked through the police in under five. He frowned sternly at a couple of officers, and they stood ready to dispel the crowd.

"May I remind you, and this is for the members of the press and for the local parents—you included, Serena Cox—that my officers will remove you from this establishment if you give them cause. This is a secure private unit, and as such, until I ask you to gather later, *in an orderly group*, you will vacate these grounds immediately."

Kinsey had never liked the heavy hand of the law, he preferred the softly, softly approach, but even he had to admit at times an arm twisted up the back yielded better results. He looked over to where Serena Cox stood, half expecting her to sullen, subdued into behaving herself after being singled out by the inspector; far from it. If anything, she looked ready for a fight. She was one of the great barrack-room lawyers of her time: no cause was too great, no argument too small for her to make her opinion known. Without warning, she made a break for the steps and managed to get within touching distance of the inspector, whereby she wagged her finger and called him a liar, a puppet of the state, a servant of the idle rich, a traitor to his class. Bill Taylor placed his enormous hand on her shoulder and for his trouble he received an elbow to the face. The gunshot crack of contact silenced the crowd.

Kinsey moved forward quickly, his headache forgotten, as two police officers tackled the woman for whom Greenham Common was a by-word for logical protest. She fell, her features twisted, framed in a moment of anger and snarling, feral abuse. Bill Taylor swayed under the weight of the assault, blood gushing down his face and onto his uniform, and all the while Serena Cox writhed like a demon possessed, disgraced and detestable.

Kinsey reached Taylor quickly, ducking underneath the ensuing fracas, the hounds of the national papers suddenly gratified by the extra element to the story that would earn them praise from their bosses. Kinsey cared little for that; his main concern was for his friend's welfare, but something deep in his stomach turned and growled. He had known Serena for some time. She always had an opinion, sometimes verging on insane, sometimes as clear and concise as someone who had studied law at Oxford could be. She was forthright, intelligent, driven certainly, not out of a need to cause the breakdown of civility but by a rigid sense of right and wrong, of wanting peace. There wasn't a war she was afraid to tackle.

At the same time, under other circumstances, she would not have injured someone like Bill Taylor. Something had pushed Serena over the edge. Her daughter was about the same age as the three teenagers found in a state of disturbed frenzy, so it shouldn't surprise Kinsey or anyone else she had reacted strongly, but the look on her face was not just one of anger—not even fear for the town's children. It was a look Kinsey had seen on a young woman many years before, not long after he had completed his training and exams—his first big break in journalism.

He had been called to a garage on the Queen's Bridge side of the town where a woman had been found along with her baby, who had been missing for a few hours. They were both still alive, but Kinsey had no idea how, especially the child. The mother had pierced the boy's skin with several hypodermic needles, each filled with enough heroin to kill the boy twice over. It was only by the grace of God, or her own drug-fuelled state, that she hadn't pressed down and injected him. Her demeanour on revival was one of confusion and chaos as she begged for someone to tell her where her child was. The mournful pity in her cries had broken Kinsey's heart. The last he'd heard was the child had been adopted by a family on the other side of the county; his mother never saw him again.

Focusing once more on the present, Kinsey winced in pain. His headache had returned in full force, making his shoulders ache and his back stiff. Leading Bill Taylor inside the building, he glanced back for McCarthy, hoping she would follow. The two officers were still trying to restrain Serena, who had lost all reason and her chance of being at home that evening. Meanwhile, Laurence Sears had regained control of the situation and had ordered the television crews to stop filming. Peace had finally descended. As the remaining police officers ushered the press down towards the main road, Kinsey knew Sam could be relied on to get a story them, to get a quote. It was up to him to get the perspective from inside the building. After all, they had broken the news, even it if was just to a small but loyal readership.

What did surprise Kinsey was Serena Cox being led into the hospital just behind him, aided by the man in the tattered suit and the two officers who had battled her earlier but were holding her steady now all the fight had left her. She seemed shell-shocked, semi-catatonic, suffering from what the services and survivor groups called post-traumatic stress, her previously wild eyes dull and half closed.

With relief, Kinsey passed Bill Taylor into a nurse's safe hands. He was no doctor, but he knew a busted jaw and broken nose when he saw them. The nurse took Bill into a side room while one of her colleagues called through to the doctor's station for assistance and prescribed pain relief.

"Poor sod. At least now he won't have to eat his girlfriend's cooking tonight!" It was a poor joke that resulted in the nurse giving him the once-over and then dismissing him as a representative of all the men who had tried in vain to make her smile. Her disdain was only broken by Serena Cox being frog-marched past the enquiries desk.

"Hasser, page Dr. Moran now," the man in the suit ordered. "Tell him to meet me in room six. Make sure he brings the straps."

It was the first time Kinsey had heard him speak, and for a man who had been set upon by the baying crowd, he sounded surprisingly unmoved by the events, unflappable, still in control. Never mind the jacket pocket dangling by a thread, the tie hanging at an angle that suggested someone had come close to throttling him or his knees poking out of his trousers. This was the demeanour of someone used to getting his own way.

"Oh, and Hasser? Please ring my wife and ask her bring down my spare suit—she'll have to use the service road, not the main entrance..." He stopped suddenly, noticing Kinsey standing close by. "And you are?"

"Simon Kinsey. I work for the local paper, but for now, I came in with the injured policeman. He's a friend of mine."

"Well, you don't have to wait. My team will soon see him cared for. I suspect you would be better off with those other animals that call themselves the free press." He looked down at his suit to emphasise the point and then carried on with his commandeered unit of the thin blue line and the prisoner in his possession.

Kinsey smiled as the man in the suit walked away, then stuck up two fingers. The nurse, unamused, turned her back on him and dialled out to the doctor as ordered by the man in the dishevelled suit. Kinsey took the hint. He knew when he had struck out, not that he cared these days. The headaches made such ideas of fun almost unbearable. Could he remember when they started? Had they always been there underneath the surface?

Realising he wasn't going to be of any use here, he headed back towards the exit, wondering where McCarthy had got to. As he approached the door, his train of thought was interrupted by a tentative, gentle tap on his shoulder. It was so light, only a cough of awkwardness alerted him that someone wanted to talk to him.

"Excuse me—you are Simon Kinsey, aren't you?" The hesitancy in the woman's voice caught him off guard, the frightened, mouse-like expression she adopted was one of pity, the cut to her eye softening the blow. Kinsey stared at her for a moment, her face familiar but out of place, the headache growling where recognition should be.

Undeterred, the woman pressed on, her voice quiet. "You came to my house once, not long after my husband had been injured. You told me that the firm were going to claim negligence on his part because he'd been seen drinking. You told me you were trying to help. I just want to say, you did help. We won. I always read your stories in the paper." She offered this last bit of information as if trying to smooth out a stubborn wrinkle on a shirt, carefully, so there was no possibility of a burr or a snag—anything that might lead the reporter to ignore or dismiss her.

A vague recollection came to him of a tidy woman, proud but unassuming—did her husband run off with another man or was that just a rumour half remembered? Something about the Birmingham pub bombings? Or had his memory embellished the story in a moment of boredom?

"I'm Fiona Frampton, Cheryl's mum," the woman offered. "The young girl who was found in the woods yesterday."

The relief must have shown on Kinsey's face, and he felt himself blush. Not three weeks ago, he would have remembered like a shot, his instant recall a trait that frightened some and impressed others. Fiona Frampton reached out as if she was going to shake his hand but instead touched him on the elbow in a fleeting glimpse of intimacy and kindness. Kinsey remembered her fully now, the memory rushing back and beating away the headache with a large stick. Fiona Frampton. Yes, her husband had caused a stir when he left with his friend, a physical therapist, and moved away to Yorkshire. Unlike many of his generation, Kinsey held with the maxim 'live and let live': an aunt of his had been ostracised by the family for having a relationship with another woman whilst at university. Kinsey had kept in touch with her until the day she took her own life. It was the only time he'd had any type of serious conversation with his father over his actions.

"Forgive me, Ms. Frampton, of course I remember you. It has been a long twenty-four hours, as I suspect it has for you. How's Cheryl holding up, is she all right?"

Fiona started to cry. "She's stable. Sedated, but she will recover. I suppose you heard about the young boy brought in this morning. You know, he...died?"

Kinsey nodded gravely. It was something he hadn't considered properly when McCarthy told him, but now, after all that had transpired in the last hour, it hit how fortunate, no matter the circumstances, Fiona's daughter and Tom Solden had been.

"Mr. Kinsey..." Fiona started nervously, almost stuttering his name, "is there somewhere we can talk? Properly, I mean, away from ear-wigging nurses and doctors. I saw something that upset me in here, I was in the room when the boy died and...my mind is a mess."

Kinsey looked around to see if anyone was watching. Satisfied there was no one, he took out a pen and paper and wrote down his home phone number.

"I usually keep the phone off at night. Nobody who knows this number will try to call me during that time. Call me tonight, and use my first name. I will know it is you. We will talk then." As an afterthought, he added, "Unless you want my colleague there as well? She might be more help."

The prospect of talking to two people seemed to horrify Fiona, who hurriedly shook her head and confirmed she would ring him later that evening.

When the phone sounded that night, the shrill ringing pulling Kinsey out of deep, troubling thoughts, he wondered if he had done the right thing.

Chapter Eleven

McCARTHY WATCHED KINSEY run towards the injured policeman and sighed—not out of exasperation at being left behind. She'd never been that type of woman, and wars were fought on many fronts. Whilst some of her friends might have pouted at being forgotten in the heat of the moment, she took it as a sign: Kinsey would be okay on his own; she would prepare the machine guns for action.

She'd known Laurence Sears since he came to the town after leaving the forces, and it was him she had made for as the pack of journalists trudged away.

He smiled at her, friendly but firm. "I can't say much for the moment, Samantha, only because I don't know anything myself. What I can tell you is what already know. A boy died this morning—I can't release his name until we get hold of his parents, but I've been in touch with our counterparts in Liverpool, who t are dealing with the situation. Other than that, I have nothing."

Inwardly, McCarthy groaned but remained upbeat. "I have a favour to ask of you, Laurence. When you release the name, I'd like the chance to interview the family first—I presume you'll be bringing them down here to identify the body. I know I'm asking a lot, but can we keep it local for just a bit longer? After all, these hounds won't care about the town. They've probably never heard of it except for seeing it on the map for the proposed motorway we're told is coming our way. Why let the vultures have yet another victory when you know I will handle it with care?"

If that wasn't enough to sway the detective inspect, McCarthy had other ways, all above board, all gifted, but she hoped it wouldn't come to having to spend money she could ill afford to waste.

"Look, Samantha...Sam, they won't be able to identify the body. There's nothing left of him. Fuck...look...I didn't say that, but you won't get your interview. This part of the story will not exist beyond you and me..." He pointed to the long trail of parents and journalists filing to the gate at the end of the drive. "And none of those with children nor the hounds, as you call them—none of them must know or we'll have a mass panic on our hands. The parents won't be coming down. We're going to prevent this from...leaking out."

The inspector had chosen his words carefully, but that didn't mean McCarthy liked what she was hearing. *Nothing left of him. Nothing? Impossible.* Suddenly she felt jealous of Kinsey. He was inside, probably with his feet up on a stool, a cup of tea in one hand, a friendly nurse hanging on his every word, and all the while he'd be sucking up the information like a vacuum on a dirt-ridden floor.

"Come on, Laurence. A young, healthy Scouse lad, full of muscle and brawn, and you are saying that you cannot...what, see a body? His face? Don't be so fucking ridiculous." McCarthy snorted, visibly scornful, though her mouth had run ahead of her brain.

"I'm going to let that one pass, Samantha, but don't push it. I've seen the mess in that room. A photograph was pushed under my nose as soon as I got out of my car, and whilst I couldn't understand what I was looking at, trust me when I say there is no body—*no boy* left to identify. Now, I need to go in and see to my injured officer. You can either wait here for Kinsey—I'll give you that much in return for now—or you can join them." He nodded towards the departing news hounds. "Perhaps you might be able to conjure a story out of thin air."

Sears looked guilty for his retort, but it was too late to take it back. Instead, he smiled apologetically.

Touché. McCarthy shook his hand, noting the warmth between them had chilled. It would take more than a couple of tickets to the theatre and dinner at Angelo's for him and his wife to thaw the tension, but it would happen. McCarthy had already lost one male friend due to recklessness. Never again. She watched Sears turn on his heels, a military man to the last, and smiled at his ease of elegance, feeling a little sick at how she had spoken to him.

As she walked down the road towards the other journalists, she realised this was what had deterred her from joining a national. Here in the town, she was able to reason, to use cunning sparingly; she got results not by being underhanded but by being trusted. If she were to join the hounds, she would have to change her style, become more aggressive, uncaring about those she tapped for information, and she didn't want that. At least not with the locals of the town. As for the hounds, that was a different matter.

Chapter Twelve

SEVEN TEENAGERS SHUFFLED uncomfortably around the large wooden table that took up most of what once passed for a small barn and sat on the bench opposite their teacher. Paul Whittle looked at each of them in turn and felt his face radiate like an untended furnace. He finally swallowed down his personal anguish and spoke to them in as friendly and calm a manner as he could muster.

"We'll be leaving first thing tomorrow, kids. Until then, I want you to keep away from the woods, and if possible confine yourself to this building. If you want to take one last chance at seeing the old windmill or the animals, then please go in pairs or more. Nobody is to go out alone, okay? I want you all back in here by six tonight for dinner. I don't want to have to come find you or worry about you more than I already am, so Phillip, I don't want any disappearing acts just for fun, all right?"

Phillip Sellers nodded in agreement, his usual high, fuelled-by-hormones spirits knocked out of him. He nudged his neighbour, Candice Fallows, in the ribs, and she nodded her agreement to their teacher with a kick in the shins for Phillip, following it up with a small, embarrassed giggle. Paul Whittle watched on, counting down the hours until they were safely back in Liverpool tomorrow afternoon.

Of course, he was also dreading it. There would be an enquiry, possible suspension—he might even have to resign—but Paul knew he had followed every guideline. Safety first at all times! The group was small, manageable, in need of encouragement and hope, and he had done his absolute best to bring that hope to these kids.

A sixth-form trip to the countryside away from the desolation of home, he was sure for some of them it would have been the best week they ever had. No bullying, no teasing, no fights, away from their families and so-called friends who ground them down and chewed away the desire to learn, to be something more—smart, successful, interested in the planet—rather than falling victim to the system and being left behind.

Paul had joined the school when this particular cohort had been in their second year, by which time most staff believed it was too late to instil in them any self-belief. Their school was failing; they were overwhelmed every day by the evidence all around them that the government had left their city to ruin. There was nothing they could do but sit and wait for the inevitable moment when a parent delivered the final smack of violence that brought the underpaid police and the overstretched social workers to the door—even an ambulance; sadly once, an undertaker.

Out of all the students he had cajoled and coaxed into taking geography and then further lessons in ecology and urban farming, it was Felix who had been inspired the most and found his calling to farm life and, if he got the grades, training to be a vet. Paul had stood by Felix's side in the family home, one hand on the lad's shoulder, hoping to appeal to the father's better nature so he would allow his son to go to agricultural college the following year. The mother had served them tea and then joined her six-foot-tall, wide-as-a-barn-door husband in finding ways to dismiss every reason Paul gave for why they should encourage their son to pursue his dreams rather than quash them.

Resolutely old-fashioned, Felix's father wanted his son to have a 'real man's job' down the docks alongside his dad— something that brought the money in, that he could be proud of. Felix's mother had been worse, hinting that Paul's interest in her son's future bordered on paedophilic. If it hadn't been for the grandfather laying down the law and handing over the cash for the trip right then and there, a gleam in his eye daring the boy's parents to defy him, Paul wondered if he'd have made it out of the house with his dignity and reputation intact.

At the memory, he shuddered with suppressed anger, hoping the kids hadn't noticed, but why would they? They were all wrapped in their own thoughts—he hoped they were of good times with their classmate. Of them all, Rachel Wassod was taking it the hardest; tasked with telling him his girlfriend had dumped him, the poor girl blamed herself Felix going missing.

In all of this only one thing was certain: Felix's parents would see Paul to financial ruin, cost him his job, make sure he never taught again. For now, he had to keep a face on for the rest of his class, they needed to be kept occupied.

"Why can't we go home now, Sir?" Candice Fallows asked, no doubt voicing the question on all her classmates' lips. "I don't want to be here."

She was looking down into her lap as she spoke, though it was still with conviction. Paul looked directly at her, willing the others to join in with the demand they leave right that minute, to punish him, hurt him; it was no less than he deserved. But he had to maintain some sort of adult reason whilst being compassionate to their needs.

"The minibus is back at the school, Candice. The footy team needed it. I've spoken to the headmaster, though, and he's arranged for Mr. Hargreaves to drive straight down after the match, so we'll be gone at first light. The headmaster and I have also spoken to all your parents, and for the moment, they're happy for you to be in my care—yes, Lorraine, even yours."

Please, please, ask me to take you back today, Paul Whittle wanted to say, but he kept his mouth shut and waited for any response. But there was none. Whilst the thought of navigating Birmingham's New Street station filled him dread, especially with seven sixth-formers in tow, if they insisted, he would do it. *Imagine turning up at Lime Street Station, miserable from the journey, devastated by the loss of a friend, to be confronted by journalists, photographers, Felix's parents understandably spoiling for a fight...*

Out of the corner of his eye, Paul saw his sister beckoning him to join her outside. Placing his hands on the table, he looked at his group and reiterated, "Remember what I said—nobody is to go out alone. Make the most of this last day, there's still plenty to see. Lorraine, I remember you saying you wanted to draw the windmills. Phillip, perhaps you could go with her? The rest of you, Miss Whittle and I will be on hand of you need us."

Paul left them to work out their arrangements and went out into the yard, where he took a packet of cigarettes out his pocket, offering one to his older sister. She shook her head gravely.

"Paul, the police have just been on the phone, they need to talk to you."

Now what? As if the day hadn't been hard enough.

Sensing her brother's troubled mind and state of condition, she spoke as softly as she could, a feat that she had never found easy, being used to barking orders, to having to be loud to make sure she was seen in a family of five siblings.

"It's about Felix," Theresa said, which...of course it was, but as the oldest of five siblings, she was used to barking orders, and her uncharacteristically soft tone and the increasingly tight grip on her brother's arm delivered the news before she finally confirmed it. "He's dead."

Chapter Thirteen

DETECTIVE INSPECTOR LAURENCE Sears looked at the space where a young lad's body should be and remarked, "Ghost Apples."

The two men standing beside him eyed him in puzzled curiosity.

Sears turned away from the scene, a vision he would never forget, and looked at the faces of the men before him. The younger one, who had introduced himself eagerly was wide-eyed, lapping up the case as if it were his first, taking photographs for posterity, cooing as though each still-frame meant something positive. The other, who had not introduced himself, was stern with cruelly set face, a six o'clock shadow despite the early morning; only his torn suit made him likeable.

"Ghost apples," Sears repeated and smiled briefly before remembering the solemnity of the occasion. "I presume neither of you grew up in the country nor had an apple tree in your garden?"

The two men shook their heads in unison, a sight that amused the policeman.

"Ghost apples occur in freezing rain. The fruit ices over quickly and is coated from stalk to bottom. When it starts to defrost, the apple being so much warmer than the outside, rots first, leaving its impression etched in ice, like a surreal sculpture. It really is quite impressive. I saw it once as a boy—my great-grandfather had an orchard at the back of his house. I used to play there, and then one year, we had freezing rain, and my step-gran took me out into the orchard to look at what had happened. Ghost apples, the flesh drained away, rotted, mulch on the floor below, leaving only the flicker of a memory behind."

Sears smiled again, not because he felt in any way superior to the two men to whom he was giving a nature lesson to, but because of the memory of his great-grandfather's orchard, hugging the cliffs of Saltash, the River Tamar adding drama and comfort below, and just across the bay, his childhood home in Southway. Sears didn't usually have time for such reminiscence, but when the memories pushed hard, he could still smell the sea air hanging over him, recall the hardship of the times eating away at his youth until he'd left it behind when he joined the army at sixteen. He'd never returned, refused to go to his father's funeral and made sure his mother had moved to live with his aunt in Bournemouth afterwards.

"This all very interesting," the man in the tattered suit said, "but how are we supposed to deal with this?" With a sense of disgust in his actions, he waved his arm over the hospital bed, the last image forever captured, a frozen block with the perfect outline of a boy who just hours before had wandered, broken-hearted, into the woods to clear his head, to be alone.

"I am sorry, I don't know your name, Mr...?" Sears prompted.

"I don't think that matters really, Detective," the man replied with a sense of ruse growling in the back of his throat.

"Well perhaps not, but if we are to have any hope of understanding this, I will require your full cooperation. Of course, I can always ask you down at the station—an old cliché, I know, but surprisingly one that always does the trick."

The man's face darkened, but he remained impassive to the request of his name.

It was Dr. Moran who broke the tension. "For God's sake, Sid. Detective, this is the facility's owner, Professor Sidney Mutton. He is no doubt concerned about his name and the facility being dragged into the newspapers. Sid, don't be an arse. The press outside probably already know, and it doesn't take a genius to ask the right questions. I am sorry, Detective, this is a very delicate matter. We should not have allowed the kids to come here, but on reflection, it was the only place they could have come."

Sidney Mutton glared at the doctor, hate and fear flickering across his shadowed expression.

Moran ignored it. He was a good man, and whilst his work at the facility was important, it was not enough to stand in the way of an investigation.

"I don't think we're dealing with a contagion," he said. "Something like this would have surely spread with ease in here."

Finally, Sidney Mutton stopped glaring at Dr. Moran. Time to put his own authority on the situation once more. "This must not get out to the press. By all means, we must keep this event between those of us who witnessed it. We shall come up with a reason for the casket to remain closed when it is returned to the parents—locked, padlocked, welded fucking shut if needs be—but they are not seeing their child as…what did you call it Detective, mulch?"

The faint outline of the boy's remains was still visible. Even with one of the nurses having diligently collected the liquid from the floor and placed it in a container, there was still the outline of what was once a boy.

"What do we do with the…ice?"

"I suggest we place that in the autopsy room for now, examine it under close supervision, nothing taken to chance, collect any samples you deem necessary and then destroy it," Mutton barked.

The three men agreed.

"It just remains to get the staff who witnessed it into my office. They need reminding of the situation and how it affects them personally. My wife should be here in a few minutes with a new suit for me—make sure it is brought straight to my office and then give ten minutes before you bring them in. Will you see to it, Dr. Moran?"

Moran nodded, shook Sears' hand piously and left the room. His small act of betrayal would not go unpunished, but as head of research, he was not easily replaced, unlike the two nurses who had been in the room when the boy had melted away.

Sears watched Moran leave and returned his attention to the man in the torn suit. "How long can we keep it quiet, Sid?"

Mutton took a step towards Sears, his eyes deep and sullen, his hands behind his back, looking as if they were tied together.

"I didn't want to be drawn into this. My facility is not here to accommodate the local health service's inability to cope with some deranged, out-of-control kids. Thankfully for them, they will receive the best treatment possible, but they will be the last ones brought here. My treatment programmes are not for the young. As for what we do here…you know only too well, Detective Inspector Sears. Just hope you never have recourse to use them, or I will make sure your stay is as…comfortable and secure possible. Now, I believe one of your officers is being treated here. As soon as his jaw has been reset, I would like you to leave, regardless of how much pain he is in. I will make sure he is transported to the John Radcliffe."

Sears nodded, not out of agreement but in understanding of the man's demeanour and his high opinion of his work. Sears had met people like him before, including several officers he had the displeasure of working under in Iraq, the odd bully on the parade ground, all full of self-importance, bile, spit and venom. He felt a grip of concern for those who were going to be pulled into the office. Still, he wouldn't break his word and would stay silent about what he had seen on the hospital bed. Who would have believed him anyway?

Shutting the door behind him, he walked stiffly towards the entrance, past Fiona Frampton sitting in a visitor's chair and staring at empty space. Had he noticed her, he might also have remembered she had been in the room at the time of the appearance of the 'ghost apple'. However, such was Fiona Frampton's lot in life, she was once again left unconsidered.

Out in the fresh air of the Wendlefields countryside, Laurence Sears took a deep breath. Whatever they were doing in that facility needed looking into, but not yet. In the distance, he noticed a car speeding along what he thought to be a dirt track. Squinting across the half mile between him and the clouds of dust, he realised it was the old forge road, which led straight to the American base, and deduced it was Mutton's wife bringing his new suit. He had no idea what type of a woman she was, but he was not impressed by her driving; even out here, it was dangerous: the countryside had many hazards that people didn't appreciate.

Sears let it go. If she had an accident, she was so close enough to her husband's facility that he could care for her himself—once he'd changed and shaved, of course. Mutton struck Sears as that kind of man.

Turning away from the approaching car, he walked down the main road towards the newshounds and Samantha McCarthy, leaving Fiona Frampton, Bill Taylor and even Simon Kinsey behind in faded thoughts. Only the squeal of brakes and the shower of airborne gravel pummelling the ground like minuscule missiles hurled in a Lilliputian skirmish caused him to glance back.

"Dangerous woman," he said out loud, not caring who heard him.

Chapter Fourteen

WHERE ARE THE children now, sir?"

Paul Whittle lifted his head from his hands and asked the police officer to repeat the question.

PC Andrea Laybourne looked upon the wretched figure in front of her and felt pity for him. He had broken down when they knocked on the farm's robust door, almost falling to his knees in a heart-breaking display of grief and penitence for the dead boy's suffering.

The tear stains had given his face a dull appearance, but from what she knew of the teacher, he was anything but dull. Alongside his sister, he had been arrested and cautioned but ultimately not charged with disturbing the peace when the public meetings were taking place about the construction of the new motorway less than ten miles from the farm. If he were a firebrand, then his sister was a nuclear bomb waiting to go off. Twenty years before, she had served time for the manslaughter of her husband, only being released after pressure was applied from the then Home Secretary.

Andrea Laybourne crouched in front of the broken man and softly asked again where the children were. This was not a time to be raising damnation against the teacher; disturbing the peace aside, he had never stepped foot on the wrong side of the law. He just wanted to see his students get on in life.

Paul Whittle forced the tears to stop and stuttered something inaudible before pulling himself as much together as he could. "Two of the children are with my sister, feeding the cows. Three are at the old windmills drawing—that would be Phillip, Candice

75

and Lorraine—and the other two should be in the kitchen preparing dinner."

Andrea's partner, who had been hanging back, stepped out of the room, returning soon after, nodding to confirm Whittle's account.

Andrea sat beside him and sighed inwardly. This was the part of the job she hated. She had joined the police to make a difference, and in a way she was, but she always seemed to be delegated the task of liaising between officialdom and those who needed the strong arm of comfort around them. If she had not been watching the news that night about the policewoman shot and murdered outside of the Libyan Embassy, she might have found a calling as a social worker—a career her mother had been much more in favour of.

Whenever she mentioned to her father that she felt hindered by being nothing more than a glorified nursemaid, he told her, "Bide your time. It will not always be this way. You will get your chance."

She was never sure if he was merely trying to give her a gee up, reminding her she had plenty of time in front of her, or as she half suspected, doing it because his own career path, blighted by rush decisions and impatience, had given him the insight to protect his daughter from repeating his mistakes.

Andrea's partner went back to the kitchen. He didn't like this—as he saw it—touchy-feely sentiment that had crept into the force. No doubt he, like Andrea, had picked up on the smell of cooking bacon: with all that had occurred, they'd missed breakfast, but with him gone, Andrea hoped the teacher might talk more freely.

"Tell me about Felix," she said. "What was his state of mind before he received the message about his girlfriend?"

"Felix was a grand kid. Open, receptive in class—bit of a tearaway when I first met him. I joined the school in his second year, you see, but there was something in his eyes—a yearning to break away from the path his father had lined up for him. Felix's mum and dad never came to the school for sports days or parents' evenings. His grandfather, though, he attended every one. He wanted the boy to be true to his nature, not go and work on the docks like his dad, or down the mines like his granddad. Felix wanted to work the land and with animals. How could I deny him that opportunity when I could bring him here for some firsthand experience?

"I was hoping he would go to agricultural college—there's one just outside of Buckingham. My sister and I talked about sponsoring him."

Despite his openness, Paul Whittle was a bag of nerves. He was not suspected of anything—three of the kids had seen him sleeping when the boy went missing—and Andrea wondered if it was the phone call he'd made to his headmaster earlier. It couldn't have been easy for him to admit that a boy in his charge was dead. He would have to stay behind, of course, but as the sooner they could get the kids back to Liverpool, the better.

Two of the teachers were already driving down in their own cars, their lessons covered by their colleagues. The news had not reached the rest of the pupils that one of their number had died on an educational visit. The minibus would pick up the kids' gear the following day, and Andrea would be there, just in case. She dreaded to think what the press would say—what they would do to Paul and Theresa Whittle.

"Did you know the girl he was involved with?"

"Only by sight, I never taught her. I always was surprised to see them together, didn't think she was his type. If anything, I thought he'd have asked out Candice—Candice Kellman, the girl who's gone down to the old windmills with Phillip and Lorraine. But what do I know about teenage hearts? It was beyond me when I was their age and remains so now!"

Andrea smiled at that, her own understanding of such matters having avoided her in the same manner.

"I'm sorry," he said. "Such a confession, I know."

She placed her hand on his shoulder. "When he was found, you were by the old windmills, I believe. What were you doing over there?"

"You will think me mad, or at least you should do I'd told the kids that the woods were out of bounds. They always gave me the creeps. A few years ago, there was that travelling community forcibly removed from there. My sister, although sympathetic to their cause, had noticed they were desecrating the area near the abandoned monastery. I didn't want the kids stumbling upon anything they shouldn't, so naturally I assumed Felix had gone down to the old mills to cool off. I obviously don't know kids as well as I should, but I can only guide them in their education, not the matters of lost love they are doomed to have at their age."

Andrea felt a burden of guilt remove itself from his body. He had done the logical thing: he had searched where he had expected to find the boy, not where he was always going to go.

"The girl who told him about his girlfriend splitting up with him—how did she know?"

"They're cousins. Large estate big families. The ex-girlfriend called her cousin yesterday evening, said she couldn't face doing it herself but didn't want him to be left under any illusion that when he returned from the trip, they were going to be 'best buds', as she put it. I didn't know what she'd said until afterwards, or I'd never have left him on his own. It wouldn't have been fair."

With a light squeeze, Andrea moved her hand away, satisfied Whittle had calmed down. He would still have to face more questions, but for now, he looked like he needed a cup of tea. Andrea stood and stretched, her uniform riding up and down and making her wish, purely so she could wear clothes that would properly fit her tall frame, that she was a plain clothes officer.

Through the window, she saw Theresa Whittle and two of Paul's students walking back from the barn where the cows had been left to feed. They seemed happy enough, not as badly affected by the morning's events as their teacher, but it would soon show as they began to relive the day.

"Mr. Whittle…Paul, why did your sister come here after being released from prison? Why did she not go back to your family home?"

Paul looked up, his eyes starting to glaze over once more. "What do you mean, Officer?"

"I'm just curious. Her husband almost beats her to death in a drunken rage, and in self-defence, she puts a knife through his neck. Spur of the moment—natural to defend one's self from an attacker. But why buy a farm? Why not go home, be with family? I believe you have several other siblings, yet you are the only one she has anything to do with. My apologies if the question is too raw, I don't mean to be unpleasant."

"It's quite all right, although I wouldn't ask Theresa directly the same question. She won't answer you. The simple truth is, I was the only one who believed her. The others, our mum and dad, they thought she had done it on purpose. They never saw him as anything but a sweet, friendly man, the proverbial life and soul of the party, but he had a vicious, spiteful streak. Anyone who got in his way or stood against him, he made sure they stayed down. If you want to know more, ask that reporter fellow who was here this morning with Ms. McCarthy. I didn't recognise him at first, but after he left, I asked my sister and she confirmed my recollection. He was beaten up badly by her husband when they were teenagers and nearly lost an eye."

Chapter Fifteen

KINSEY RETCHED INTO the toilet bowl one more time and slowly lifted his head to face the dots that were dancing in front of his eyes. Leaning back against the tiled wall, he allowed his body to feel the benefit of the chilly evening as he breathed deeply, taking in the oxygen his body craved. *I promise to mend my ways*, he thought and felt his stomach lurch once more, giving up with watery applause.

The headache had reached a crescendo and seemed at last to be subsiding, the dots fading into the background, joining the onlooking crowd rather than taking a star turn on the dance floor beneath the revolving glitterball. Kinsey struggled to his feet and sent the contents of the pan downstream. Splashing cold water on his face and then rubbing it dry with a clean towel, he examined his reflection. No doubt about it, McCarthy was right when she said how rough he looked when he'd re-joined her at the gate.

The walk from the facility to where the car was parked, and where over-inflated opinions were being voiced loudly, was no more than two hundred yards, yet Kinsey felt as if he had walked through acres of marshland carrying a rucksack filled with concrete. His legs had given way as he'd reached the gate, and he was thankful that one of the broadsheet journalists was on hand to steady him. A voice in the background, muffled and coarse, said something that was inaudible to Kinsey but drew a cacophony of sarcastic laughter from those at the rear of the group. Kinsey had asked the man who was holding him up if he could help him sit on the ground; his head was swimming, and his vision was blurred. He'd felt nauseous often enough—the after-effects of the night before a recurring reminder of his taste for alcoholic numbness—but this was different. This was pain.

McCarthy had reached him and thanked the journalist by name. He'd insisted it was no problem, raising another loud sheet of laughter from the group. Kinsey neither knew nor cared if it was about him. His head throbbed as if under attack from an out-of-control boomerang, and that was his only concern.

"Kinsey, I'm going to take you home, you look like hell. Can you stand?"

He'd just found a comfy place to sit and contemplate death, now McCarthy wanted him to stand again—did the woman have a heart?

Groaning under the pressure of having to move in any direction other than downwards, Kinsey stood on unsure legs in what was surely a display of absolute heroism and self-sacrifice made.

McCarthy leaned close and murmured, "I know you haven't been drinking, so I'm chalking this up to something else. I'll get you home and make an appointment for you at the doctor—if you're not back to your condescending best by the morning."

***

Holding Kinsey up with one arm around his waist, McCarthy bulldozed her way through the jeering crowd. Only Andrew—the journalist who had helped Kinsey earlier—showed any compassion and dropped his bag to assist in taking her sick colleague to her car.

Once inside, and with a seat belt around him, Kinsey breathed hard and closed his eyes. With a wince, he cried out in pain.

"I think he needs to go to the John Radcliffe," Andrew advised. "He's in a lot of pain."

"He'll be all right. Tough as they come, this one," was McCarthy's dry response. But deep down, she was worried.

He'd looked awful that morning when she got him up, but she had put that down to the lateness of the night before, lack of sleep, lack of a decent meal. By the time they'd come out of the woods, he'd seemed brighter than he had been for weeks, even years, in good enough spirits to crack a few crude jokes on the way to the facility and give some serious insights into what was occurring in the town. Now he looked helpless, a sick dog cowering in the corner of the room as it watched its owner remove their belt and walk slowly towards them.

She shut the door and thanked Andrew again.

"When are you going to come and work for us, Samantha? You know you are wasted here."

"Not the time, Andrew." She smiled at him broadly. Were it not for this story or Kinsey's health, she might well have dragged him into town, found a table at the Green Man and discussed the idea further.

Andrew returned her grin. "You can't stay here forever." Turning serious, he said, "Get the lad home. He's no good to you in this state."

***

Lad, Kinsey mused as the car moved off. He was almost thirty-six, but to many in the town, he would always be 'that kid'—the child staggering down the Baneberry Road with blood coming out of his eye and a bruised, swollen face.

Another stab of pain caused him to breathe deeply, inhale, exhale…a coin over the eye…a shilling on a railway track stood on its edge, a bet, a dare between friends over which he got into his first ever fight—hardly a fight, jumped on by a gang of boys as his terrified friends ran away, only returning when they noticed he hadn't made it back to school. Why was this memory returning now?

Inhale…exhale…inhale…exhale…

Kinsey opened his eyes, relieved to find his vision was no longer blurred and he could the road clearly, although reading the road signs and mile markers was a non-starter.

"Boss? What happened?"

McCarthy turned her head but kept her focus on the road. "I don't know. But I've been thinking back over the past few weeks. You've not been yourself—even your usual high spirits have felt…I don't know…like a mask. Like you're putting a brave face on something you don't want to confront. I initially put it down to your drinking habits, but I haven't really seen you touch any recently. The odd glass perhaps, but nothing like I know you can put away. And then there's this morning, when I found you in that clearing in the woods. You seemed calm, serene, like a weight had been lifted off your mind. If I didn't know better, I'd say you'd been smoking weed, but there was something else about you, and I can't put my finger on it."

Inhale…exhale…inhale…exhale…

The image was fading now, disappearing into the past; the miles between that moment of agony and praying for death had passed. He wondered who he had annoyed so much that they took pleasure in sticking pins into his effigy; he hoped they got the hair right and the patches on his jeans.

"I'll be all right, boss. Just get me home."

Several hours had since passed, it was now evening, and Kinsey was pushing hard at the memory of such a long, confusing day. Again, he vowed to change his ways and was about to go back to his bedroom when the phone rang. Cursing under his breath at his missed opportunity to pull the plug for the night, he remembered the girl's mother was going to call him.

"Simon Kinsey," he answered carefully. The static on the line made it difficult to hear the small, timid voice at the other end. "Is that you, Ms. Frampton…Fiona?"

"Hello, Mr. Kinsey," she replied more confidently, now she'd been given permission to talk. "I didn't wake you, did I? You did say to call this evening."

"No, no, I was awake. Just…a very long day."

"One of the nurses overheard the professor's wife say she'd seen a man collapse outside the building. I wasn't sure if it was you, but then I phoned your boss at the office, Ms. McCarthy, and she said she'd taken you home—a headache. Are you feeling better?"

"I am, thanks," he lied. Kinsey hated idle small talk, especially with someone he didn't know, but Fiona seemed sincere. "You wanted to tell me something at Wendlefields—you said you saw something odd?"

Fiona Frampton cleared her throat. "It was the boy—not the lad from the town, Tom Solden, the other one from up north they brought into the facility this morning. He…sort of melted into nothing."

Kinsey wasn't sure if he'd heard correctly and had to wonder if it was 'Pull a Joke on Simon Kinsey Day'.

"Fiona…I'm not sure what you mean. Can you start again from the beginning?"

Fiona Frampton drew in her breath and told Kinsey, from the beginning, what she had seen take place inside the stark small room, the panic on the nurses' faces, the sheer incredulity of the attending doctor and the shock all round as the boy at first froze over, a thin layer of ice covering his hospital gown, and then the revulsion of seeing him silently scream one last time before slowly dissolving into what looked like curdled blancmange that seeped out of the ice shell onto the floor. All this, Fiona recounted matter-of-fact. Whether out of shock or out of ghoulish intent, she seemed to have coped remarkably well with seeing the body liquify—if she was telling the truth—like soup in a blender. But seeing the image of the boy's face imprinted on the ice, his torso carved in the unnatural freeze, had finally broken her.

Kinsey listened dispassionately, not once butting in nor asking her to clarify. That didn't mean her believed her. How could he? It was just too fantastic. But after what he had witnessed himself over the past couple of days, it no longer surprised him to hear such a tale, and Fiona Frampton didn't strike him as a woman to tell lies. To conceal the truth, yes, but to make up something as bizarre, as incredible, as this, just wasn't in her nature.

He asked her to repeat the story, this time jotting down all the salient points, making sure he got a description of the nurses and the doctor in attendance, what the room was like, what the boy was screaming before he turned to blancmange, whether she'd been spotted, spoken to, ordered to stay quiet. He wrote all her answers on the pad and was pleased and relieved that the last question he put to her was one answered in the negative: nobody paid her any attention, not even the police officer who had met with the man in the tattered suit and the doctor afterwards.

Kinsey thought he should enquire after her daughter; after all, it was part of the story. Fiona seemed overwhelmed that he'd asked and gushed, her words becoming muddled as they passed into the open air. Finally, she pulled herself together and told him her daughter had been brought out of sedation that evening and would be okay to leave the facility in the morning.

"I've not told her about the boy—do you think I should?"

Kinsey considered the question. It might be interesting to gauge her reaction, but why put the girl through further trauma? It would probably do her more damage. In any case, he'd be better off only sharing this information with McCarthy. He thanked Fiona for calling and warned her not to tell her friends or neighbours what she had seen. Her response nearly broke his heart.

"Who is there to tell, Mr. Kinsey? People haven't spoken to me in years. Most of my neighbours avoid me since my Ken left. They don't know how to treat me."

She thanked him for listening, telling him it was nice to be able to talk to someone other than her daughter, and then the line went silent.

Kinsey was still holding the phone to his ear long. after Fiona had hung up. Such was his life that he genuinely didn't know how to respond to a painful cry for acceptance, for a call for company. He had only felt that way once, the stranger on the edge of town looking into the eyes of passers-by and seeing only distrust, wariness and suspicion. The doctor who treated him told his mother to keep him indoors for a few weeks until the bruising of the savage beating had ebbed away. His mother had ignored that advice: she wanted the town to see what her son had been reduced to. The doctor told them both that he had been fortunate to not lose an eye.

Kinsey pressed down on the cradle of the telephone, switching the call-disconnected pip for the burr of an open line. He dialled the newspaper office number, assuming McCarthy would still be there, putting together an extra piece, and received no answer, just a constant ringing. He put the phone down on its cradle once more and then immediately picked it up again, hesitating for a second before dialling McCarthy's home number, something he hadn't done in years.

Not McCarthy: a younger voice, slightly higher pitch, nicer.

"Hello, Rebecca McCarthy speaking."

Kinsey wasn't sure how to respond. There was a time she'd have called him Uncle Simon.

"Hello...who's calling, please?

"Hi, Rebecca, it's erm, Simon Kinsey. Before you put the phone down, I wouldn't have called if it wasn't absolutely necessary."

For half a minute or more, nothing was said. Only the sound of her furious breathing confirmed she hadn't hung up on him.

"What do you want, Kinsey?" She almost spat his name. It was probably all she could do to restrain herself from telling him to fuck off, and he wouldn't have blamed her if she had.

Kinsey kept his response civil, no need to add further problems to the relationship, or lack of, between them. "I need to speak to your mum about a story we're working on."

Again, the line went quiet, only the increasing sound of buzzing in Kinsey's head telling him he had not gone deaf.

"You have a nerve calling here."

"I know. I'm sorry, Rebecca, I really didn't want to disturb you, I just want to speak to your mum, and it can't wait till tomorrow."

"Do you think I give a damn what you want.?" The girl's voice was cold, relentless. "You were my *friend*—my parents' friend. I live every day knowing my mum, after all you did, is still your boss—that you still have a place in our lives. I hate you so much, do you know that, Kinsey? I hope you do."

Kinsey agreed, trying desperately to get Rebecca to listen. His voice echoed; he could hear himself talk down the phone, and when he looked down at his notes, the words swam like frenzied fish. Rebecca was still talking, years of pent-up frustration tumbling out, all what her father had told her and not the truth of what had happened between Kinsey and her mother. Was this how Sam had been dealing with this? The constant urge to just tell Rebecca to shut up and listen to her side for once? It certainly was how Kinsey felt at that moment.

Feeling dizzy, he put out his hand to steady himself against the wall, his fingers barely touching the plaster and sliding down and fell forwards with a hefty bump.

"Are you still there?" Rebecca asked, and then with a greater sense of alarm, "Are you okay?"

Kinsey heard the question in the far distance as the headache came screaming back...*a sharp elbow to the face, a shilling on a railway track, another blow.*

"Kinsey, are you there? Simon?"

***

Rebecca McCarthy yelled down the phone, terrified that the man she playfully called Uncle Simon when she was younger had had a heart attack. She hung up so she could call the emergency services, but the line was still connected at Kinsey's end. In a blind panic, she ran to the next-door neighbour's house and then phoned 999 and requested an ambulance to the journalist's address, hoping he hadn't moved in the years since she'd last spoken to him.

Chapter Sixteen

THE TWO TEACHERS who had been allocated the task of driving down from Liverpool to pick up the children that morning arrived at the farm just after seven p.m., a combination of a two-hour tailback on the outskirts of Birmingham and getting lost in the Oxfordshire country lanes, twice finding their way back to the town but somehow completely bypassing Lynnsford, all taking their toll on the nerves of Paul Whittle and his students.

Seeing them at the farm gate, Paul Whittle let out a sob of relief. He had got the students to pack their belongings after the police had left and had spent a quiet dinner in their company, all the time casting weary, tired eyes on the clock.

Two teachers, one male and one female, under orders to get the children home safely—the same instruction that had been passed to Paul Whittle before he climbed on board the school's minibus only a few days before hand.

The headmaster had shaken his hand and wished him well but had also drawn him closer in a symbolic embrace of brotherhood. "Let them enjoy their time, but don't let them out of your sight. Make sure you bring them back in one piece—no scratches, no broken arms..."

Paul Whittle would have killed for a broken arm right now, for the young lad he had taken under his wing to be heading home with nothing more than his arm in plaster and a tale of youthful misdeeds.

"So sorry we're late, Paul. Traffic was bloody awful."

"Don't listen to him, Paul. Robbie can't navigate to save his life. We've been roving around the countryside for what seems several days."

Paul managed a small smile and opened the gate to let them both in, noting there was some ice on Robbie's windscreen.

"It's not that cold, is it?" He wiped his index finger across the glass and showed his fellow teacher the result.

Looking perplexed, Robbie Singh got out of his car and copied Paul's actions. "I swear that wasn't there ten minutes ago—is yours the same, Carol?"

Carol Stevens had already locked her car and seemed in a hurry. "Are the kids ready, Paul? The sooner we get them in—*after* I've made sure I don't piss myself—the sooner we will be home."

Paul pointed to the open farmhouse door. "Straight through, up the stairs, second on the left."

Carol thanked him and made a beeline for the house.

Turning his attention back to the ice on the screen, Paul arranged absent-mindedly outlined the travel arrangements. "Robbie, you take the boys, Carol will take the girls. I'll be tomorrow as soon as the school minibus comes for me." He rubbed his finger over another part of the windscreen. It was still cold, but slimy rather than icy.

Four of the children appeared at the farm door and walked towards the cars, each carrying the barest minimum in their school bag and armed with sandwiches Paul's sister had made.

"Come on, you lot, shake a leg. Boys with Mr. Singh, all in the back—no room in the front as you know—and girls with Ms. Stevens. Will one of you please go and ask—no, *insist* that the others join us."

One of the group spoke up, her voice laced with fear of being called a snitch. "They're not here, Sir. They snuck out about an hour ago."

Robbie sighed. "Who did, and where did they go?"

"Candice, Phillip and Lorraine, Sir. They went back to the windmills."

"What on earth for?" Paul asked.

The girls giggled at the question, and the lads shifted uncomfortably on the gravel. The two teachers looked at each other in despair. Carol Stevens appeared at the door.

"What's going on? Why aren't you all in the cars?"

"Ms. Stevens," Paul called, "Would you get the children back inside and ask my sister for the two torches in the cupboard under the sink, please. Girls, that's enough!"

The two girls stopped giggling, and for the first time since all this had begun, Paul felt as if he was back in command of the situation.

Robbie Singh raised an eyebrow. "They aren't off doing what I think they're doing, are they?"

Paul didn't know what to think. Or rather, he knew *exactly* what he thought but didn't want to admit it to anyone else. A scandal in the countryside, as well as a death—this was not what he'd signed up for.

He noticed his sister coming towards them and carrying three torches. "No arguments, Paul. I'm coming with you. I know that stretch of water a lot better than you."

With Carol Stevens supervising the main group in the farmhouse, the trio walked towards the river, following a well-worn path through long grass and overgrown banks, each step highlighted by the cold light of three industrial-use torches, each footfall crunching down on the earth below. All the while, the river ran past them, quiet for the most part other than the occasional crash as it hit the rocks that jutted out like islands caught in the wake of tsunami.

The windmills were not far from the farm, but in the darkness, they may as well have been several miles away. Paul remembered coming here as a child. It was a popular location with people from the town during and after the war and had been *the* place to go for a day out. A travelling fair had called the area around the windmills its own during the summer months, children had played out in the countryside, all happy and content...until Sally Witherton's body was found in the rushes a few yards from the first of the windmills.

If Paul knew his students at all, that was where they would be. The other two windmills, whilst still working examples of how nature was harnessed, were not as easy to access. The farmer who owned the field had made such a noise about local kids trespassing that he'd managed to place the windmills under a kind of structural quarantine, protecting them with fences, padlocks and warnings of prosecution.

As they walked, Paul glanced across at his sister's silhouette, knowing she would be thinking of the girl who drowned. Almost anybody of a certain age did whenever they found themselves on the wrong side of the woods. The young of the nearby town only saw it as place of urban myth and somewhere to make out. Paul had been too young to come here as a boy, though he was certain his sister had, when her dead husband was still finding his way to being a terror to those who got in his way.

The windmill loomed out of the dark, large and imposing, the raw power of the light wind enough to make the sails sing their obscure love song, a frightening tone of influence when heard at night. Crossing the boundary between the two farms, Paul's torch began to fade, and he looked at his comrades, thankful theirs seemed to be holding out. He turned his off, hoping it would conserve the remaining battery for the walk back.

In the distance, he thought he saw a figure watch them as they approached the windmill. Too tall to be one of the students, the figure was motionless.

"They're here," Theresa whispered. "I can hear noises coming from inside."

Paul nodded. "Does your neighbour—what's-his-name, the one with the flashy car—often come out to inspect his fields at night?"

"Who, Yobe? Not at all! He doesn't even live on the farm. He prefers the comforts of the new house he had built on the road to Wendlefields!"

"Then who's that?" Paul pointed at the distant figure, the cold air seeming to illuminate their outline, making it shimmer, then radiate brightly. Paul couldn't make out any features, but a disturbing thought played havoc with his mind—that the figure was grinning at him. Then with clarity, he saw the figure slowly lift a hand and place a finger over its deeply terrifying, snarling grin on a face which could not be seen.

Theresa turned her attention back to the windmill's wooden door. "Well, if it is Yobe out there in the dark, he probably heard some kids were mucking about on his land and wanted to scare them. He saw us and thought better of it. He'll be round tomorrow to lay down the law on me, though, rotten bastard."

Paul let that topic of conversation go; it was not for Robbie Singh to have any part of. Find the kids, get them out of the building and get them home; anything else they'd deal with when no one else was around to hear the concerns of the past catching up with her. It wasn't even as if she was directly involved. It had happened to someone else; she had found out and killed the disease stone dead.

When at last the windmill door swung open, the scene that before them shook Paul to the core—he could only guess what it did to Robbie and Theresa. He averted his gaze, but the image was still there, burned into his mind, where it would stay until the day he died. Stepping in front of his sister, he blocked her view, her mouth wide open in shock like a cartoon character, whose jaw hits the floor.

"Go back to the farm," Paul told her. "Run if you have to. Tell Ms. Stevens to take the other four kids back home immediately and then call the police." He shoved his sister hard, urging towards the door and away from the act being carried out in front of them.

Theresa took a few steps backwards before she turned and fled from the building. She was not a young woman, hardly in the best of physical condition, but for the next fifteen minutes, she ran harder and faster than she had done in her life.

Paul watched his sister leave and then shook Robbie hard, his face wrapped in a mask of disgust and disbelief. "Robbie... outside now. We must *not* be in here when the police come. We'll lock the door and wait for them. There's nothing we can do now—Robbie!"

Robbie stumbled backwards, his cheeks ballooning, eyes watering as if he was about to throw up, and Paul could understand why. In all his years, he had never seen anything as cruel or horrifying as the image playing out before him. As teachers, they saw kids turn equipment into weapons—compasses, cricket bats, even their school ties—but this? This was leagues beyond classroom bullies.

Paul pushed Robbie again, bundling him out of the windmill. Once they were both clear of the door, Paul heaved the wooden block back onto the metal hooks in the doorframe.

"Nothing and no one gets out of here. Let the police deal with this."

Chapter Seventeen

ADAM YOBE WAS enjoying his later years. All those times of stress, of scrabbling around for money to pay the bills, threatened with closure more times than he cared to remember, was lost to the past. He could sit back and relax, watch his bank account become healthy, a jet fighter that rained down hard cash instead of missiles with a salute and the stirrings of Uncle Joe singing his favourite anthem.

Pouring himself a whisky, he walked over to where his wife sat on the leather sofa and kissed the top of her head, nestling his nose in her abundant hair, breathing deeply. Yes, life had been good, and he owed it all to his wife introducing him to several interested parties who took some of the redundant, fallow land off his hands, clearing a huge amount of debt and allowing the farm over at Lynnsford to diversify, to change the way it had been run since his grandfather had won it in a horseracing bet. Calisdale Farm had never made money; the ground was sickly, failing year after year to yield a good harvest. He didn't want to lose it, though: there was his pride at stake.

All those days of scrimping and saving, only to be kicked where it hurts were behind him. Yet he wasn't happy, not truly. He had a new house, his wife adored him, all eyes turned in admiration or jealousy when he drove through the town, and still he felt as if he were at the bottom of the barrel looking up at the faces of those who had once belittled and ignored him—especially that woman in charge of the local paper. He had tried to get her onside and when that failed made enquiries into her position, searching for scandals, but aside from her divorce, there was nothing he could use against her. She was so well liked by the paper's owners it was nauseating.

Out of the French windows, he could see the remains of the river that had been diverted so he could sell the vast majority of the land. All he kept now were his prize cows—one of the best decisions he had ever made. The company that bought the land had been recommended to him by the owner of the manor house during an evening when, financially at least, he had finally arrived. He had returned his rented tuxedo the following day and replaced it with a made-to-measure tux, which now strained at the seams. Fat cigar in his mouth and brandy glass in his left hand, he had shaken so many hands that evening that by the end, his wrist ached. He didn't care what that company did with it; he made a handsome income from the land at both Wendlefields and Lynnsford.

Yobe returned to the soothing leather reclining chair and watched the television, his wife napping on the sofa, her breasts moving in time with her occasional gentle snores.

Guiltily, he recalled watching the professor's wife drive past earlier that day. He'd been surprised to see her using the old army camp road, its existence forgotten by most in the town, and it had taken her past the house. He concluded she had come that way purely for his benefit and felt another flush of lust course through his body before nestling in the warmth of his stomach. She was a good-looking woman with shapely, tanned legs, and the way she smoked a cigarette drove him crazy.

His train of thought was disturbed by the telephone. His wife looked up sleepily, and he smiled at her, answering the phone on the fifth ring. A distant voice but recognisable came down the line—one of his farm hands who lived in the cottage over at Lynnsford.

"What is it, Dennis? It's a bit late to be calling me about a problem."

"It's the kids up at the Whittle Farm again. I saw them down by the windmills this morning and managed to chase them off, but as I was doing my final round before tonight's delivery, I saw them again."

Yobe counted to ten and let the news to filter through his mind. Dennis was hard-working man, prone to jumping the gun where his temper was concerned, but it meant, as far as Yobe was concerned, that he could be relied upon to deal with most situations and leave him to enjoy the spoils of his deserved wealth. But there were occasions when it would have been simpler to bark himself.

"Dennis, it's a protected site—local interest and all that. I can stop them getting in, but I can't stop them from going to look. As long as the top field is fenced off, what do I care about some stupid kids?"

"I understand that, sir, but there are police down there. I think there's been an accident or…something worse. The gossip is rife. There's talk of…" Dennis's words trailed off, and for the first time since he'd sold out, Yobe felt under pressure. The police up at the farm? He would have to cancel the delivery tonight.

"Okay, Dennis. I've got this," he said with just a little too much confidence. "I'll call the courier now, get them to postpone the delivery for a few days, and you, my friend, you keep the police away from the building until I get there. Just make sure the fence is intact. That way, they have no reason to come over to us until the morning." Yobe was doing what he did best—taking command—but what Dennis said next blew all sense of control away.

"Marcus went down the hill to see what he could learn, sir, and a couple of coppers were talking. They said it looked like a ritual had taken place inside the windmill. Three kids involved, one dead."

Yobe replaced the telephone receiver. He'd heard about the commotion up at Sterhan Close and the girl found in the woods. He wondered if there had been any other problems, any connections closer to home. His wife knew all the latest gossip in the town, thrived on it, but she hadn't mentioned anything. But then, he'd hardly been in the mood to notice, too busy looking at ways to expanding the business to care for the whys and wherefores of town life.

She was fully asleep now; if he woke her to ask such a question, he would pay for it for a few days. *Never disturb the wife when she's asleep. That way, she's only spending money in her dreams.* It would have to wait. First things first: cancel the delivery. More than likely, it would not have left the depot yet. *This is just a bump in the road. It happens, just go with it.* He smiled, relishing the thought of being in control. He placed the call and waited patiently.

Eventually, a man's voice answered. "Hello?"

"Marbon, it's Yobe. Listen, there's trouble up at the farm. Police are at the windmills—apparently, some kids have got themselves into a bit of bother."

"No problem. I'll get the message across. How many days do think you need? We can't afford to fall behind. It would just mean more deposits building up."

"Two days, maximum. The windmills are on common land, so the police will rope them off, but they have no reason to come over to the farm. I'll find a way to keep the workers away for a week, apart from a trusted skeleton crew. Arrange for the next delivery to come at one on Sunday morning."

"Okay, that's workable. Keep me informed of any developments."

With that, Marbon put down the phone, no need to exchanging pleasantries. They would share a bottle of whisky and talk over simpler things the next time the farmer was due to come and visit his boss.

All was good in Yobe's world. Even the presence of the police was a minor inconvenience. He looked across at his sleeping wife, whose moans of pleasure in her dream state stirred up his resentment. He had not elicited those sounds from her in what seemed like forever.

In annoyance, he picked up the keys to the house and the car, gripping them so tightly they left a deep impression that throbbed all the way to Lynnsford. What he wouldn't give to be in the car with that professor's wife right now. He had the urge to turn around, go back and smother his wife where she lay. Oh, to feel the life drain out of her gasp for gasp, each moment ticking away as her arms waved helplessly, furiously, grasping his wrists.

If Yobe had waited a couple of minutes, if he had hung around and collected his thoughts for a few minutes, his wife would not have been awoken by the telephone and would not have heard the soft, cotton-like voice at the other end telling her exactly what her husband had been thinking while she slept.

Chapter Eighteen

LISTLESS, KINSEY CRIED out, complaining to the empty house. The headache was relentless, but he was convinced the cause this time was the sudden appearance of a bruise around his eye and the dried blood matting his hair above his ears. He was brought to his senses by the banging on his front door.

Pulling himself up on his feet, he returned the phone to its cradle and took a moment to marvel at having not broken any bones when he'd met the floor. The last thing he remembered was talking to Rebecca McCarthy, the girl's pent-up fury finally to breathing free instead of being buried deep within her.

The banging recommenced, rattling the door in its frame. Gingerly, Kinsey walked down and looked through the spy hole, surprised to see two paramedics on his doorstep. He opened the door wide.

"Hello. Can I help you?"

"We received a report of an accident at this address. A young woman called it in."

Kinsey chuckled inwardly. Rebecca may hate his guts, but she still cared enough to make sure he was all right. He would get her some flowers, or perhaps find out from her mother what music she was into these days. A small emotional connection would be a better start than flowers that ultimately die.

"I fell over, but I'm fine. Too much work, not enough sleep. I'll be as right as rain by the morning."

The two men shared a suspicious glance. They'd know when someone was covering for a deeper issue.

The older man took charge. "Can I take a look at your head?" he asked, already pulling on latex gloves.

"Sure."

The paramedic lightly prodded at the distended skin around Kinsey's eye and then the cut on his temple. "Let me put something on that for you, sir, and while I do, you can tell me again what happened." He nodded to his colleague, who returned to the ambulance.

"What do you do?" the older paramedic asked as he tended to Kinsey's wound. "Work-wise."

"I'm a journalist. I've not eaten much this past couple of days. not enough time to eat. Long hours, you know? The workload is exhausting, and it doesn't leave much time to look after myself properly...shit, sorry. I sound like an arse. I know you guys work hard, I shouldn't be moaning."

The paramedic smiled. "No need to apologise. My wife's a postwoman, my eldest daughter works in a bank, and my son, who you just met, is a trainee paramedic. If we aren't on shift together, we don't see each other from one week to the next. We all have busy lives, no more or less than anyone else's."

"Still, you do great work. Important work." Kinsey could have kicked himself for his lack of tact.

"As do you, Mr...?"

"Simon Kinsey. Call me Simon."

"Simon, it is. I'm Craig."

"Nice to meet you. Well..." Kinsey rolled his eyes and winced. "You know what I mean."

Craig chuckled. "I do. So, now that we're friends, Simon, can you tell me the real reason you fell?"

Kinsey lied once more but made a joke about it. If he told Craig the truth about the headaches and the way he'd been feeling of late, he'd be blue-lighted all the way to Oxford. *Not now. Too much going on.*

The other paramedic arrived with a medical kit.

"Simon, meet my lad, Dave. He doesn't work as hard as us," Craig winked, "but he's still learning the job. Wants to be a doctor. I keep telling him he should stick to the ambulances, get to meet far more interesting people."

Dave shrugged, obviously used to his father's good-natured putdowns, and handed over the medical kit. "Message from dispatch—as soon as we're finished here, we're to make our way to the windmills up at Lynnsford."

Craig frowned at his son. "Okay." He turned his attention back to Kinsey. "Right, Simon, I'm trusting you to get something to eat and get some rest—"

"Never mind, that," Kinsey interrupted. "Any chance of a lift up to the farm? I think this is connected to the story I'm covering."

"No can do, I'm afraid. Aside from us not being a taxi service, you haven't been truthful with me this evening. It's your right to refuse treatment, but—"

"What if I guarantee you an interview with the paper—a four-page piece in which the people of this town get to see how you work over the course of say, a week? I won't get in your way, but we can consider this the start of the interview." He'd have to run it past McCarthy, of course, but he didn't foresee any problems.

The two paramedic exchanged glances again. Craig was still doubtful, but his son's eyes lit up with the promise of earning local celebrity status.

"All right," Craig said reluctantly. "You've got two minutes. If you're not out before we've packed everything away, we'll go without you and there'll be no interview."

Kinsey saluted and tore up the stairs to change of clothes, grab his Dictaphone, notebook, bag and pens, his headache forgotten in the blink of an eye. No time to lose—he would have that chiselled into his tombstone—he was climbing into the ambulance before the paramedics had finished putting their equipment away. True to his word, he started gathering background information on the way to the incident, soon discovering Dave was a talker.

"I have a couple of weeks off soon," he said as the ambulance raced through the narrow roads, overhanging tree limbs scratching eerily against the roof. "I've got an invitation to study at Wendlefields—just to observe, follow and learn. I'm psyched to get started. Then back with the ambulances till September and then off to university. When do you think the piece will be out?"

"Before you leave for uni, I would think," Kinsey said. The lad was keen but hardly the stuff of legend. Craig, on the other hand, was more reflective. He'd been in the job a long time and had encountered everything—suicides, car crashes, house fires, old people stuck in their house day after day with no one to care for them suddenly passing away and not being found for weeks. Before that, he'd attended sporting events as part of a St. John's crew, he explained whilst laughing. "I hated the uniform—I was fresh out of the army then."

As they approached the Whittle farm, Kinsey saw a car blocking the way, three police cars had parked up behind it. For the ambulance to pass safely, they would have to square off against the limestone wall that ran parallel to the road.

Theresa Whittle came scuttling out of the farmhouse, a torch bobbing up and down in time with her movement. "Thank God you're here!"

Her country accent was extenuated by fear and alarm as she explained her part in what had taken place. Out of earshot of the female teacher and the remaining kids, she'd called the police and asked for immediate assistance with a problem involving the kids at the farm. As soon as she'd put the phone down, she'd implored the teacher to take the four teenagers back to Liverpool. The teacher had argued at first but relented when she understood the police would be on their way. She'd left only five minutes before the first police car turned up.

"I couldn't move my brother's car," Theresa explained apologetically. "I can drive tractors easy enough, but cars—too fiddly for me, and my brother's still up at the windmill."

She looked at all the vehicles blocking the lane up to the farm. If this story was as big as Kinsey believed, by tomorrow, she would be a virtual prisoner, her farm an island surrounded by sharks holding microphones, television cameras and flashbulbs.

"They're all up at the windmill," she said, pointing in that direction. "An officer said they'd stay with me, but I told them not to bother—I only came out when I saw your lights coming up the lane.

Kinsey stared at the flustered woman. He'd noticed her earlier in the day, but with everything else that had happened, he hadn't probed too deeply. Now his mind was racing, attempting to place the woman, to remember her story. Her name hadn't been Whittle, that much he was sure of.

Theresa Whittle caught his stare, and he saw the fear shift to resignation, but he shrugged it off, exasperated that his memory had let him down. It was the thing he relied upon most.

The paramedics had already gathered their equipment, and he set off with them for the windmills. Glancing back towards the farm, he saw the Theresa make her way back inside, an air of defeat hanging around her like a black cloud. Kinsey understood the toll of a tragedy happening on your own property, and she was obviously distraught, but her brother would be back soon; he'd be able to deal with the fallout when it came.

Even with the path having recently been beaten down by police officers trampling their collective size nines, the way past the river and on to the windmills was difficult, and it wasn't until they saw the flashing lights of torches and heard the hurried sound of officers running towards them that they knew they were on the right track. One false step and they would have been in the river.

The two officers slowed as they approached, hailing them as they did so. Kinsey recognised them both. They nodded at the journalist but didn't address him.

"Is it only the two of you?" Craig asked.

"We're heading back to the cars. We need more equipment and people up here. It's a right mess—might be a good idea from one of you to come back with us and call for another crew."

Dave didn't wait for an instruction from his father. He handed his gear to Kinsey and jogged away with the police officers, two torch lights floating into the distance and then disappearing, the darkness consuming them.

"You ever been out here, Simon?" Craig asked as they continued on their way.

"When I was a kid. I think most of us did at one point or another, although the days of the fair were winding down by the time I was old enough to appreciate it."

"My mother stopped bringing me out here after they found that little girl in the river. I begged, of course—the fair was the highlight of the year for me—but my mother was a formidable woman, there was no shifting her on the subject. She never believed it was an accident."

The question formed in Kinsey's mouth, a wisp of detail in his hands, but it was forgotten with the sight of two men sitting on the grass in front of the windmill, their heads in their hands, a police officer standing with them, horror deeply ingrained in his face. The windmill door was open, and several figures were illuminated by dancing torchlight.

A shout cut through the fear that was creeping out from inside. "Here she is—what's left of her, anyway." Squinting through the open door, Kinsey could make out a police officer crouched on a high beam. "She's still dissolving, but it's got to be her!"

One of the men on the grass looked up, and Kinsey saw it was the teacher he had seen briefly that morning—Theresa Whittle's brother. The man attempted to stand, his legs buckling under the weight of grief, and the police officer steadied him. Kinsey put the equipment on the ground and walked over, his hand outstretched.

"Mr. Whittle, isn't it?" The man before him seemed to have aged ten years in a day, his thick mop of brown hair now spotted with white, dried blood running from his temple down the side of his face. There was more blood on the man's jacket and mixed with mud and hay on his shoes.

"It's not mine," the teacher said. "It came from in there." He gestured to the windmill and then to the police officer and other man still sitting on the ground. "We've all got it on us." He turned away slightly, his eyes full of questions and terror. "If you have the stomach, you need to see it for yourself before they close it off."

The teacher returned to his former position on the ground and leaned across to place an arm around the other man, who was weeping.

Kinsey turned away, glad to have witnessed such compassion, and in doing so saw two figures looking down on the scene, their silhouettes lit by the headlights of what appeared to be a large truck. If he'd thought he could make it up the hill without falling, he'd have done so and…then what? Confronted them to ease his troubled mind? A familiar sense of dread enveloped him, and instead, he focused on the windmill. Craig was already in there, and Kinsey walked up behind him, preparing to face the images illuminated by torchlight.

High above him, suspended from thick rope, hung the body of a boy, his throat cut, his stomach open, his entrails and guts hanging out. What blood remained in his body was slowly leaking down onto the hay-scattered floor below, a constant steady drip that marked the seconds ticking by. The boy's head lolled to one side, his half-severed neck under the strain of being ripped from the rest of the body. Kinsey's eyes followed the ropes up to a pulley system and back down to the boy, suspended in ghoulish, Christ-like serenity as if he understood he had to die, and they, the witnesses to this crucifixion made of rope and metal.

The scene was one Kinsey always imagined when he read books on ritual murder. A torch swept over the windmill's interior woodwork, picking out chalk drawings of otherworldly worship and unintelligible writing scrawled on the beams and in small pockets of clear floor. Below the boy—a ten-foot drop when they went to lower him down—was an image, slowly disintegrating as blood dripped upon it, of a pale-faced man, a snarl of a grin emerging on either side of the man's finger pressed to his bulbous lips. Written underneath his image was a single word, scrawled in block capitals and ingrained into the fabric of the building: DISEASED.

Kinsey tore his eyes away from the macabre altar and saw Craig climbing a ladder to where the police officer had shouted earlier that he had found a girl.

"It's impossible," Craig shouted down to Kinsey. "I'd suggest you come up and see for yourself, but it's too dangerous in your state. There's no girl, just pale goo trapped inside an...ice coffin like an Egyptian—what's it called? Sarcophagus."

Craig sat on his haunches, shaking his head. Kinsey admired him for not giving way. He just took it in, contemplating what could have taken place here. Of all the tales Craig had to tell about his job, this one topped the lot. Some would accuse him of embellishing the facts; Kinsey hoped he would be there to set them straight.

The sound of a scuffle behind him made him turn around. A young girl, slight in stature, roared with anguish and venom and charged at him. One of the police officers—a sturdy man who could have taken on a pro-wrestler—grabbed her, pinning her arms to her sides, yet somehow she got one arm free, and as she straightened it in front of her, Kinsey saw the glint of a kitchen knife. Before Kinsey could warn the officer, the girl swung her arm backwards, slamming the blade into the officer's thigh. Blood spurted from the wound, but the officer kept his hold on the girl.

Above him, Kinsey saw Craig move along the beam and down the ladder with the quiet grace of a gazelle.

Unsure what to do, Kinsey stood motionless as the girl worked the knife out of the policeman's leg and then sickeningly plunged it in once more, this time connecting with the man's groin.

One of the other officers sprinted to his colleague's aid and managed to catch the injured man as he fell backwards, his screams rivalling the girl's in intensity, though his were ripped from his throat in pain, while hers was demonic, seized by the devil and rejoiced in its anger. She charged forward again, knocking Kinsey off balance, and fell to her knees, her palms sliding in the mixture of hay, mud and the boy's blood. Dipping her head, she licked at the congealed mess, her tongue digging ravenously into the grooves in the floor.

Craig approached her subtly, quietly, from one side, while the uninjured officer came from the other, holding back until Craig signalled he was ready, at which point the officer leapt on the girl and held her down while Craig slammed a syringe into her arm. Slowly, unremarkably, the girl's body went limp and still. The police officer was taking no chances; rolling her onto her front, he cuffed her wrists. All the while, the boy's blood dripped down between them, replenishing the pool the girl had started to lick clean and Kinsey stood motionless, an uninvited guest at a frenzied feast.

The commotion inside the windmill had alerted the teacher and the fourth police officer, who warily stepped inside. By then, Craig had moved away from the unconscious girl and was tending as best as he could to the fallen police officer, who was losing a lot of blood. Kinsey tried to speak, but the words came out in a flood of stuttering nonsense. Before he could even take a breath and start over, a crack sounded above him, the wooden beam gave way, and the remains of the other girl came crashing down, the icy tomb cracking open as it hit the floor feet first, wood splinters showering the scene and embedding themselves in the after-image of the girl like stakes into a monster's heart, before the sarcophagus toppled and fell onto its side.

Whatever was left of the girl, the residue, the dissipated soul, seeped out like wet candy floss on the circus floor, sticky, foul-smelling, inching its way towards the unconscious girl. It was the final straw for the group of men inside the windmill as they watched the mixture crawl up the girl's shoulder and across her chin, and she opened her mouth and lapped at it like a kitten enjoying its first taste of cream.

The officers who had met Kinsey, Craig and Dave on the path from the farm returned soon after and carried their fallen comrade to the ambulance, commending Craig on his work. He'd tied a tourniquet around the leg and pressed his entire stock of bandages over the stab wound in the officer's groin. Neither they nor Dave believed the tale of what had happened in the short time they had been away.

Once they were all out of the building, the officers taped off the scene, closing the door carefully and respectfully on the boy still hanging there. Not until the scene-of-crime officers came with their cameras and evidence bags would the door be reopened, and by then, what had transpired would seem impossible. Kinsey looked down at the stretcher and the prone body of the girl who had attacked the police officer, the substance like curdled strawberry yoghurt dribbling from her mouth.

He forced himself to remember that she was once an innocent young woman on the threshold of adulthood with dreams of her own. Even in her unconscious state, something about her struck fear into them all—the surge of animalism, of crazed brutality—and Kinsey realised it was the second time that day he'd witnessed it. Serena Cox had surprised and scared half the crowd outside the facility at Wendlefields with her violent display.

Paul Whittle broke the silence. "Would it be okay if I took Mr. Singh back to the farm? I don't think he can take much more of this." Without hesitation, the senior police officer, only by virtue of age, nodded in agreement. There was nothing more the two teachers could do. Paul shot a look at Kinsey, who took the hint and offered his services.

"I'll walk back with you," he said.

When they were out of earshot of the officers, Paul Whittle thanked him. "I couldn't have carried Mr. Singh to the farm on my own."

"Not a problem," Kinsey assured him. What he didn't say was that he didn't want to be around that girl anymore. He felt his headache start again. Arms draped around both their shoulders, the grief-stricken Mr. Singh stayed silent, shell-shocked and unable to comprehend the savagery of the attack.

As they crossed the low fence that acted as a boundary between the two properties, Kinsey looked up once more at the hill. The figures were gone, the light of the truck extinguished. All seemed normal at the other farm, and he thought that strange. Surely someone, if not to offer assistance then out of sheer curiously, should have come down to see what the trouble was?

Chapter Nineteen

REBECCA McCARTHY GRUMBLED to herself as she walked through the rapidly darkening town. She had tried to get hold of her mother, but all the phone numbers she had for her mum's friends were either busy or had rung off the hook. She knew that she had done the right thing by calling an ambulance for Kinsey, but she didn't want to seem uncaring; despite all he had done to her family, there was a part of her that loved the man she called Uncle Simon.

The mismatched pavements bled through the ever-expanding estate of which she had once known every corner and nook. Gone forever was the quaint, old town filled with local people who had never experienced the delights of Oxford. Vanished was a way of life in which children took over their parents' shops and continued on doggedly through every season, every harsh winter, every stifling and joyless summer. The town had grown, stretched out beyond the two estates at either end of the high street, its winding passageways forlorn reminders of former glories.

There was talk at council meetings of the wetland farm just beyond the train station being drained and turned into 500 houses. This was commuter belt within striking distance of London, and further estates were planned plus a new shopping parade on the large field where the local football teams played every Sunday morning. It would not be long before it encompassed the outlying villages and places like Wendlefields, Long Lillis and Redmond Buck were hemmed into the town's borders, a growth uncontained, eating away from the inside, reaching outwards like tendrils. The town she had loved and known was changing, and it didn't sit well in her heart.

The air was cold and damp, and a thin layer of mist clung to the pavement as she walked downhill towards the small playpark, where she cut across the back of the estate to Kinsey's street. Pulling her coat close around her, her tight jeans gripped her legs, she mused that both showed off her figure but did little to keep out the cold. She wondered if she should go home, but to what? There was little warmth in the house since her father had left and her mother was working all hours. Even when she wasn't in the office or chasing a story to fend off bankruptcy, she was never truly at home.

Rebecca understood her mother's desire to keep her distance, knowing she had wrecked something fine, yet she could not bring herself to look her mum in the eye and have that one argument that would clear the air for good. She sulked, slammed doors— anything but hear the make-or-break admission of her mother's part in the destruction of the family home. Rebecca had instead taken all the hatred, all the hurt and despair, and turned into a ball of unforgiving disgust and loathing for Simon Kinsey.

At least I don't have it as bad as Karen, she thought to herself as she reached the corner of the playpark, the swings moving slightly in the callous, icy wind picking up around her. Karen was a former school friend who had come close to dying after a failed overdose on badly cut heroin. Even before the suicide attempt, her life had been one of rotten luck and ill-considered choices, all covered up by an abusive father and a mother who enabled her husband to keep performing acts of cruelty and disgusting advances on their daughter.

The thin layer of mist clung to Rebecca's ankles and numbed her feet. Overhead, the last train from Banbury slowed as it approached the station. Many a school child had scrambled their way to the top of the steep embankment and hidden in the bushes, cheering as the train raced past them.

They had found Karen, unconscious in a drainpipe exposed to the rain and the elements, six days short of her sixteenth birthday. Hers was not the first death that September. A total of twenty young adults and teenagers had been found with that toxic sludge in their systems: drain cleaner and rat poison mixed into the heroin imported by evil men and snatched up by the alienated and estranged. Karen was fortunate, if survival could be considered a blessing. Some had died; others were sent mad—the worst was the woman in the lock-up garage who had stuck needles in her baby. The photo, taken by Kinsey, had made Rebecca want to vomit. For weeks afterwards, it infected her dreams and her waking moments. It took hold of her ability to concentrate, and as she approached her mock exams in the November and December, she felt, like others in her year who had known Karen since infant school, that there was little point in continuing to do their best.

Karen had been found by an old woman walking her dog. The woman had thought it was just a bundle of rags that someone playing silly buggers had thrown down—"Causing mischief ahead of firework night," according to the newspaper article Rebecca's mother and Kinsey had put together.

Mischief...is that all it boils down to? A generation on the verge of neglect, nothing to do, no money to spend, no place to be, all decisions made by those who come straight after the war and who reaped the economic benefit?

Rebecca turned the final corner of her journey; Kinsey's house was at the end of the lane, but even at a distance and in the gloom, she could see there was no ambulance outside. Had it come and already taken Kinsey away? Or had they arrived and, receiving no answer to their knocking, assumed it was part of a hoax and returned to the station?

She felt like the girl in the song—she couldn't remember the title, but the lyrics were of wallflowers, the Magdalene and missed appointments—is that what she was doing here? Was she a lost soul in need of comfort from the older man, the one who had ruined her idealistic picture of family life and replaced it with cold, unfeeling torture? Was he the one who would turn back on a light in her life? She had never thought of it that way, but why else was she here? Up until tonight, she couldn't have cared less if Kinsey lived or died, but something had twisted in her gut when she'd heard him fall to the ground.

Uncomfortable in this new revelation of self, she stopped still and watched the house, trying to make sense of her feelings. The only reason she could find—and it was one that did nothing to dispel the unease in her mind—was that she was fulfilling a petulant wish to get one back on her mother.

The house remained in darkness, no sign it was even lived in. Had Kinsey ever brought another woman across that threshold? Someone to look after him, care for him, scold him, screw him—Rebecca wasn't sure, but she kept looking just the same.

A light came on in the porch of the house next door to Kinsey's, a silhouette unknowing of Rebecca's voyeurism until she took a step too far and crossed an invisible boundary.

Rebecca smiled and waved, such bravery from the nosey, and poked out her tongue, unsure whether she was any more than a ghost at this distance.

How much fear did Karen endure at her father's hands? The times she'd arrived at school caked in make-up and other girls had thought she was being cool, rebellious, flirtatious, a slut and a whore—she became a warning for others. Don't be like the strange girl in heavy eye make-up. When she returned to school after her overdose, there was no sign of childhood left in her. She had lasted out the school year, taken no exams and lost interest in all but daily survival. On the day her father was imprisoned for his crimes, she smiled for the first time in years; when her mother committed suicide, she rejoiced then checked herself into a facility where she could work through the pain, and she had been there ever since, comforted by illusion.

It was the playpark that Rebecca had walked through earlier in which her friend had first tried heroin with a group of strangers bound by guilt and damage, a small dose, just enough to blot out the pain. She had tried to influence her friends, told them about this secret club. Some tried; most kept out of her way; none broke her confidence.

By comparison, Rebecca had been lucky. She had managed to avoid sharing her friend's downfall because of her own problems during that tricky time but had also stuck by her, visiting her in hospital, holding her hand and seeing through the façade of her joy when she heard her mother had looked into the train driver's eyes as she stepped off the platform. Rebecca had mourned with her at the graveside and helped graffiti the house Karen had lived in before the council tore it down.

Rebecca shivered, angry at her own place in life, but she still had both parents, and they both loved her. So why was she here?

She made up her mind to turn around, walk back home, hoping her mother was there when she walked through the door. If asked, she would tell the truth—that she had been worried about Kinsey—and ask her mum to call the hospital and see how he was. Then she would go to bed, no arguments, no drama.

It was then that she felt a hand on her shoulder, a firm unexpected grip that made her heart miss a beat, and she screamed.

Chapter Twenty

BILL TAYLOR OPENED his eyes. He felt as if he had survived a car crash and couldn't understand why. His jaw ached, and he couldn't move his arm without a tight discomfort, but he was alive. He had no reason to think otherwise, but the force with which the woman had hit him…well, he was surprised. A friend in his third year of school had been hit on the head by a heavy, wooden boomerang as he walked across the playing fields, and although Bill didn't hear the sound when it connected with the side of his friend's head, he felt the sickening crunch as it met and knocked him to the ground with tremendous force, killing him instantly.

After that, Bill had become over-cautious when it came to playing sport, first dropping out of rugby, then football. He countered the sports master's anger at losing a good team member by declaring he wanted to play table-tennis—a sport the teacher liked to play but had no opponents. He also took on responsibility as lead long-distance runner for the school; anything to avoid being hit on the head and befalling the same fate as his pal.

Joining the police force had been a different matter. There were more chances of being put in a situation in where someone might take a swing at him, where he would be put in some type of physical danger, but the urge to be part of something bigger, to give something back to the community that had taken his family in when they had come from the Caribbean with just suitcases in their hands was too much of a pull to ignore. Still, he avoided playing contact sport, kept his head and thought of his friend often.

Bill raised himself up as far as he could manage and looked down at his arm. An array of tubes and wires were attached to him, sticking out like porcupine quills. He tried to remove them but found he was unable to move enough to get his arm across and pluck them out without causing untold harm. To be in hospital was bad enough, but to feel as if he was in chains, a prisoner under self-harm watch—he didn't want to endure that for too long.

With effort, he managed to swing his arm across his chest. An electrical monitor started to beep; Bill supposed correctly that an alarm had been triggered and that he might not have long before someone came to check what the problem was. Already, there was movement outside the door, a female voice, low, conspiratorial.

Ripping off the last of the electrical monitors, he cautiously sat up. His head felt heavy, and he put one hand up to his face. A hard shell covered the right side, and when he tapped it, it sounded like solid plaster. Then his fingers touched something metal, a prong sticking out, several others across his jawline; they had wired his mouth shut. If he had wanted to call out for help, to raise the alarm—hell, even enquire where the toilet was—he was out of luck.

It was only then he became fully aware of the room in which he had awoken.

Surrounding him on all sides were machines, and large metallic lamps shone down on him. At the end of the bed was a metal table, on it a container full of surgical instruments—the blade of a scalpel glinting in the harsh light. He put his feet on the floor, and the shock of cold made him wince. Someone had removed his boots and socks whilst he had been out of it. Then he remembered the plaster and metal wire across his face; surely someone would have had to give permission to do the surgery? He certainly didn't remember giving it himself.

The whisper of a woman's voice came again, this time with the tentative push on the door. Bill stood to his full height, the cold floor giving him extra incentive to run as hard as he could towards the person and catch them off guard. A woman popped her head around the door and asked with a fair degree of suspicion, "Mr. Taylor, is that you?

Bill stayed quiet, not only because of his jaw. It had already been a day of the unexpected and he didn't want to add an element of treachery to the list of things he had to tell his girlfriend the next time he saw her.

The woman asked again, "Mr. Taylor? It looks like you. See—I am unarmed." She put both her hands through the gap and turned them over, revealing nothing but empty palms. "I won't hurt you."

Through the metal wiring keeping his mouth shut, Bill managed to get out the words, "Who are you? Where are we?"

The woman walked into the room and turned around so that Bill could see she was not concealing a weapon. She was dressed in a hospital gown of basic material, pure white, but as she turned, Bill noticed that there was a small logo above the pocket.

"My name is Serena Cox. I'm the woman who got you into this mess. As for where we are—well, we haven't moved. We're still at the facility at Wendlefields."

She walked over to the bed and looked up at his face with shame. "I did that. No, don't try to open your mouth. Just nod or shake your head. For what it's worth, I really didn't mean it. I mean, yes, I hate you lot, the police, but I would never intentionally hurt someone. I wasn't thinking."

Inside, Bill wanted to grab her by the wrist, put a pair of handcuffs on her and charge her with so many offences she'd be in Oxford Crown Court from now until the turn of the decade. Instead, he sat on the bed. His jaw hurt, he was tired, and he didn't want to be accused of anything that might come back to bite him later.

"Just listen and do the thing with your head if you understand."

Bill nodded slowly. He could see the woman's face perfectly now, but she too was covered in bruises—on her face, arms and legs. He couldn't fathom what had happened. They were supposed to have taken him to the hospital in Oxford to get his jaw reset and then perhaps some time off work to recover, hopefully at home. If he got lucky, he might be able to swing it until well into the World Cup, watching television, even if it meant drinking milkshakes. Instead, this crazy-ass woman with elbows of steel was telling him things that he didn't want to know. Bill set his frustration aside and urged her to continue.

Serena Cox smiled, though she looked like she'd lost a fist fight with a soldier from Upper Heyford. No doubt, she was intimidating when she fresh-faced, and that was okay, but that elbow—he didn't want to get on the sharp end of that again.

"I turned off the alarms—there's a control switch outside the room. Did you pull out all your wires? Show me your arm."

Bill did as he was told. He turned his arm over and showed the campaigner that she was right: every wire and tube was out, just the residue of restraints, no blood.

"Good. They've been monitoring you." She looked down at the multitude of hanging wires almost brushing the floor and bent down to pick up a silver lead, giving Bill a broad grin of triumph, and then proceeded to explain the injection procedure and what it carried into Bill's nervous system.

Once she had finished, Bill looked her in the eye and told her, to the best of his ability, that she was a loon, a fruitcake, although with his teeth almost clamped together it came out as a small, indecipherable moan. He believed he made his point though when she stepped back, but her hurt at his disbelief didn't last long. It never did with Serena Cox. A hard-line socialist, she was a mentally tough woman who had camped outside American army bases, been to Woodstock in her youth and come back with great ideas and noble principles, but also left her child with her parents for months at a time when the call came.

"You don't believe me, Mr. Taylor. Okay, come with me, and I will show you what's going on here." With that, she pulled Bill off the bed and led him by the hand, her grip vice-like with no chance of escape.

Serena stopped at the door, opened it a few inches and smiled. Seeming satisfied, she motioned to her new captive to follow her out into the white-tiled hallways and the powerful stench of bleach.

"There were three children brought in here. One died—you probably know that—one girl has recovered and is resting. Her mother is keeping vigil by her bedside, so she won't be tampered with. Then there is the local boy, Tom Solden. He's unconscious, and I don't know if he'll recover." She talked as she walked, her footsteps quiet. "I'll show you him first. The nurses will be back around in about fifteen minutes, so we have to be quick. Understand?"

Serena looked back at Bill, who despite having a good six inches and at least five stone on the woman, was having trouble keeping up. Her grip on his arm intensified as she spoke, the excitement of her discovery fuelling her mania.

"Understand?" she asked again a little more forcefully.

Bill nodded. Although he thought she was crazy at best, dangerous at worst, he wanted to see with his own eyes what was going on. Down one corridor, past doors that were all painted with the same bright white, turning into another corridor and slowing as they came to one room that was open, and on the bed was a young boy, a teenager who looked sick but at peace. Serena ventured into the room, letting go of Bill's arm as she crossed the threshold.

"You don't have to come in, but you won't be able to see from there what this tube is collecting." The suggestion was almost hypnotic, and Bill wondered if this was how she'd become a trusted figure on the picket lines and in the campsites. It may have been her spirit, her loyalty to her cause, but Bill surmised it was because she smiled—a lot. There was a seething volcano of hate and vengeance in that woman, but there was also a lot to love, and if you were in pain, who did you turn to? The one who smiled and told you how the war could be won.

Bill stepped into the small, almost forgotten room, no furniture except for the bed the boy lay upon and a small machine with several wires coming out of it, including a silver one similar to the one Serena had identified in Bill's room. The other end of the wire appeared to enter the boy's head.

"What's it doing?" Bill managed to push the words out between his teeth, the action making him sound a lot tougher than he felt.

"Try not to talk, Mr. Taylor. You will only hurt yourself further, and I don't want that on my conscience, not when there is this to sit there unhappily." Serena pointed to the machine. "This is keeping Tom alive. If it were not for this machine, he would have rotted from the inside out by now. That's what happened to the other boy. He just dissolved, liquified, and all that was left was goop, juice and pulp."

Bill had seen his fair share of unbelievable moments in his time. He had arrested paedophiles and been on duty when the Queen opened the sports centre. He had helped in the search for a local criminal who had absconded from jail and taken his father hostage. The everyday and the unreal, side by side. Yet before him, he saw liquid, brown and thick, being pumped from the boy's head and collecting a plastic hospital bag, and he could not believe it.

He tried to talk, but his mouth strained, the words caught between his teeth. Frustrated, he wanted to rip the wire off and scream. Serena saw his agitation and took his hand again, shushing him gently.

"From what I've been able to gather, the poison,—if we can call it that—is what they're collecting, nothing else. No brain matter, no blood. He will survive. He wasn't protected like the girl—don't ask me how I know that. It's just a feeling." She released Bill and turned her attention back to the boy "What you should be asking, Mr. Taylor, is what they plan to do with this collection of bad dreams and body sores."

Placing her hand on the boy's temple, she brushed back his hair and caressed his cheek with what Bill could only describe as a mother's touch.

The seconds ticked by. The building was asleep; the boy might survive, but Bill felt his reality crashing down, Joshua's trumpet declaring war on Jericho and then playing a sad lament for the fallen.

"You see it, Mr. Taylor, don't you? You had the same silver lead in your arm. That was not the monitor, it was a tube so you could receive the goop from his body into yours."

With a Herculean effort, Bill asked how she knew this.

An unexpected female voice from behind him to jump.

"Because, Mr. Taylor, I have already done the procedure on her.

Chapter Twenty-One

MARBON HAD NO intention of delaying the next shipment to Yobe's farm. To do so meant questions would be asked, and whilst he didn't mind taking the responsibility for a greedy fool such as Yobe, he refused to associate his name with any type of screw-up or delay.

The day had got away from Marbon. He had no memory of getting back home after walking through the woods earlier. He looked down at his hands, still dirty from his fall, and at his trousers, torn across the knees, smudges of blood congealed on the surface, the hems hanging like twigs caught in a storm.

Trying to retrace steps is normally an easy task. Even under the influence of a few shots of whisky, you can make an educated guess of where you've been—unless, of course, you were absolutely hammered, and that hadn't happened to Marbon for many years.

Concentrating harder than he had done as a young man when handling explosive devices or learning how to handle a gun, he remembered falling and catching his foot as he made his way to collect the papers and then nothing until the phone rang and the mist cleared.

He strained to think beyond that. His right ankle felt stiff when he tried to turn it. His mind went back to the woods—had he knocked himself out as he hit the ground? If so, how did he manage to get back home? The master wouldn't have left the house, not on such a cold day. His wife was too frail, and they wouldn't have called the police; they wouldn't have wanted to make a fuss.

He was sure there was some painkillers in the kitchen. If he could hobble through, maybe by the morning, he would feel better and be able to resume his duties.

Marbon went to stand up, but nausea flushed through his stomach and smacked angrily against his head.

Marbon sat back down carefully, the very motion easing the pain. Images swarmed like hungry ants gnawing inside his brain, of a girl dying in a hotel bathroom, a hit of heroin coursing through her system, and he had watched her die. He saw himself looking down at her as her soul slowly ebbed away, her breathing slowing, became faint, barely registered. Panic rose in his stomach, his alert mind quickly going through all the options. This was the biggest personal crisis he'd had to endure, one that would be eclipsed in the future, but for now, it felt as if the sky wasn't just falling in, it was fracturing, splintering, shards of blue piercing his skin as they fell to earth, turning black then dirty red as they sliced him into pieces.

Marbon had done the only logical thing: he'd left her there on the cold floor as the drug in her system did its corrosive work. He was sure he hadn't been seen on the way out of the hotel; there was evidence that he had been in the room. If someone dared point him out in a line-up, he would say he had taken her to the room, and she had thanked him for a pleasant date, but she was tired and closed the door without a kiss goodbye. *I swear upon the bible and the patron saints, Your Honour, she was alive when I last saw her.*

He *had* been seen, though, recognised by one of the commander's 'eyes on the street'—or in this case a hotel worker who reported back after the body had been found that Marbon had been there. That girl, that pretty, young woman—how she had entranced him. But he wouldn't have gone near her had he known she was a drug user. He may have been many things, but he refused to sanction the abuse of narcotics.

That was the beginning of the end. The ants bit down harder, the silence of their noise deafening, the instructions passed between them as they dug deeper through every mistake, every error of judgement, nibbling at the connections, the motion of their labour making him anxious. Prickly heat rubbed at his arms, and the pain in his ankle became unbearable. He couldn't remember if he had ever felt such unease, such restless apprehension. He wanted to call the master, but what would he do? Anonymity at all costs, the barest of contact with the town, only a favoured few being given access to his time and even less to his funding. Marbon tried to pick up the phone, but his arms felt like fire.

Why had he fallen? He knew the wood, every pathway, every hidden hole; every tree was indelibly stamped in his memory. He kept the trails free of the encroaching vines—they were his woods in essence. He treated it as if it were his own personal kingdom. The pathway had been clear...

The clock on the mantelpiece chimed, a sweet serenade for the bereft and floundering. With renewed vigour, he overrode the fire in his arms and dialled a number. Whoever answered the phone did so too quickly, catching the Irishman lost for words, and when he did speak, they sounded strange, metallic, robotic, certainly not his own dark tones and the linger of whiling away afternoons down on the River Liffey that had cultivated both his lilt and his temperament.

"Who's this?"

"Dennis, is that you? It's Marbon!"

"Yeah, it's Dennis. You all right? You sound awful." Dennis wasn't wrong; he sounded like one of those insidious aliens that inhabited that television programme the kids watched and their parents pretended they didn't.

"I'm fine. Now, listen, there's a delivery scheduled for tonight. Yobe has asked me to cancel because of some trouble up at the farm. I want you to deliver it anyway—straight in and straight out. We can't afford to have it hanging around. There will be someone still up at the farm—let them deal with it. We need it off the books as soon as we can. Do you understand?"

Dennis confirmed that he did, and the phone went dead. No messing around, simple instructions followed to the letter, such should be the response everywhere. There were too many people who believed they had to ask questions; Dennis was not one of those people.

With searing pain so intense Marbon could well imagine it left scorch marks on the inside of his body, he dropped the phone handset. It clattered against the base and bounced, its cord acting as a bungee cord, swaying side to side until the receiver finally came to a rest a couple of inches off the ground. Marbon looked down as best as he could at the resemblance to the Hanged Man in a Dali-esque Tarot.

One more second of agony in his arms, and then his body became still, his heart still beating, He closed and opened his eyes several times. Nothing changed. The wallpaper pattern didn't morph into the glistening purity of heaven; more importantly, it didn't transform into the fiery pits of hell. It was just the same wallpaper that had been slowly fading and revealing the crumbling walls beneath.

Marbon slowly moved his left arm, waiting for a surge of pain, but it didn't come, and the simple actions which yesterday, he took for granted, now returned to him. He straightened out his arms and felt relief of being able to bend them again, as if all he had suffered was a bout of intense cramp. At worst, he wondered somewhere in his mind, if he had experienced a mild stroke. Recalling an aged aunt who had danced as a young woman in her kitchen with Eamon de Valera, then, following a stroke, refused to uncover her face for the rest of her short life, Marbon rose with the intention of looking in the mirror. His ankle was still tender and stiff, and he sat again and bent over to remove his shoe, noticing that beneath the torn, frayed trouser legs, minute flecks of broken bark and wood had embedded themselves in his flesh.

Lifting his leg up and placing it precariously across its partner, he took off his sock and examined his ankle. It wasn't broken, of that he was sure, but around the bruising, there was a yellowish ring, raised and bumpy to the touch. He felt what he thought was a strange scab and was surprised by the tackiness. On closer inspection, he saw that the yellow tinge had attached itself to his fingertips and glowed slightly, the skin underneath pulsing with life.

Bringing his fingers to his nose, he sniffed and immediately recoiled against the smell. It reminded Marbon of rotting flesh, meat that had spoiled. A vague childhood memory of childhood, a group of young children in the Irish countryside exploring an off-limits building. One of the boys, Sean maybe, had dared him to crawl through a gap in the metal covering that once housed the building's boiler. The inevitable shouts of 'chicken' followed, accompanied by arm flapping and squawking noises that gathered strength the more the young frightened child shook his head.

Finally, out of shame of being thought a coward, he relented and crawled through the metal opening, finding his way blocked by a rusted fan hanging off its hinges. Beyond the fan were slivers of light and male voices shouting, one singing a local tune, another asking if he knew any other song because that one was recorded by an Englishman. As the two men argued over the rights and wrongs of song-writing, he plucked up the courage to kick through the remainder of the hanging fan and then lowered himself gently to the ground.

From the outside, the building was a blot on the village's landscape. His parents had always forbade him from even coming this far down the hill. If he was playing with his friends, he should go up the hill or out towards the park. The trouble was, the park was as rusty as the villagers' thinking; even as a young boy, he was aware there needed to be change. He had not yet learned the word radical, but his aunt had encouraged him to listen to stories of a time before the war, of her own grandmother's fight to survive the famine and losing three of her four children to those desperate times.

The smell was intense. Marbon wanted to throw up, and he held his nose and breathed through his mouth, his lips only slightly open, acting in his mind as a gauze between him and the unnameable stench. From outside, he could hear the faint tones of his friends, an excitable babble of noises and that sneak Michael declaring he was probably hiding in the vent and crying for his mammy. Someone banged on the outside of the metal air vent, and his friends laughed, until a louder, deeper voice shouted at them, bringing an end to their fun.

"*Now* who's crying?" Marbon asked himself absent-mindedly as he studied his fingers some more.

The young Marbon moved from his spot and took refuge behind a steel container to catch his wits. He couldn't hear his friends now; the noise of industry overpowered them, metal grinding on metal, the concrete floor vibrating violently as he hid in the shadows. He couldn't turn back now; he guessed that at least one of his friends had dobbed him in under the threat of a good, hard slap. The only way out, it seemed, was through the front of the building.

He believed he may have ten minutes at the most, to get to the front door and scarper. Naively, he thought if they didn't see his face then he couldn't be recognised. Even if all his friends were subjected to a thrashing and named him as part of the enterprise, he would just say, "*You didn't see me—how could I have been there?*"

He was about to leave the shelter of his hidden position when he heard a phone ring. His parents didn't have a phone, neither did the vast majority of his neighbours, but his aunt had one, and the complex system of wires and structure of the machine had fascinated him, an early attraction which would serve him well when bombs became his natural home. The phone rang again, and this time, Marbon ran. The phone would attract attention, calling out to the workers in its shrill voice, *"Here he is, follow my tune, here he is. This way, man who sings English songs. This way."*

The building was large, but it was laid out methodically, each twist and turn bringing him closer to the goal of freedom. The door was not that far away when he heard a shout. He'd been seen.

Marbon panicked. On the walkway above the steel vats was his father, a hard hat covering the remains of once-golden locks of hair, his features revealing surprise and alarm at seeing his son running around a building he had expressly forbidden him to be within a mile of.

"Stand still! One of my men will collect you and lead you to safety. Just please stand still, son."

The words were lost on Marbon. The panic rose in his stomach, fear and concern strangely alluring bedfellows. Across the narrow gap, he saw some stairs and ran for them. He reached the bottom as a man in blue overalls rounded the corner, warning him to stand still. Marbon ignored the request and climbed, each step taking him into the darkness above his head, where he could scurry like a mouse through the labyrinth until he found another way down.

He reached the top of the metal stairs and heard the phone ring again. He wondered how many phones such a building needed. In the darkness, he couldn't see more than a couple of steps in front of him, but he could still hear the man behind him manoeuvring up the stairs. Marbon turned to see if he could jump to a different level and saw there was a small walkway not five feet across from his location. He could easily jump that: a short run up and he would be across. From there, he would continue his escape. Avoiding his father later would be out of the question, but at least he wouldn't be caught in here.

He took a couple of steps back onto the ledge that hung above the metal vat and saw the head of the pursuing man. He closed his eyes and said a small, childish prayer to a god he wasn't sure existed. Opening his eyes, he realised he needed to back up further to gain enough momentum. At the last second, his pursuer stopped and held up his hands. "Don't take another step, *please.*"

The man's scream was lost in the cacophony of noise, machines and tools, steamers and pistons clanking. Later, Marbon wondered, as he nursed a backside whipped raw by his mother, what had caused him to lose his balance and fall into the mixture below. Whatever it had been, the fall was relatively short, but the liquid he had pulled him under, the stench of the dead clogging his nose and filling his mouth, and he was sure he was going to die when a strong hand dragged him out and back onto the platform. He had fallen less than a foot into the uncovered remains of the dead, an exposed pressure cooker in which melted fat and carcasses was being drained, ready to be turned into glue in another part of the building. He was fortunate that the vat was only being primed and hadn't yet reached full heat.

His father was reprimanded, but he didn't lose his job. Another of the men wasn't so lucky. Michael's father took to drink in shame of his son's part in the betrayal of trust, and within a year, Marbon, his mother and father, and the rest of the village attended the man's funeral. He had committed suicide with his own father's rifle that he had found on the floor of the Dublin post office in 1916.

"Still crying, Michael?" Marbon heard himself say unkindly as he focused once more on his fingertips and the yellow tinge that was turning to slime. From somewhere, a man's faint voice crept out of his dreams and into the waking world. Realising it was coming from beside him, he bent down and tentatively picked up the phone. "Hello?"

Nothing; no sound. Marbon felt a moment of foolishness and went to replace the handset on its cradle when a voice said, "Marbon, I'm so glad to meet you."

Chapter Twenty-Two

U PON THE RIDGE which led down to the river and windmills, the two figures watched impassively in the darkness, the lights of a truck shining down on the field below and the sound of mayhem filling their ears. Dennis lit a cigarette and offered his companion one from the packet. The man refused firmly but politely, adding sage advice on how each drag took a minute off your life. Dennis smiled. After all the shit he'd had to deal with, the refusal of compensation from Her Majesty's Forces for the damage to his face and chest as a result of burns when his ship was torpedoed in the South Atlantic, a smoke every now and then was hardly a concern.

He removed the cigarette from his lips and blew the smoke out into the cold air. "Marcus couldn't get anywhere near the coppers down there. They told him in no uncertain terms to back off! What do you think they're doing? Looks serious, doesn't it?"

His companion on the ridge shrugged. "Does it matter?"

Dennis agreed, to an extent. Being nosey by nature, and in other circumstances, he might have wandered down the hill and offered to lend a hand so he could glean information which might serve some purpose later.

"Come on, we have got to get this lorry unloaded and out of here before your boss turns up," his companion said, slapping Dennis on the back. Dennis traced the sky with the tip of his cigarette and plunged it into the surface of the moon, imagining it puncturing the celestial body, deflating it like a football caught on the pike of a metal railing, or a head on show on Traitor's Gate.

"How much is there tonight?"

"Twelve large barrels—less than an hour if we put our backs into it."

"He'll be here by then."

Another shrug; another unsaid *"Do I care?"*

Dennis flicked his cigarette out in the night. The moon, happy to still exist, shone down on the men as they walked back to the truck. Dennis's companion climbed into the cab and turned off the headlights.

"No sense giving the crowd below a reason to come up the hill tonight. Let's get these barrels into the barn."

Dennis and the driver worked for twenty minutes before a car's headlights were seen at the entrance to the farm.

"What do we do?" Dennis asked.

"What can we do? We've already unloaded six. It won't take much longer, and besides, as far as you know, I didn't get the message in time. There's nothing to worry about."

Dennis worried. He obeyed orders and followed instructions because that was how he had always operated. From the barracks to war and into the misery of civilian life, he had toed the line, but that didn't mean he would never worry.

The two men were lifting the seventh barrel down when Yobe's car pulled up alongside. His face flushed with anger, he started to shout but quickly realised he had wound up the window to keep out the cold. Dennis's companion hid his amusement by turning his back on the owner of the farm and rolled the barrel down the gangplank, Dennis bringing it to a halt just a couple of feet from Yobe's driver's side door.

"What the hell is going on, Dennis? Why is he here?" He glared at the driver. "Didn't you see all those police down by the river?"

The driver climbed down from the lorry and held up his hands. "I am sorry, Mr. Yobe. I only got the message when I arrived. Dennis told me you'd telephoned him and our mutual friend, but my radio is damaged—a wiring problem, I think. Won't be able to get it fixed until I get back to the yard. Anyway, we're nearly done, another twenty minutes out in the open, another twenty to get the barrels inside, and I shall be on my way. I will note your concerns, but they don't care about us up here. Whatever obstruction to the law they're facing down there, I'm sure it will take up all their time."

Dennis helped Yobe out of the car and handed him a pair of gloves. "I'll park the car for you, sir. I thought you might have been here quicker, though." Dennis openly admired the vehicle.

Yobe stopped him curtly. "No, I will do it. I had to run another errand along the way. Something else came up, and I don't want the item broken. I will move it. You get those damn barrels inside before the whole of the Oxfordshire constabulary descend upon us."

Chapter Twenty-Three

"WHO THE HELL are you?"

The man who had gripped Rebecca's shoulder stepped back and raised both his hands in the air, turning them around slowly to show he meant no harm and wasn't carrying a weapon.

Rebecca's scream had been loud enough for several of Kinsey's neighbours to poke their heads out of their doors but not enough to get involved, although one brave old man shouted across his front garden to ask if she was all right.

"Please, I will not hurt you. Just tell him you are okay. I will explain, and I will not take another step near you."

There was no way she was trusting the stranger, but she also didn't want to give the old man an excuse to get involved. The man in front of her had at least one hundred pounds on her, but he was in no physical condition to catch her if she ran. She also had a large kitchen knife in her bag.

"Sorry. I didn't mean to disturb you," Rebecca called to the old man. "Just a friend jumping out on me."

He seemed to take exception at her reply and shouted at her for disturbing the peace as he shut the door with a slam and a final curse word.

As Rebecca fumbled in her bag, the man lowered his hands and thanked her, begging her pardon for any distress. When he caught sight of the knife being held up in front of him, he took another step backwards and started to utter words that made no sense to her.

"What are you doing? What are you saying?" Then, remembering he hadn't answered her initial question, she repeated, more calmly this time, "Sorry, who are you?"

"Please, I don't want to get hurt. I only wanted to talk to you about your friend Kinsey."

Rebecca lowered the knife, not all the way down, but enough to show she was prepared to listen. The man visibly dropped guard, giving Rebecca a chance to properly look at him: piercing blue eyes; short hair that matched the faded glory of a bushy, grey beard, which covered what might have been a strong jaw; he was tall but carrying more weight than looked natural on his frame. His coat was shabby, but his shoes looked brand-new, even if they were covered in specks of mud and dirt.

"Had a good look at me have you, miss?" he asked, his face a mixture of amusement and scowl, as though he had been scrutinised a thousand times before and now, instead of making him angry, it merely confirmed his suspicions that people didn't like what they saw.

Rebecca apologised and in a show of faith placed the knife back in the bag. Taking a gamble that the man would not see detail in the dark, she made out she had zipped it up; she wanted quick access to the blade if he suddenly turned on her.

"Thank you, miss. You asked me a question. My name is Silvanus."

"What do you want, Mr. Silvanus? Why did you grab me like that?

"Silvanus is my first name, my only name—the only name that matters to me. I also suggest we find somewhere less out in the open to talk. The curtains are still twitching, and despite your lie, someone will surely see that I am too old to be a friend and will call the police, who have too much going on at the moment as it is."

"I'm not falling for that. What do you think I am—a ten-year-old being shown a bag of puppies?"

"We could talk inside your friend's house. I know he's not in. He left in an ambulance earlier and forgot to lock the door."

However much the idea of getting out of the cold appealed, Rebecca wasn't about to put herself in a situation which would leave her alone in the company of this man, even if she was confident she could cause more damage with a knife than he could with his hands.

"There's a fish and chip shop back up the road, no more than five minutes. It has a table and a couple of chairs. If you're not there in ten, I'll call for a taxi and then call the police—you might be surprised how creepy and dangerous you'll come off when my imagination starts."

The man stared at Rebecca. She thought he might have been calculating the risk—if he was one of those men who liked to prey on young women—or perhaps he was impressed by her courage and quick thinking. Every bone in her body screamed at her to run, every muscle taut and ready to flee, but something made her focus on something else, something he had said about Kinsey's house.

The man who called himself Silvanus told her he knew the place she'd mentioned and started walking off up the road. No further explanation, no sign of drama; he just ambled on into the night. Rebecca felt in control, a nervous appreciation for a feeling she had barely been able to register over the course of her life. Still, she would take no chances and kept a hand over the top of her handbag, the zip open and ready to deal with anyone who attacked her.

For a little over ten minutes, she followed the man at a safe distance, cutting him some slack. She hadn't noticed his limp before, but as they passed numerous streetlights and cars whose headlights drowned him in fleeting silhouettes, she noticed he was struggling. Of course, it could have been a ploy; her mother had taught her well, and Kinsey and her father—when one was around and the other cared—had given her lessons in self-defence. Whilst she didn't like the idea of hurting anyone, if it came down to the assailant getting four fingers in the throat or her being attacked, then she was punching whoever in the face and kicking them where it hurt as many times as it took.

Finally, they had both arrived at the chip shop. She let him sit down before pushing the door open herself. The smell of vinegar and battered fish hit her nose, and she suddenly found herself salivating at the thought of food. She smiled at the woman behind the counter, someone she recognised from school but who had been a couple of years ahead of her. The woman's dad sat on a stool, drinking a cup of tea.

"Hello, Sandra. Fish and chips, please." Raising her eyebrows at her unexpected guest for the evening, she enquired, "Same for you or would you prefer something else? My treat."

The man smiled respectfully at her and nodded, shifting uncomfortably on the plastic seat as he asked if he could also have a cup of tea. Rebecca returned the nod and ordered their food. Sandra told her to sit down, that she would bring it over in a few minutes

Rebecca paid and joined the man at the table, realising why she had never seen anyone sit there before: both chairs had seen better days.

"The food is miles better." She offered an apologetic smile as if she were to blame for the poor fixtures. In the bright, unforgiving light, she could scrutinise him with greater ease than she had out in the darkness surrounding Kinsey's home. He looked older—nearer sixty rather than the late forties she had guessed—and his beard was, long and unkempt, though his hands though were spotless, even under the nails.

"There you go again, sizing me up, making a profile of me. I guess your mother taught you how to do that. Good woman, she is."

"I'm sorry, truly. But when someone scares the life out of you, you try to remember any detail about them just in case the police need to know later. And yes, my mother did teach me to be observant." Rebecca glowed at what she felt was a compliment from the strange man.

"So observant that you didn't even notice the car behind us, the driver keeping an eye on us just in case something came out of the dark—in case the mist came down?

Rebecca felt awkward, even a little stupid. Of course she hadn't noticed; her mind had been set on keeping a relative distance between her and the man

"Don't worry. It was my daughter. She's out there now, look—underneath the lamppost on the other side of the road, smoking one of her foul cigarettes. She won't bother us. What I have to say is for you. She already knows the story—she was there when it all kicked off by the river."

Rebecca looked out the window and across the road to the woman bathed in light, smoke from a cigarette punching at the barrier between the man-made radiance and the fear of what lay beyond. Her hair, wild and exotic, tumbled down her back, a purple trilby covered her crown, and her clothes seemed to have come straight out of the flower-power days in which Woodstock was a dream and hope was eternal. Rebecca's gaze was interrupted by Sandra placing down two plates of fish and chips in front of them, followed quickly by the tea. Rebecca said thanks; the old man, obviously not one for social niceties, simply grunted through a worrying grin.

Not bothering with the knife and fork, he picked up a chip and bit into it, his eyes lighting up at the taste. "Haven't had chips in ages. Rosa won't let me eat them—bad for my heart."

"Mr. Silvanus, are we going to discuss your health, or do you want to tell me what this is about?"

Silvanus' grin disappeared, but not before he grabbed a handful of chips from his plate, crammed them into his mouth and knocked on the window to catch his daughter's attention. Rebecca could see her swearing under her breath and in that instant began to warm to the old man. Anybody who could still have a streak of rebellion in them at that age couldn't be all that bad. Silvanus chewed with delight, vinegar running into his beard. He didn't seem to care. Rebecca gave in. He would talk when he wanted to; she may as well eat her meal.

She got halfway through her fish when the old man belched his appreciation and held up his now-empty plate for his daughter to see.

Cackling like an errant schoolboy, he said, "I'm going to pay for that later, not just because it will play havoc with my stomach, but because she will not allow me to eat anything except strained rabbit for weeks." He laughed again, wiped his mouth and then leaned forward, his whole demeanour changing in the blink of an eye.

"Your town is in danger. You, your mother, Kinsey, your friends—you have been warned but you paid no heed. We tried, my family, to protect you, but your police forced us off the land. We kept the monster at bay, and now it is at its strongest."

Silvanus sat back, the sudden rage of his face swept away as he laughed once more, whilst Rebecca could do nothing but stare at him. Her fork tilted sideways, and the piece of fish she had speared fell back to the plate and broke apart under the weight of its fall.

"Sorry for the dramatics—serves you right for keeping your hand on the knife when we were walking here."

Rebecca put her knife and fork down on the plate. She wanted answers more than nourishment. A line of Jim Morrison's poetry came to mind: "All games contain the idea of death."

"What was that?" the man asked. "I saw you mumble something, but I didn't quite catch it."

"Do you not miss a thing? It's a line from a Jim Morrison poem. I never quite understood it, but it seems apt—you telling me we're all in danger, breaking rules when your daughter who only wants to keep you alive, creeping around in the dark, and, by the way, how do you know Kinsey's door was unlocked—unless you went in after he left? Not nice that, gaining entry into a sick man's house."

"He didn't look sick. He sprinted out to the ambulance as if he'd been compelled by God, and he got in the front."

"What?"

"That's not to say he hasn't been sick. I have no doubt that the piece of skull threatening to tear into his brain is causing him a fair bit of distress, and if he doesn't see someone about it soon, it will be too late—if it isn't already."

Rebecca held up a hand, her palm facing the old man. "Okay, stop there. Can you please tell me what is going on? I hear rumours of three kids being taken seriously ill and suffering violent hallucinations, so unless there's a new strain of drug going round brought in from the army base, I have no idea how to help my mum." Rebecca didn't realise just how concerned she was until that moment, but saying it out loud made her begin to cry.

Sandra asked if she was all right whilst glaring at the old man. He smiled softly and handed his dinner companion a tissue that had seen better, and cleaner, days.

"Just some bad family news, my dear. She will be all right, I promise." He returned his attention to Rebecca. Reducing his voice down to a whisper, he leaned in and spoke quietly.

"Kinsey is dying. Something that happened years ago is giving him these headaches—a bit of fractured skull has become lodged in his brain. But that is nothing to what's coming. These sightings, the kids—it will only get worse. I know because it has happened before, but I managed to stop it. We thought we'd stopped it by clearing a place in the woods and giving the evil that you have allowed to fester a spot to be contained. By clearing off the land a few years ago, the evil has had chance to regain its strength, and now it has a different, nastier edge to it, thanks to the way you farm."

"What do you mean, it's happened before? I would have heard something."

"Oh, but you did, and you ignored it. You believed what your mind wanted you to believe. You see the best in people—unless you're carrying a knife of course. Your friend, the one whose parents abused her?"

"Karen? She overdosed on heroin. We were lucky it didn't kill her."

"Yes, very lucky, but she would have been better off dead."

Rebecca stared at the man before her. Anger flushed her cheeks. She wanted to leave the sad excuse for a restaurant and go home, half-minded to report the man for bothering her and breaking into Kinsey's home. But the old man's hand settled on hers, and he looked deep into her eyes and quietly implored her to hear him out.

"Let me explain, and then, if you still want to report me to the police, I shall gladly hand myself in. I don't have much strength left to fight this evil again."

Chapter Twenty-Four

KINSEY HAD HELPED Paul Whittle get his colleague back to the farm and was now drinking a hot cup of tea. With his sister's aid, the teacher had led the man upstairs, taken off his shoes and thrown a blanket over him.

"He's asleep for now," Paul said as he returned to the kitchen where Kinsey sat on the wooden bench where, only a few hours before, he had told the children to be safe.

He sipped his tea, his mind racing, his headache a distant drone in the background, a bluebottle circling a room in search of shit to land on. Theresa Whittle came down the open stairs; he still couldn't place her, but it would come to him, even if he had to force the issue.

The teacher was still talking, his shock manifesting as an uncontrollable urge to scratch at the scene the three men had witnessed.

"What was that? Some sort of ritual, an adolescent game gone horribly wrong?"

"That was no game. That was death, sacrifice...insanity."

"In all my years, I have never known..." Paul trailed off. No words could adequately describe what they had seen.

"I don't think any of us have," Kinsey said. "Sure, I have seen death. I have witnessed the terrible aftermath of it in court. But this was something else, and I cannot explain it. I don't want to even try." Kinsey peered down at his tea, the steam rising pleasantly into his face. *In the end, time is short, games lead to death*...he couldn't remember the exact quote, but he was sure he'd read it once.

143

Theresa joined him at the table and placed her head in her hands. If the evening had been hard for Kinsey, he wondered what effect it had on the woman. Visibly distraught, she began to sob. Her brother came up behind her and gently placed his arms around her, telling her it would be all right, that she would not have to suffer anything alone again. He would resign his position at the school—it would be imposed anyway, after what had taken place—and return to help her run the farm.

Kinsey saw the scab forming and decided to pick it before it hardened completely.

"Ms. Whittle, I'm sure I know you from somewhere, but I can't think where."

The woman said nothing, but her body language told him plenty. She knew him too.

"I don't think this is the time, Mr. Kinsey," Paul protested, his voice raised to the level he probably used to scold a classroom full of pupils hell-bent on destroying his lesson plan. Then he immediately apologised. "That was uncalled for. It's been… a long day."

Kinsey took no offence; it was only to be expected that recent events would play with people's nerves. He apologised also for his question and was surprised when the farmer told him there was no need; he was right. They had met before, and that it wasn't right what had happened to him.

She shrugged off her brother's arms and sat up straight. Her eyes were almost black from crying, but Kinsey sensed her need to unburden and resolve the mystery.

"You knew my husband when you were children. He was good few years older than you, but you crossed paths, and he made you pay for it."

"Theresa…I'm sure Mr. Kinsey will understand if we leave this for another day. It was so long ago and not relevant to what's going on now."

Theresa shot to her feet. "Don't you see, Paul? It *always* comes down to the kids. This town—it has eaten away at them and offered them nothing but damned lies and misery. Those who leave—they are the lucky ones. Those who stay—they become just as rotten as the fruit that goes unpicked in the orchard."

Paul backed off, though Kinsey sensed the man's dread at what his sister was about to reveal.

"You knew me as Theresa Flanagan, Mr. Kinsey. Paul was also a Flanagan. We changed our names when we returned—when I was released from jail for what they reminded me every day was the murder of my husband. But that's not where you know me from. I was there when you confronted the bastard with your theory about the girl who drowned in the river."

Kinsey's mind was numb. He had a vague recollection of a family called Flanagan, of a murder, but it was different time. His head hurt, and the more he pushed, the faster the maggots hatched...became a swarm of bluebottles trapped inside a jar. *Never mind the murder, what was this about confronting someone about a girl that drowned?*

"I don't remember," he admitted. "I know the story of the girl— she wandered off from the picnic, and her parents discovered her body by the riverbank, drowned in just a few inches of water."

Theresa sat back down and directed her brother to go to the cupboard and get a bottle of whisky and three glasses.

"I believe you like a drink, Mr. Kinsey. Tell me, does it ease the pain in your head? I've seen you rubbing your temple and trying to concentrate the last couple of days, and I hear you've been blacking out. Do you remember the railway line? An elbow smashing into your eye?"

Paul returned to the table, three semi-decorated whisky glasses pinch-gripped between the fingers of one hand, a half-empty bottle of ten-year-old Scotch in the other. He placed the glasses on the table and emptied the whisky bottle into them, looking at his sister for a brief second before picked up his glass and swallowed the liquid in one gulp. He remained silent for the rest of the story, eyes closed, occasionally flinching as memories resurfaced.

"My husband killed that little girl. He kept his hand on her head, pushing her under three times, until finally her body went limp. Then he walked back to the fair whistling a tune, no remorse in his soul. He would have been nine at the time, and you, Mr. Kinsey, would have been a bit younger than the girl. Back then, as now, asking too many questions was your downfall."

"What questions?"

Theresa took a sip of her own whisky, and another tear trickled down her cheek. Kinsey couldn't tell if it was out of remorse or because the memory of the girl was too much.

"My husband—who was at the time my boyfriend, even though I was barely old enough to understand the meaning of the word—was messing around on the railway, placing shillings on the metal line, trying to flatten them with each passing train. I guess he and his friends were bored. I know I was, standing there watching him whoop and holler like a monkey in a zoo, but where else was I going to go, Mr. Kinsey?"

Another gulp and her glass was empty. She looked down at the whisky that had been poured for him. Kinsey shook his head and pushed it across to her, their fingers touching for a moment. Unlike the movies, there was no spark of connection, no meeting of minds; just cold, heartless, relentless pain being shared.

"I watched you walk along the bottom of the field. You were small back then, but you were persistent. I think you'd been reading up on old cases—I'm not surprised you became a journalist, but you would have made a better history teacher. I gather your knowledge of the subject is good enough to teach.

"So, there you were, all cocky and demanding. You said you'd solved the mystery of the girl that drowned, but you made the mistake of talking to the suspect instead of going to the police."

The woman began to shake, her fingers losing their grip on the glass. Kinsey gently removed it from her hand and set it down on the table. Memories began to swim in his mind, repressed thoughts returning, given form, and making his head hurt further.

He saw himself running down the side of the field, the railway line high above him. He had found out a truth; he had seen a picture in a book about the fair, and there was a date on one of the three plates, a glossary adding flavour to the story of the town. The picture was of the fair, and even in a black-and-white facsimile, you could almost feel the sun blazing down on the townsfolk who had made their way to where the three windmills kept vigil over the countryside. The photograph had been taken from above the crowd, a tryptic of what Kinsey supposed was intended as a panoramic view but with each being set up individually. He was thankful the photographer had made the effort.

On the first plate, there was nothing out of the ordinary: a crowd of people waved at the camera above them, the war forgotten, the entire town out on a summer's jolly, work left for a day, children hooking for goldfish, the smell of candy floss fluttering across the fields, and in one corner, a young boy holding the hand of another child. The second picture showed a farm in the distance—the one in which Kinsey was now sitting, but back then, it had been ruined by war and driven into disrepair, making it a perfect hideout for teenagers who couldn't get into the windmill for some fun. However, it was in the third picture that the young Kinsey had found something missed at the time.

He had sat on the information for a couple of days, until he was absolutely sure, then, following a group of lads and a couple of girls one day, he took his chance. He was going to expose the boy in the picture for what he was: a child killer.

Unseen by the photographer, at the edge of the frame was the boy and the girl in the water. Though the image was blurred, it was possible to make out that the boy was standing in the shallows, while the girl was only seen from the neck up, her dress submerged. To the naked, uncritical eye, it looked like two siblings having fun in the river, except it wasn't fun; it wasn't a game. He was drowning her.

The book had been out for a few years, but it hadn't sold well, and Kinsey had been fortunate enough to find a copy at a jumble sale, donated by the photographer's mother not long before she moved to a retirement home on the south coast. It was only by borrowing his father's magnifying glass that he had stumbled upon the moment, but that was all it took to reveal a murder in progress.

"If it helps, I kept the book," Theresa said reticently as if she had read and knew she was interrupting his thoughts. "I left it with Paul while I was in prison. He didn't know why I wanted him to keep it. I don't think my parents did either, but I was no longer part of the family by then. I had destroyed the name. They eventually moved away, all of them. Only Paul kept in touch. When you leave, you'll find it on the bookcase in the hallway— it's yours. You should get the credit for it, your big case solved."

Kinsey's mind returned to that afternoon, not a cloud in the sky, a beautiful Oxfordshire day, the only sound the rumble of trains that shook the ground every half hour, one up, one down, as they connected Birmingham and London with day-trippers, businessmen and secretaries, school field trips and the freight. He had confronted the boy about what he had found—a rookie mistake—and shown him the book. The boy's friends didn't budge an inch; the expected recoil of finding out their friend was a killer didn't happen. Only one of the girls reacted, turning on the boy, jabbing a finger in his chest. He ordered his friends to hold her still whilst he dealt with Kinsey. One of them pushed her to the ground and put his hands over her mouth to dull the scream, not that anyone would have heard, sitting on her back to make sure she didn't move.

Was it arrogance? Was it childish ego to think nothing would happen to him when he stood up for the memory of the drowned girl? Why hadn't he gone to the police? He suspected it had a lot to do with pride. The case was his, as Theresa had just reminded him, and if he had gone to the police, they would have stolen it from him, taken the credit and left him with ruffled hair and a ten-bob note for his trouble.

The punch to the face came first, knocking the young Kinsey to the grass at their feet, then the savage beating, limbs held down. He tried to call out, but another blow, this time to the stomach, caused him to splutter the cries of help. The boy climbed on top of him, forced open Kinsey's jaw and hawked up a large gob of spit, letting it drain from his mouth into Kinsey's and then forcing him to swallow.

The gang laughed, hyena-like, rabid, urging their leader on. How dare this kid come up to them and make accusations!

"I'm going to make you forget what you were doing here today, but first, I'll give you something to remember for the rest of your life." The boy sneered in his face, his nose mere inches from Kinsey's blood-soaked own. His tormentor sat back and rolled up a sleeve, taking him time to line up the distance between the sweep of his elbow and Kinsey's face. Then in one swift move, he brought the elbow crashing down just below Kinsey's right eye.

The pain was intense, like fire in his mind, and his whole being shook with the sheer force of the blow. The boy seemed to enjoy that even more and brought down his elbow several more times until Kinsey was sure his face was nothing more than mushy pulp.

He couldn't remember anything else. He wasn't even sure how he'd got home. Blood seeped from his eye and congealed around his chin, large red stains on his jacket that his mother showed in anger to anyone who would listen over the coming weeks. Just thinking about it caused his headache to roar back into action.

"You see it now, don't you?" Theresa said. "No one could know what he had done to that girl—that's what I thought at the time. He wanted to burn the book, but I managed to keep it from him, told him I'd destroyed it." Her voice became flat as she tried to absolve herself of the company she had kept that day. She was tired, but she still had more to reveal.

"This is why I cannot go through it all again. I live here, the children died here. How long before someone, one of your kind, Mr. Kinsey, starts digging into the farm's history and recognises me as a killer? Fingers will point, tongues will wag, and then will come the questions…relentless, bloody questions."

She stood up and walked across the kitchen to a wooden cupboard that hung on the wall, talking as she went. "I killed my husband, Mr. Kinsey, because I caught him trying to kill my baby brother. Another couple of minutes and he would have throttled him to death. That poor girl suffered, and I did nothing. You could have bled to death alone in that field had I not asked the other girl for help to get you on your feet and point you in the right direction. I was able to stop him a third time, but I couldn't own up to it, not the real reason. I hoped to start over. I should have known it was just…fantasy."

She unlocked the cupboard and turned back with a smile for Kinsey. "Don't forget the book. I'll give you five minutes' head start. That way, your conscious will be clear. You won't have to lie. You left me and my brother in peace—he will attest to that."

The farmer's gun shone like a newly polished guitar, and its size overwhelmed Kinsey. This was not a bluff, a cry for help. She intended to kill herself, and Kinsey was no hero; self-preservation was the name of the game now. He rose and walked slowly to door, hoping that any members of the police force would be close enough to hear the gunfire and come rushing to the brother's aid.

In the hallway, Kinsey quickly scanned the bookcase and saw what had been hidden from him for over twenty years. He took it from its place and held it aloft to show the farmer he had found it.

She nodded, a faint smile of acceptance crossing her face as she urged him to leave.

Out in the open, he marched down the path and was overjoyed to see a young police officer standing by farm gate. The officer greeted him, asking if everything was all right. Kinsey lied and said all was fine, that he had come out for some air and to find out if there was any news on the officer who had been attacked earlier that evening.

Before the officer could answer him, a gunshot shook the air around them. Kinsey instinctively ducked for cover. Then a second gunshot came, and Kinsey lowered his head in prayer. He was covered as she had promised. It would be ruled a suicide, but she had taken her brother with her to save him from the accusations and inevitable damning questions from the children's families; secrets and lies taken to the grave.

The police officer sprinted into action, only slowing when Kinsey shouted that there was a third person upstairs—better be sure he was all right first. The officer gave a thumbs up—a reliable witness to the fact that Kinsey was not in the building when the gun went off.

Chapter Twenty-Five

McCarthy had been in the office all evening. The phone was off the hook; her fingers typed methodically and with care, the story taking shape and the quote from 'a private source' given prominence in the headlines. She didn't have much choice but to give the local side to the news happening on their doorstep, especially after the tip-off she'd received whilst waiting for Kinsey to complete his snooping inside the facility.

This was not for her readers' eyes only; it was an exclusive, a compromise between her values and the release of a demon inside of her. Accepting money for a story had never been a consideration before; her ethics, her integrity meant much more. Yet every man, every woman, had their price, and hers was information on Adam Yobe, a man for whom her dislike over the years had turned to disgust.

As she typed, she understood what this could mean for her—either a fast-track to the paper where her fellow journalist worked or obscurity if it turned out to be false. She would, of course, look after Kinsey, but his erratic behaviour of late had forced the issue. He was not well, and she felt a large part of that was down to her—the long hours, their one-night love affair—not all of it was Kinsey's fault. In the dim light afforded by a single bulb, she had come to realise that.

It was only after she had made sure Kinsey was in bed and asleep that she started thinking over the conversation she'd had with Andrew outside the facility. Taking the chance on using the reporter's phone, she scrambled through her bag and found her diary, in the back of which was Andrew's phone number at the newspaper. She dialled it and waited. A female voice answered, giving her name and the newspaper's with a cheery welcome that defied their reputation for the hard sell and the ability to bring shame to the government.

After being put through to the newsroom and explaining who she was, something that didn't seem to faze the person on the other end of the phone, she was given the name and number of the hotel where Andrew Fillus was staying. She thanked the person and ended the call; a plan began to form in her mind. She looked up the stairs and made sure Kinsey had not stirred whilst she'd been talking. Satisfied he was out for the night, she crept out of the house, locking the door behind her with the spare set of keys he'd given her. She hadn't noticed the Volkswagen parked further up the road or the bearded man who watched her drive past, her mind on other matters.

Wary of his reputation as a womaniser, she arranged to meet Andrew Fillus at the hotel within the hour. There, over a glass of beer, he told her all that he had found out about the facility—its drug rehabilitation programme and its sideline role in research in the fight against HIV. He confirmed that the man who had been attacked on the steps of the building, Professor Sidney Mutton, had bought the land from Adam Yobe for an undisclosed sum even though the books said the land was a gift. It was all basic stuff, but it was enough to rekindle McCarthy's interest in the investigation she had tried to keep Kinsey from pursuing as part of his personal vendetta against Marbon.

Once again, the offer had been made of a job in London, and initially, she turned it down. She couldn't leave the paper, not now, when something big was happening on their doorstep. Then came the counteroffer—a manoeuvre so smooth it could have been made of marble.

"One piece, a local angle, ask the question which I can't. A thousand words by tonight. Send it over to my office by ten, and I guarantee it will be in the paper tomorrow. Plenty of time for you to wrestle with your conscience, but it will be your by-line, and it will give your paper a shot in the arm, national recognition. You deserve it, Samantha."

There was a knock at the door, and through the dim light, she could see the silhouetted outline of a man.

She came to think of that moment later on—whether it was her belief that Andrew had come to check how far she had got with writing the article that made her abandon her usual sense of caution. The streetlight outside the building flickered off, leaving nothing but a shadow where the man stood.

She walked to the door and flicked the latch. Too late, she realised what she had done, what her daughter had always said was her biggest downfall: she was careless. As the man stepped into the light of the office, she knew with certainty that trouble had found her.

Chapter Twenty-Six

I T WAS ONLY the duty sergeant being indisposed that evening
that saved Lorraine Doughty from being taken straight to
the facility at Wendlefields. Escorted by two policemen,
and with two others standing by in case she turned violent
again, the reward for her slaughter in the windmill was a cell
and not being plugged into a machine under the watchful eye of
the professor's staff.

By the time the police car reached the station, she was docile
but confused, unsure why she was in handcuffs, but she was
also no longer acting—according to the constable—like a raving
lunatic. That was enough for acting Desk Sergeant Wilcox to
place her in a cell, pending removal to Oxford the following day.
He raised his eyebrows when he learned what she was accused
of, and for her part, Lorraine gave an anguished, heartfelt denial.

After reading the girl the reason for her arrest, logging the
packet of condoms and purse in her possession, he ordered
that some different clothes be brought down for the girl, as she
couldn't stay in what she was wearing. He couldn't look her in the
eye; he had never heard of anything so gruesome, such a grisly
act. He was even more shocked when one of the officers who had
been present at the time went into graphic, though somewhat
understated detail of what had taken place.

***

Alone in the cell, Lorraine Doughty couldn't take in what
had been said at the desk. She had little memory of the journey,
waking up as the car approached the town. She tried to put

together what had happened that evening. The police said she had killed Phillip—that she and Candice had tied him up and crucified him, slashed open his guts and performed some weird ritual while he bled to death. If it was true, why hadn't Candice been arrested too? Or maybe she had been, and they were being kept separately. That made sense.

Conspiracy to commit murder... Conspire with whom, though? The last thing she remembered was Phillip's arm around her, Candice's hand on her thigh, and them both whispering the same line, the exact same eight words: "Let's have some fun before we go home."

Lorraine shivered at the thought of how easily she had been enticed into their game. She would have done anything for Phillip. Strong, athletic, imposing, he was a boy for whom she would have gone to watch Everton even though her heart was always red. All the way through senior school, she'd had a crush on him, and him noticing her was just the best feeling. It didn't matter that he'd been going out with Candice on and off since third year; in her heart, Lorraine believed she was the one for Phillip.

Sitting by the river, the air had been cold, but Candice's hand had been warm, the heat of her palm transferring through Lorraine's tights and firing an unfamiliar glow in her stomach.

"The mist is crawling in off the water, look. Let's go inside the windmill and see where this leads."

Candice and Phillip had pulled her up from the grass...and that was the last thing she remembered, her mind hiding from her what she needed to recall. She began to cry, a steady flow of silent tears, of agitation and frustration turned in against itself.

"Lorraine?"

A small, whispered voice floated under the cell door and caught her attention.

"Candice, is that you? Oh, thank God! I was beginning to think I wouldn't hear from you again." Despite the horror of the last hour, she was genuinely happy she wasn't alone in the darkness.

"Keep quiet in there!" an authoritative male voice called. "This is not a playground, you know."

Lorraine gasped at the rebuke. Her father used to shout like that when her mother came home late.

"Shush, Lorraine, be quiet now. We don't want to upset the policeman, do we?"

Lorraine shook her head, daring not to speak.

"That's a good girl," Candice praised softly. "Look under the gap in the door, but remember, just whisper when we speak."

Lorraine lay on the cell floor and peered through the minimal gap. She could see one of Candice's eyes looking back at her. "Have they told you what we're supposed to have done?"

The eye remained impassive. Only the voice, even in a whisper, was strong. "Don't you remember, sweetheart? How could you forget such a night?"

"I don't remember anything," Lorraine lied. "Nothing from the moment we left the farm.

The eye sparkled, and Candice's voice gently purred, "Liar. I know you, Lorraine Doughty. I've known you for such a long time now. I know so much about you, like when you're telling me fibs to save your blushes."

Lorraine swallowed hard, the action creating a feeling of nausea in her throat. "Okay, you win," she hissed back. "I remember right up to the moment you and Phillip led me into the windmill."

"That's right, good girl."

This meant nothing. What she wanted was an answer, not teasing, not a drawn-out confession of how much she'd enjoyed the feeling of Candice's hand on her leg.

"Candice, just tell me—have they told you anything? Have they rung your mum and dad? Is Mr. Whittle here?" And then, acknowledging the fear she felt trapped in the cell, "I want to go home, Candice."

For a while, Candice didn't reply. Her eye watched, unblinking, from the other side of the door. Lorraine grew frustrated again and sat up, wiping the dust off the clothes the policeman had ordered her to change into.

Eventually, Candice spoke again. "Would you like me to get you out of here, Lorraine? You only have to ask—you only have to be nice to me."

"Why should I?" Lorraine snapped, not caring this time if any of the police heard.

"Because you love me. Because Phillip knew it, and we wanted you to be part of our club. Can I tell you a secret, Lorraine? If you look under the door, I will tell you a secret, and then, if you are nice to me, I will get you out of this cell. We can be together, Lorraine."

Lorraine banged her head against the metal door. She didn't like playing games; her parents' relationship had been built around that destructive pattern. With a groan, she rolled onto her front and skewed her head to the side so she could see under the door. Candice hadn't moved; that eye still stared directly into Lorraine's.

"That's better, I can't help you unless you give yourself to me. That's what I wanted at the windmill. I wanted you to give yourself to me. I love you, Lorraine, and I know you love me. Phillip—he was nothing more than a boy you wanted to be seen on the arm of, the big man who'd take you out to clubs, spend all his money on you. But that isn't love, that's settling. That's denying your true feelings, and it's wrong, Lorraine. It is wrong."

Candice's words dripped with honey, but they sounded off, as if delivered without meaning or understanding what it meant to be confronted about her feelings for another girl. Despite that, Candice spoke the truth. Yes, she wanted to be with Phillip Sellers, but she didn't love him. She would have done anything at that moment to kiss Candice, to hold her in her arms, share a bed with her.

"Do you want me to get you out of here, Lorraine?" the voice asked once more.

"Yes."

The eye disappeared from Lorraine's sight, and above her, the lock turned. Through the door, she heard Candice's voice say, "Tell me you love me. Tell me that you and I are destined to be forever entwined."

Lorraine stood up slowly. Such words and endless possibilities—she could do nothing other than agree. "I love you. I never want to be apart from you."

No reply, no sound other than the lock turning. The door opened gradually, but where Lorraine expected to see the welcoming face of her friend, there was only a wall. She poked her head out into the corridor and saw no movement, no Candice—no policeman at the desk.

"Candice, where are you?"

"This way, my love. Just keep walking. Look straight ahead, don't look around. Just follow my voice."

Lorraine did as she was told, cautiously covering the short distance to where she had been confirmed her name and home address earlier. She didn't even look down when she passed two policemen who lay in a heap on the floor, their throats cut, their blood mixing together like an absurd cordial waiting for a measure of water. If she had dared peek over the counter that separated the presumed guilty from the first stage of justice, she would have seen the desk sergeant cowering, frightened beyond wit and comprehension as his own life ebbed away as the pocket through the small, self-inflicted incisions in his right wrist.

Lorraine walked past the three men and on towards the external door. The station's phone kept ringing, but nobody answered it, as if the building was unoccupied.

"Where is everyone? Shouldn't I wait to be formally released?"

Again, there was no physical sign of Candice, only that voice as clear and tender as she had ever known. "They knew you were innocent, so they just decided to let you go. Don't you remember?"

Lorraine thought hard as she walked down the uneven steps out of the police station. She remembered talking to Candice, and then…

Candice must be right. They've let me go.

She walked on, the voice directing her.

***

WPC Andrea Laybourne was not meant to be working that night, but with all the trouble in the town and the growing sense of unease, DI Sears had asked her personally if she could step up and fill the void. She'd agreed immediately, not only because she needed the money, but because she was ambitious and didn't want to stay in uniform all her life. She wanted to be part of something bigger. As she drove into the station car park with the duty solicitor to whom she had given a lift from the train station, she noticed the doors to the station were wide open, light streaming out as if someone had shone a torch through the gaps of a skull.

***

Lorraine saw the policewoman get out of her car and wanted to go back and warn her what was inside, but Candice said no. The policewoman would have to deal with what she found.

Chapter Twenty-Seven

BILL TAYLOR STOOD his ground. Behind him was the woman who had given him the broken jaw; to his side was the slowly fading life of a young boy; and in front of him, blocking the exit, stood a woman in a sharp, pinstripe trouser suit. Her long, flowing hair, tied back and bunched on top of her head, added four inches to her already impressive height; she was slim and elegant with a touch of unfulfilled desire colouring her face.

She could have been wearing a sequinned dress and make-up for a night out in London; or a single, well-placed fig leaf. None of it mattered to Bill Taylor. No, what mattered was the gun in her hand pointing at his chest and was the expression on her face that told him she would kill him if he took one wrong step.

"How is our patient?" she asked the woman who only a short time before had—so Bill thought—rescued him from an operating room.

"He is almost drained. He will begin to freeze soon." Serena's voice had changed, taking on a slower, more deliberate drawl that Bill associated with drunken old wife beaters, and when he glanced her way, her head was down, slumped against her chest as if the fight had been kicked out of her.

"I can see it your eyes," the armed, suited woman addressed Bill. "You think she led you into a trap. You already know Ms. Cox is not a fan of the police, and I have to say, who can blame her? To put your mind at ease, let me assure you, her intentions were noble, but she was always going to betray you. It just takes a while for the body to absorb the pulp. I was surprised, really, that she absorbed the nutrients—the best of the boy brought in earlier—in just over an hour."

The woman smiled as she spoke, and Bill changed his mind: she was not just dangerous; she had all the markers of being psychopath. Throughout her explanation, the gun remained perfectly still in her hand, cool, calm and one quick finger-press away from putting a hole in his chest.

Behind him, he heard Serena fall to the floor as her body succumbed to the foreign matter pumped into it.

"Well then, it seems I have fifteen minutes in which to secure you and get our friend here back to bed. I don't want her leaking everywhere. My husband will not be pleased if he comes in tomorrow and finds a mess to clean up."

Bill tried to talk, to ask a question and stall for time. Whatever had been put in Serena Cox would either kill her or change her, and if he knew her at all, she would rather die as the woman who fought battles and threw as much shit as she could at the establishment than become something she didn't recognise, who wasn't even really her anymore. The wire holding his jaw together, though, had different ideas, and his words came out in a grunted, stilted, closed-off manner.

"Don't try to talk, you fool. Your jaw was broken. Doctor's orders—try to rest. It will do you good." The woman laughed scornfully.

Bill had only one option: escape. He wanted to believe Serena had a chance, but whatever they had put in her, he was going to refuse anyway; he could not suffer the same fate. Raising his hands as if making a sign of compliance, he closed his eyes and prayed quickly, bargaining with his mother's god, that if he escaped, he would go back to the church he'd walked away from when his brother decided he could no longer live in the town, his worries about the unease he felt there unheard.

Bill moved quickly, and whilst he caught the woman off guard, she still managed to get a shot off. The bullet tore through his shoulder, causing him enough pain that he struck out at her, and for a fleeting second, he wished he and the journalist Kinsey could have swapped places, not only for the story to be in the right hands but because he thought he should not be the one being shot.

As his shoulder twisted, he became aware that he was falling. He'd planned to shove the woman out of the way but instead found that as he fell, he was able to connect the metal frame holding his jaw together with the woman's face. The sound was sickening, her nose exploded, and though he was not in the habit of enjoying violence, in this circumstance he made an exception. They both fell to the ground, him on top, her screams echoing down the hall and no doubt alerting whatever staff were in the facility that her plan had gone awry. Despite the burning pain in his shoulder demanding he pass out, he raised his head once more and butted the woman, knocking her out cold.

He got up on his feet and listened. In the quiet of the building, he could hear commotion, raised voices of people asking questions. He quickly scanned the hallway: no sign of any closed-circuit television down here, but he had noticed some in the entrance and by the nurses' desk. Perhaps it was not as open a secret as he had initially believed; that or they hadn't got around to installing cameras down here. Whatever the reason, he had to think on his feet. He took one last look at Serena Cox, who was still breathing but her skin was grey and sickly. He didn't look at the boy on the bed, the one who had been raving inside his shed, talking of a translucent man. The machine had stopped; the pulping had taken place, and—Bill guessed—the boy was longer be part of his world.

He didn't put stock in his mother's faith; he also didn't believe her warning about his father's family past—that they had practised voodoo and had the capability to bring the dead back to life. Still, he didn't want to hang around to see what happened next. Placing a hand on his wounded shoulder, he ran down the corridor haphazardly, trying an occasional door in the fruitless hope of finding one open. He made it to the end of the corridor before he saw another person.

Chapter Twenty-Eight

D R. MORAN HAD heard gunfire as he was writing up his notes. Immediately on edge, he walked out of his office and saw one of the nurses trying to usher Mrs. Frampton back inside the room where her daughter lay asleep. He had hoped the girl wouldn't come through her experience, but she had fought back; something had kept her alive. If the mother had only gone home when he had suggested, if she had understood there was nothing she could do, then the girl might have developed further complications. *I'm so sorry, Mrs. Frampton. It seems your daughter had a relapse. By law, I am duty bound to perform a post-mortem. Her remains? Of course, in due course...* But no such luck. It might have come in handy to have insight to determine if it was natural or—as one of the nurses had suggested when she didn't know he was listening—down to other outside sources.

He wasn't sure what he had missed; neither was Mrs. Mutton. All the screening for the agent had come back negative. The two boys in their care had both shown elevated levels of imagination on a resonator. Their brains were wired to such a point that whatever had scared them had stayed with them and could not be reconciled, each passing minute subjecting them to greater terror. The girl, though—it was if she suffered from some type of aphantasia and her experience relied on facts only. She might have had the scare of her life, which was why she went into shock, but her mind found a way to reason with it, to blot out the source of fear.

All children had imagination. It was, in Moran's opinion, only adults who lost the ability to see what wasn't there. Sometimes remnants remained, fragments of a distant soul, but it was enough to get them to do extraordinary things, to create new worlds. The problem was keeping that imagination going, not burning them out or sending them mad. After all, every artist suffered burnout; it is what made them so beautiful.

Mrs. Mutton understood, even if her husband didn't. He had no idea how much the facility could help better the understanding of the problem. It was just a matter of finding the right subjects.

Last year was when it started to become a little dangerous. Moran had noticed there was a natural tail off in the younger adults, the teenagers being caught up in the drug craze in the town. As a charity, it was their privilege and responsibility to help the victims of the scourge of heroin, cocaine and other lethal drugs. And so they ran their tests and gave guidance; they helped some recover. Those who kicked the habit and returned home to their wealthy families, and they forgot what they had undergone in the facility.

A few remained, some could not cope back out in society, their minds continually processing the sheer volume of visual stimuli they were receiving. For those poor unfortunate wrecks, a new process was developed, one that would make use of the images they were seeing. They became the artist's easel, the potter's wheel—such beautiful minds creating a new and better future.

And it had worked. Private patients kept the money rolling in and ensure they could also treat children from less well-off families in the town, but it always built upon the sanctity of healing. Professor Mutton would have it no other way.

Moran walked away from the argument taking up his nurse's time. He had been wrong about Mrs. Frampton. He thought when he first saw her that she was pitiful, meek and compliant. But in the last two days, she had become stubborn, wilful, and refused to leave the room even for a simple blood test to take place. Moran wasn't sure if she had learned anything. His head nurse told him he was being foolish, that she had tried to push Mrs. Frampton's buttons in the staffroom, and she had run away like a frightened child. Moran didn't know what she meant by that; he wasn't sure he wanted to.

The sound of gunfire had come from the new wing, the furthest from his office. He noted there were only six people working that night: himself, four nurses and a male orderly. Six people, none of whom should have a gun on them. Moran trod carefully as he walked towards the new wing and remained calm; it might be nothing.

Finally, he reached the beginning of the corridor where he believed the gunshot had come from. By this time, a nurse had caught up with him and was asking questions. He told her firmly to be quiet, a sharp rebuke which he wasn't known for. He normally left that to the professor.

"Go and check every room. We should have twenty patients all together, including the policeman and that woman—the eco-warrior. Make sure they're all accounted for. Get Brill to help you, and send the other three nurses to the entrance door just in case. Lock the door. Do you think you can do that?"

The nurse's face was one of scorn, but she nodded and set off back the way she'd come.

A few feet along the corridor, Moran saw a body slumped outside one of the side rooms, and he called the nurse back. She returned to his side and confirmed his eyes were not deceiving him. It Mrs. Mutton, the professor's wife, but she wasn't due to be here. How had she even got inside? The nurse caught hold of Moran's arm and directed his attention to the bed in the room. There was a child in it attached to one of the machines. It was Solden boy; even at this distance it was unmistakably him.

"He was in his own room earlier," the nurse said. "He was attached to saline and a heart monitor. How the hell did he get there?"

167

Moran ran, no time to answer the question. If he had, he was sure he would have only been able to surmise that the professor's wife had been conducting an unauthorised experiment.

He reached the bed first, followed quickly by the nurse. One of the machines attached to the boy was such a weighty piece of equipment that the only person who could have done it was Brill—all muscle and no brain. Moran had tried to move it once with two of the nurses; they'd barely budged it a foot before conceding its weight was too much for them to handle. Brill was an ox of a man, well over six foot in height and just as impressive when you looked at his reach. He had been chosen because he had little in the way of communication and always did as he was told, especially when it was one of the nurses.

"Is that internal phone working yet?" Moran barked, his sense of inadequacy poking through the façade of doctor calm. He looked around the room, and as he did so noticed slumped Serena Cox also slumped against a wall. Her breath was erratic, she had lost all colour—she was in shock. Whatever private experiment Mrs. Mutton had been running that evening, it had got out of hand.

"Hasser, I asked if the phone was working," he repeated in panic.

"No, Doctor, they haven't been connected yet."

"Right." For the first time in his career, Moran was at a loss. Everything had been so well controlled for so long—the setting up of the facility, the lack of exposure thanks to military-style planning. It wasn't until around a year ago, when that idiot of a farmer got drunk one night and blabbed he had sold part of his land and the offshoot of the river been diverted, that anyone nearby even heard of the facility. Now it was unravelling. The horrible thought crossed Moran's mind that he would blamed for this. He had fought against keeping the social anarchist in the building, but Hattie Mutton had overruled him, convinced Serena Cox had somehow become infected with whatever was attacking the children, that something locked away in her genes would aid them. Mrs. Mutton cited Cox's irrational behaviour outside the building, the way she had furiously attacked the policeman causing his jaw to break: *"Doesn't this all add up to finding a link? Perhaps she has been up to the airbase. Perhaps they sprayed her with chemicals—I wouldn't put anything past our American friends."*

Hattie Mutton had the power, thanks to her husband, to vote him down, so he had let her keep her new toy but on the strict understanding that they would not attempt anything until they had more data. Now, as far as Moran could tell, she'd gone behind his back, and not for the first time. If that were the case, then the woman they had brought into the facility didn't have long. Had Mrs. Mutton used some of the extract from the Liverpool boy to conduct her test?

Moran looked at the glass container beside the local lad's machine, it smelled obnoxious and was certainly full. He made a decision: the woman was going to die regardless. He would have to arrange for her to be found out in the woods, make it look like an attack. It might even work to their advantage; after all, they had a policeman on their side. However, Hattie Mutton was only unconscious. Bruised, battered but still alive, and he needed her to stay that way if he was going to make any sense of this.

"Nurse Hasser, help me carry Mrs. Mutton. We need to get her to my office. I can treat her there. We'll get Brill to deal with Serena Cox later—after Mrs. Mutton has told me what the hell happened in here."

Nurse Hasser complied, and between them, they were able to lift the unconscious woman and make their way back down the corridor. In all the drama, Moran had forgotten what had alerted him to the room in the first place.

***

The sound of footsteps falling away into the distance came as a relief for Bill Taylor. Each door he had tried had been locked, leaving him only the briefest of moments to run back to the room from which he had escaped and find a place to hide. He had picked up the gun and a couple of towels that were on a chair in the other corner and ducked inside a cleaner's cupboard. He had no idea what he was going to do if they found him. His only option might be to shoot or at least threaten them with the gun. He didn't like weapons of any type; they felt bad in his hand. They reminded him of his father.

The cupboard was just large enough to house the policeman. It had been a tight squeeze, especially as he tried to keep the towels firmly in place against his shoulder and the gun pointed outwards should he be discovered. He waited, sweating harder than he ever had before, concentrating with absolute conviction so that he, like the woman he had headbutted, didn't fall unconscious from pain.

He counted to twenty before carefully extricating himself from the cupboard and looked down at the woman who had been the cause of his stay in the facility. As he watched her fade, become cold, a layer of transparent film covering her body like frost creeping up the inside of a window where there was no double glazing, he did the only thing he could think to do. He forgave her, and then he shot her.

He looked down the hallway, nobody to be seen, but it wouldn't be long before they found him. He checked the barrel: three more bullets, but he was a lousy shot at the best of times, and with his shoulder, he would more than likely miss three times.

I can use the gun to break the window. It might trigger another alarm, but what the hell.

He dropped the towels onto the floor, and taking the gun by the barrel, he smashed the grip against the glass several times and watched it finally shatter, the larger pieces staying in place against the frame so he had to take them out one at a time.

If an alarm had been triggered, he couldn't hear it, and with no time to second guess, he climbed out the window and into the night. His arm caught on some of the remaining glass, adding further pain as shards impaled themselves. By way of distraction, he recounted the names he had heard, keeping the information fresh in his mind until he found help. As he slid off into the April twilight, he kept repeating *Serena Cox* in his head, lest he forget her.

171

Chapter Twenty-Nine

REBECCA SAT BACK in the plastic chair and blew out a long deep breath. Regardless of the genuineness of Silvanus's story, it was quite a tale. Yet somehow, all that he had told her made sense, as much as her mind could accept anyway.

She gazed at her dining companion. He had fallen silent, his eyes closed, and she wondered if all the talking had exhausted the poor man and he had simply fallen asleep. She looked out the window and saw that woman Silvanus had called his daughter was still there, bathed in light from above, a small cigar hanging from her mouth, occasionally removed and the ash flicked away into the darkness.

Silvanus's story had been incredible, but it tied with what Kinsey had said about the so-called illegal campsite in the woods that had been disbanded by the police several years back. It had divided the town in opinion: some, such as the radical group made up mostly of bored teenagers and led by a woman called Cox, had formed a barrier against the wave of attack from the police. Kinsey had captured a great picture at the time of the protestors singing songs of defiance, Serena Cox at the forefront, two fingers raised and spittle coming off her mouth as she lambasted the officers for their lack of human decency, for their great betrayal. Like Orgreave and Greenham before, they would not be forgiven.

The man's voice startled her as he asked her a question.

"Tell me, Miss McCarthy, where a good dumping ground for animal waste would be?

"I don't know. I suppose the two farms—Mrs. Whittle's and the other one with the ringed fence around it?"

"I believe you are right, though not about Mrs. Whittle. I know she had us removed from the land, but it was done out of trying to protect her name from the past. No, the real culprit here is Mr. Yobe. His name won't appear on any paperwork, but it is his farm to which the waste is delivered, the by-product of death being fed into the system. We protected ourselves, we sought to protect the land. We didn't know about the river. We didn't know about the evil that had been committed upstream, but we saw him, the figure. We wanted to protect the town, but we didn't know what we were fighting."

Silvanus grabbed Rebecca's hand roughly, his nails digging into her skin, fear crossing his face. Out of the corner of her eye, Rebecca saw daughter look her way and shake her head, suggesting he wouldn't hurt her and she should let his actions take hold. Within moments, his grip lessened, and she glowered at him as he leaned back in his own chair. He closed his eyes once more.

"That's a hell of a story," Rebecca heard Sandra say. In the intensity of the moment, she had forgotten the chip shop owner's daughter was behind her. "What is it? Some sort of play you're writing, Rebecca?" Her Oxfordshire accent made the words sound dull, unintelligent.

Rebecca simply smiled and said it was something like that. Before Sandra could interrogate further, her father shouted from the back of the shop to leave the customers alone—that if she was bored, she could come and batter some sausages for the rush at closing time. Sandra harrumphed and stomped away with slouched shoulders.

"Thought she'd never stop earwigging," Silvanus said, smiling at his own words, his eyes still closed but his wit sharp and alive.

Rebecca smiled back unseen. "One thing I don't understand… okay, there are many things I don't understand about all this… but how has it happened so quickly? Surely, we would have had warnings, some sort of sign that the river was polluted.

The environmental lobbies would have been up in arms. Fishermen would have noticed."

Silvanus opened one eye and fixed her with his gaze. She was unsure if it was a look of contempt or one of silent disbelief.

"Evil doesn't appear overnight. It festers, gathers strength and feeds off the weak at heart. I admit there is something else at play here driving the madness—something I cannot see—but it all stems from Yobe's farm, I'd swear to it. He probably thought it was a good way to make money. After all, he was close to bankruptcy. He did what he believed was right for the business, but that's how it starts—a favour here, a turning of a blind eye there—and before you know it, people are dying, children are born malformed, old people lose their minds, and all because one person said they could deal with the small consequence, that nobody would truly get hurt."

Rebecca thought on this. Her fourth-year history teacher once wrote down a blackboard a quote by Edmund Burke that haunted her for the remainder of her time at school: *"All that is necessary for the triumph of evil is that good men do nothing."* It was this that had spurred her on to help her friend as much as she was physically able, to stand by her when her innocence had been lost. Even then, Rebecca had not done as much as she probably could have done. It had been exhausting, spirit-sapping, and truth be known, when Karen booked herself back into the clinic, Rebecca was relieved that she was longer be responsible for Karen's care. She had, in her eyes, become that bad person who cuts themselves off when they can no longer cope with another's problems. Her mother had told her not to be silly, that Karen knew how much Rebecca had done for her and would have wanted her to get on with her own life.

As she sat on the plastic seat, as the first trickle of those who had already had their fill of wine, women and company for the night staggered in humming the last song they had heard on the juke box or argued with a friend over the chances of Oxford winning the cup on Sunday, she began to wonder if there was anything she could do to stem the evil brewing in her home town.

Silvanus stood up, looking at the queue forming to order their fish and chips and attempting to chat up Sandra whilst her father stood behind her with his arms folded.

"When good men do nothing indeed, Rebecca." Silvanus winked, but it was of sadness, not joviality.

The pair walked out of the shop and left the smell of vinegar to those with more urgent need of salvation. They crossed the road, and Silvanus patted his daughter on the back.

"Anything?"

The woman shook her head. "All quiet. I feel nothing."

This seemed to placate Silvanus, and his mood lifted slightly. "Rebecca, would you like to come with us—see for yourself the evil that men do when left unchecked?"

"Yes, please," Rebecca said, eagerly jumping at the chance. "Where are we going?" she asked, hearing the thrum of pleasure in her voice after an evening of hard-hitting facts and suspicions.

"You said it yourself—the only place to go would be Yobe's farm."

A young girl in ill-fitting clothes shuffled past on the other side of the road, her shoes scraping the dirt and dust on the pavement, her face blank of expression, but her lips moved as if she were silently conversing with a ghost.

A girl walked past the fish and chip shop. She paid no attention to the wolf whistles, nor to the young idiot who banged the window a couple of times as he tried to garner a reaction. She kept walking onwards, up the street and into the darkness.

The old man caught his daughter's eye. "Are you sure?"

His daughter nodded. "She stinks of it—the same stomach-turning smell of decaying flesh. Whatever it is, she's caught up in its web, and she has given herself willingly."

"Do we follow?"

"We follow. I'll get the car—but we keep a discreet distance. Whatever is guiding her, we don't want it to know we're on its trail."

This time, it was the daughter's turn to slap her father on the back, and Rebecca couldn't help but notice that it was a slap rather than a pat. The daughter ran a couple of hundred yards down the road, got into a car and started the engine.

"I know what you are thinking, Miss McCarthy, and you're right. She is angry with me. She wanted to have nothing to do with this. But you see, she has a talent for picking up the smell of certain things. A gift or a curse, take your pick."

Rebecca decided it was safer to say nothing. She wasn't going to put herself in the middle of a family dispute; not again.

The car drew level with them, and they both got in, Silvanus taking the front passenger seat, Rebecca sitting directly behind him.

"Good men…Father?"

"Good men, Daughter!"

With that simple exchange, the car sped up until they could see the girl once more in the gloom, and they waited to see where she would lead them.

Chapter Thirty

ONCE MCCARTHY RECOVERED from her shock, she ushered the police officer inside the office, locked the doors behind her and pulled down the blind. Taking no chances, she turned off the lights and led him by the hand into the back room.

When she had opened the door, the sight had scared her immensely. In the darkness and the semi-bright back light provided by the nearby lamppost, she could not comprehend what stood before her—a vision from teenage nightmares when her father took her to watch ghoulish B-movies mixed with the memory of having read *The Man in the Iron Mask*—and it took a huge dose of mental strength for her to not look upon the figure as some sort of punishment for past deeds and failures.

The figure had held his hands out in front of her, imploring silently for her to not scream—a strange visual indication of passiveness, of requiring assistance—but it had worked and brought McCarthy out of her own darkness.

In the bright light of the back room, she surveyed the man who had given her the fright of her life. She recognised the dishevelled figure in front of her, half dead on bare feet covered in cuts and bruises that needed washing and tending to. His shirt was ripped in several places, and he was freezing to the touch. It was the sight of the metal cage around his face that made her skin crawl; she had never seen anything so barbaric, but as Bill Taylor grunted through clenched teeth the words "Broken jaw," it all made sense.

McCarthy tended to the wounds on Bill's feet the best she could, picking out thorns and gravel with as much care as she could, but she admitted she was not the best person for the task. He shook his head softly and grunted again, and after several attempts to be understood explained that he had seen the light on and knew that either she or Kinsey were in the office—they were the only ones he could trust.

It was when she went to remove his shirt that she noticed the full extent of his injuries. The blood had stopped pouring, but it was no wonder he looked drained. He must have lost at least two pints.

"Don't speak, Bill. Just listen. You need to go to a proper hospital. I'll call a friend, and he'll drive you to Oxford—no ambulance. I'll get him to bring a change of clothes and some soft slippers or something, but while we wait, please write down as much as you can for me, tell me who did this to you."

She walked back into the office part of the small building, groping her way to the phone in the dark so nobody else would think of knocking on the door at such an hour. The town had become a scary place in the last few days; she had no need to add any more to her own sense of unease.

From memory, she dialled the number of the hotel, her finger sensing the next number needed on the rotary dial, and asked to speak to Andrew Fillus. She could almost hear the receptionist's exasperation as she asked McCarthy to hold whilst she tried to connect her. A few minutes passed before the receptionist came back to her and told her that she was unable to raise Mr. Fillus, almost taking a shred of delight in the fact. "I can take a message, but if he is asleep, it is not our policy to wake a guest unless it is a family emergency."

McCarthy ground her teeth together in annoyance, the sound connecting down the wires and through to the ear of the young woman on the other end of the phone.

"Would Madam like for me to take a message?"

"Please, just this once, would you mind checking again? Mr. Fillus did say he would wait up for my call. Did you check the bar?" If McCarthy gave off an expression of annoyance, then she had good reason. The girl, and she sounded all of sixteen—was sticking to the company script and clicked her tongue audibly as she put McCarthy on hold once more. The tin rhapsody serenade was enough to make her explode with rage, and it was only the dulcet East End tones of Andrew's voice that stopped her from laying down a journalistic curse on the poor girl doing her job.

"Well, that was quick, even for you, McCarthy!"

"Andrew, shut up and listen, please. I need your help. I have an injured policeman in my back room—the one who was hurt outside of the facility earlier today. He's been shot, his shoulder is in a terrible state, and I think he's lost a lot of blood. And he's wearing some awful contraption around his head to stop his jaw from coming loose. He needs some sort of soft shoes or slippers and a change of clothes, and I need you to take him to Oxford. We can't trust the facility or a local ambulance crew. I don't know who's involved."

McCarthy had relayed the information and the request quickly, grateful that Andrew Fillus a proper old school journalist who knew shorthand and always had a notebook in his pocket.

"Ten minutes," he said. "I'll get someone from the news crew to drive me to your office. Have him ready to leave as soon as we pull up outside. Bye, Sam."

Short and to the point: those were characteristics Sam admired, and she couldn't help herself saying goodbye softly to the whirring sound of a call that had ended.

After she had groped her way to the back room, she found the exhausted policeman heroically still writing down details. She looked down at the notebook and then at his face; he was starting to fall asleep. She stroked his good arm and told him he had to wake up, now was not the time to fall asleep. To his credit, Bill roused himself and did his best to smile at her before jotting on a new page: *I've come this far. Run barefoot through fields and across roads. Not giving up now.*

McCarthy squeezed his hand and told him to put down whilst she relayed the conversation she'd had with Andrew.

"He's going to ask you for the story at some point, once you can speak, of course. Whether you tell him is up to you. I'd like to think Kinsey or myself would be your go-to for that interview though, keep it local. I know you and Kinsey are friends. I hope I've earned your trust tonight."

Soon after, she led Bill by his good arm to the front of the building, where they waited behind the locked door. Within ten minutes, a car pulled up outside. Only when she'd seen Andrew get out of the car did she unlock the office door.

"I couldn't find any of my crew," Andrew explained, "but this guy was in the hotel bar—he volunteered. I know you said no ambulance men, but he says he's a fan of you and Kinsey. In fact, he had a conversation with Kinsey this evening. It seems someone called for an ambulance for him, and somehow, they ended up at the Whittle Farm. There's a story both of us don't know yet—I suggest you get up there, Sam. Craig and I will look after our friend here."

McCarthy bent down to look at the smiling driver. "Craig, I presume?"

"That's me, and don't worry, Mrs. McCarthy, I won't do anything to jeopardise the interview with Mr. Kinsey. You can rely on my discretion."

Despite the seriousness of the situation, McCarthy smiled back at him. She didn't know what arrangement Kinsey had made, but she approved wholeheartedly.

"It's a right mess up at the farm—never seen such a thing. I had to drop my boy off once we'd taken the other policeman to hospital. I think what my lad saw tonight put him off wanting to be a doctor."

Bill Taylor was safely in the back seat of Craig's car, Andrew Fillus got in beside him and through the open window he shouted to McCarthy to get herself up to the Whittle place. "By the sounds of it, Kinsey will be able to give you all the details. I'll swing by later, once we have this brave chap safely at the John Radcliffe." With that, the car's engine revved, and McCarthy watched the three men disappear from view, not before acknowledging Bill Taylor's silent gesture of thanks that was signalled in a single salute from the heart.

She went back inside the office, closed everything down and picked up the notes Bill had written. If he survived the night, this would be a huge story. She was surprised he'd lasted as long as he had; the sheer will of the man was immense. He impressed her as much as the names in his scrawled notes disgusted her. For one, Laurence Sears could not be trusted anymore. All that time and effort cultivating what she had believed was a good working arrangement, dismissed by the seven slanting question marks after his name.

Andrew Fillus was right: there was more going on than she could begin to understand, but it had never stopped her before. She pulled on her coat and checked that the car keys were in the pocket before leaving the office with Bill Taylor's note in her handbag. She hadn't noticed the cold in the air before, when she had waved the three men farewell, and she certainly hadn't seen the mist covering the pavement. *Such was life*, she thought, *that we only see something when it is under our feet.*

Chapter Thirty-One

MARBON HAD LISTENED to the voice on the phone talk of secrets, rage, guilt, memories of dishonesty, broken glass and smashed dreams. All bundled together, it was enough to make any other man turn his head away from what they had done and repent to whatever god might listen. To Marbon's ears, the words were gospel sent from on high, the whisper of a deity who required only that you observe silence and disregard those who would ask you to feel shame.

Shame for that time in the factory where they were pulping down the dead animals for glue, where he had discovered his father's deceit and his mother's furious temper. Shame when he was caught masturbating over a picture of local Dublin girl and his aunt shamed him into apologising to the girl so he wouldn't go to hell. Shamed by the schoolteacher who swore he was a devil because he picked up a pen left-handed…because he wouldn't recite the Lord's Prayer during Mass…

It was shame that had brought him to this point, to a place that wasn't home, and he felt his blood burn.

Something else was clear: that journalist, Kinsey, had found out about Marbon's connection to the Republican cause. How he had found out? Was it from higher up the ladder? Had those bastards finally sold him out?

All his strength had returned. He felt invigorated, and he was angry. He would find that reporter and beat the living breath out of him until he gave up the name of his informer. Then he would go to Ireland and shoot the dog who thought enough time had gone past and kill him as well.

The voice down the phone returned. "I bet it was O' Dougal, or Ó Dochartaigh or even that traitorous bitch Shea. Christ, it could've been all three, the whole cell, the damned lot of them. They just couldn't wait to screw you over, Marbon."

The voice had it in one. They'd heard he was doing all right for himself, gained some authority, and they were jealous. *Ahh, that Marbon. Let's hand him over to the English, but not the authorities. No, let's drip information to a journalist with a grudge, give him the rope to hang him for us.*

Marbon brain was going to explode. The dirty sell-outs, the bastards. All because he had warned against that one job. Shea had promised revenge at the time, and how she crowed when the news had come in, when the papers were full of the names of the dead.

The voice down the phone changed, rough from years of cigarette abuse, her Belfast accent highlighting the mockery, her loathing for the man who had once put a knife to her neck and threatened to gut her like a pig because she refused to sleep with him.

"How you doing there, Mar? Stuck in the middle of the countryside of a country that hates you. If you came back here, you'd just be as hated, wouldn't you?"

"Shea, you bloody bitch. I should have just let that knife slip into your neck."

"What you going to do about it, little man? Ahh, right, that was the reason. God, it feels good to tell you that now. I wonder if that English journalist will quote me when he exposes you. Little man, afraid of his own shadow—call yourself a patriot, call yourself a loyal member to the cause. What was it, Mar? Why did you not want me to arrange the Birmingham job? Was it because secretly you love those English bastards? Because deep down, you want to keep those country robbers in place. You're a traitor, Marbon."

"Now look, Shea, I hate the fucking English as much as you. But wouldn't have won us the war. It was reckless and stupid. There were other ways to hit out at the English over Christmas."

"English lover. It's all right. No hard feelings. After all, when we finish giving details of your movements during that time, you'll come out as the hero. It will all be down to you. I might even throw in proof you killed that girl—you remember the one. It's funny—don't you think she has a resemblance to the girl you saved in the woods? Won't that make for a great picture on the front of every paper—you in between the two striking girls? Did you like girls then, Marbon? Was that the problem? Was I not cute enough for you? Was the skirt just a little too long? Was I too…mature for you? Is that why you threatened me, Marbon—I wasn't young enough for you to control?"

Shea spat out the questions, each vowel an accusation, each pause an allegation. Marbon raged at the smears on his name and his sexuality.

"Shea, I warn you. When I finish with that interfering bastard Kinsey, I will come back to Ireland and I will make good on that promise to slit you from Belfast ear to Belfast ear. You want to be reminded of the past? What about that fourteen-year-old boy you shot in cold blood? What was his crime again? Refresh my dull old memory, Shea. Was it because he kissed your sister, got a bit too hot and steamy—you didn't like seeing her tongue down his throat? Poor bastard didn't know what hit him, did he?"

The line was quiet for some time, and the voice that spoke next was more reasonable, affable to Marbon's situation.

"Do you want a way out of this, Marbon?"

"Ó Dochartaigh, is that you? What happened to Shea? Has she run off scared back to Belfast?"

"Just listen, my friend. One job, one small favour, all right? Deal with Kinsey and all will be forgiven."

"I don't know where he is, the bloody nosey—"

The voice cut him off. "He's on his way to the woods—you know where. All you have to do is *deal with* him and you can come back home."

"What about Shea? I won't have that witch talk to me that way, Ó Dochartaigh."

There was no answer. Marbon knew what he had to do. He could walk there quickly enough, and he would see to it that Kinsey and all his questions stopped. He got out of the chair, not noticing that the telephone wire had come loose when he originally dropped it—that all he'd been holding was the receiver, and the voices were all in his head. He put on his shoes and went to the gun cabinet, removing the Remington shotgun—a gift from a grateful sponsor in 1969—and a box of bullets that had been patiently waiting since before he arrived in the town.

Chapter Thirty-Two

H E PUT IT down to the pressure of the long night. The gunshot confirmed that the farmer and possibly her brother were dead, but inwardly he knew something was happening underneath his skull. The pain had increased whilst he had been out in the open; now, the still air began to close in and made him nauseous, a radiating sickness that grumbled away above his eye and kicked out like an aggravated donkey. As he watched the policeman come back out of the house and reach for his radio, silently gesturing for back-up from any officer close by, he felt the urge to vomit hit him and made a run for it, spilling his guts between the parked cars littering the lane.

The feeling of sickness abated, slowly draining away as if someone had released a tightly wedged plug in a bath full of bile. He wiped his mouth on his jacket sleeve and looked down to the ground in self-pity.

"Are you all right, sir?" came a voice of concern a few feet away. He looked up and saw the policeman who had sprinted into the house standing a few feet away, not daring to come any closer.

"I'm fine. Just been too much of a night," he lied awkwardly. "Are they both dead—the farmer and her brother?"

The policeman shook his head. "Mr. Whittle is alive and well. He says his sister pulled the gun on him, fired a warning shot and then turned the gun on herself." He hesitated briefly. "But the woman—her gun misfired, went off prematurely, and she took buckshot to the arm. Ballistics will be able to tell, but she'll be okay. Although she'll have questions to answer."

"So why did you come out screaming blue murder?"

"Ah...that. I received a message from my colleagues down by the windmill. There's been an incident at the station—I think you met WPC Andrea Laybourne earlier, not that it matters whether you did or you didn't. Anyway, she found two of our colleagues dead and the desk sergeant bleeding out, a knife in his hands. Laybourne said at first it looked like Sergeant Green had lost his mind and attacked the other two, but the girl we took into custody earlier has gone missing. Surely, she couldn't...I mean... she wouldn't have had the strength to do such a thing."

Kinsey thought back to the moment in the windmill where it had taken several men to subdue the girl, to get her to stop lapping at blood and hay from the floor. Like Serena Cox earlier at the Wendlefields facility, the girl's rage was like nothing he had ever seen, but the policeman didn't seem to understand that girls were as prone to outrageous acts of violence as boys. Still, Kinsey nodded and said nothing.

"We're down to our bare bones," the officer continued. "There's me, the two officers by the windmill, the officer who took Watney to the hospital and WPC Laybourne. No one's heard from PC Taylor all day—not since that women's lib lady cracked him in the jaw—and no one can get hold of the inspector. Laybourne's all alone...well, she has the duty solicitor with her. I don't understand it."

Kinsey straightened up, walked through the congealing mess and put his arm around the young, scared policeman. There was nothing he could say to help the man. He was out of his depth. They all were. Kinsey felt he had little choice but to take charge.

"I suggest you go back inside the farm, lock the door, and until you hear from a figure of authority or you recognise someone, you don't open it again. Look after the three people in the house, they are *your* responsibility now. Call for an ambulance. I'm sure Ms. Whittle will be fine, but make sure that you or her brother are in constant sight of her. Radio the men by the windmill. Tell them to get back here as soon as possible. There's nothing they can do until morning, and if evidence gets tampered with, so be it. I don't think we're dealing with an ordinary situation here. There's something terribly wrong in this town, and especially here by this farm."

The officer accepted the command without question. He was far too young to be involved in something like this.

What Kinsey wouldn't have given to have Bill Taylor here at this moment. Dependable and passionate about the job, he would have taken the lad by the shoulder and told him straight: *we do our duty son; we do our duty.* Kinsey couldn't help but worry where Bill had got to. Surely, he couldn't still be at the facility—he should have left there hours ago. If he was at the Radcliffe, someone at the station would have known, and by default in a town where everyone knew everyone's business, Kinsey would have eventually been given the nod on his friend's state of health.

His head began to pound with greater urgency, a series of SOS messages which knocked violently against his mind. He'd heard the first signs of madness were when you could hear someone hammering *save me* over and over again on your skull.

"Go," he urged the officer again. "Go inside and deal with the problem at hand. You'll be safe there."

With that, the policeman strode away, given purpose once more: to do his duty. That was, after all, what he had sworn an oath to do.

Kinsey watched him go inside and then let the pain dictate what he should do. He wanted to go up the hill to the other farm. He felt in his gut that some of the answers could be found up there, but he couldn't withstand the pain much longer. Whilst his heart maintained that he must do his duty, it was to his head he listened and found himself remembering the only place in the last few months that he had been at peace, where the agony in his head had subsided. He needed to go back to the spot in the woods and sit down on the quiet, contented earth.

***

Kinsey trudged out of sight of the farmhouse, away from the watchful eyes of Paul Whittle, who had managed to remove some of the buckshot from his sister's arm, and who would stick to the story of how it came to be until his dying day. Damp powder, dirty gun. It was believable because his sister was a poor housekeeper. Paul doubted once there had been an investigation, when everything about the untold tragedy was researched and locked away, that few people, if any, would ask for a more concise answer. He wished the reporter well as he disappeared into the trees.

***

Kinsey wasn't sure where he was walking. He could hear the bustling river as it ambled somewhere over to his right, the sound acting as a kind of compass, keeping his faltering steps on the path. His hair caught in twigs that reached down to him, tangling their early blooms in his neck-length, peculiarly cut mop. He stumbled, and the pain in his head swelled, causing him to squint and fumble the way so that he was going by memory rather than the ability to see the route he was taking. One of his shoes became snared in the muddy path, and he kicked them both off in annoyance, the cold air biting at his socked feet, his ankles feeling the bitter chill of April's seduction. Yet he ploughed on, almost blind with pain as he groped at every tree and kept a sharp ear out for the river, until beneath his toes he felt a sharp pain where he had blundered his way to the edge of the circle.

Lowering to all fours, crawled through the ring of trees and herbaceous shrubs, to the safe haven where he believed he could lay down his head and forget his life, rest awhile before another battle commenced.

The flowers were fresh and cool against his palms. He lifted one to his nose and sniffed; the fresh scent set his nostrils alight. A calming effect quickly followed.

IAN D. HALL

The unmistakable sound of someone treading on twigs caught his ears, too heavy-footed for the spectre he'd seen earlier. He forced himself to move into the circle, the flowers acting a buffer against splinters from the branches strewn across the clearing. He couldn't see a thing, the pain in his head overwhelmed him, yet he had never felt so alert, ready to act should the stalker pounce upon him. He listened, but nothing came except the rustle of the wind catching the higher branches, causing them to sway reluctantly in its breath. He wanted to believe the pain had caused him to imagine it, that it was all in his head, and for a second, he dared to hope it was just a fox or a badger come to give him a scare.

"Kinsey, I know you're here. Your friends in Ireland told me where you 'd be!" The loud voice broke the near-perfect silence that Kinsey had sought. If there had been any animals close by, then the anger in Marbon's voice would have had them skulking back to their dens, their back legs trembling and their young whining softly.

"Where are you? No point in hiding—show yourself! Be a man!"

His voice edged closer, and thanks to the near stillness of the woods, Kinsey could tell Marbon was coming up behind him, from the wooden bridge that crossed the river. He shifted into a better position to gauge how close Marbon—how long it would be until he was face-to-face with the man who had completely lost his mind.

"Marbon!" he shouted finally when he estimated he was about a hundred feet away. "Is that you?"

"I see you there, sat in the clearing, you English fuck. Perhaps you should get on your knees and pray. There's a chance I might not blow your head off."

"I don't know what you're talking about. I don't know anyone in Ireland. Yes, I'll admit I've been digging into your life because there's a story to be told. I'll even admit I don't like you. You're a

190

conniving, thieving bastard. But is that really a reason to shoot me?"

A glimmer of light flickered over Kinsey's face, followed by the full beam of a powerful torch, and he squeezed his eyes shut.

"What are you doing here, Mr. Kinsey?"

"I could ask you the same thing, Marbon—aside from threating to shoot me."

Marbon laughed cruelly. He took another step closer to the circle and stopped. Kinsey listened, the pain once again subsiding. Whatever magic was at work in this circle, whether it was down to a placebo effect or some sort of incantation, he welcomed it.

"Shea—you know her, don't you, Mr. Kinsey? Well, said you'd been asking questions, and that she gladly told you about my part in a lot of nasty business. But I'm curious. You don't work for a national—you're just a local man reporting on local news. What were you going to do with my story? Turn everyone against me, get me barred from every public house in the town, have me tarred and feathered, a sign hung around my neck proclaiming me for what I am? Or were you going to swallow your pride and sell the story to *The Mirror*, *Express* or the BBC? You'd be a hero, Mr. Kinsey. Is that what you wanted?"

Unheard by the ranting Marbon, a sound of breaking water came from the river, and Kinsey tilted his head to listen, the torchlight now longer shining in his eyes. He opened them slightly and to his amazement found he could see perfectly. The sound he recognised as someone shifting from water to land, but nobody in their right mind have been out swimming at this time of night, certainly not in April.

Marbon's exasperated voice drew Kinsey's attention back to the intense glare of the torch, though this time, Kinsey found he could focus his stare without too much bother. Marbon was still a couple of yards outside of the circle, but Kinsey noticed the gun for the first time, and he swallowed hard on the tension in his throat. He shifted his gaze to look the man in the eye, and whilst it was still the obnoxious face of the man he detested, there seemed to be a shifting in the way he looked. Like a two-headed coin being spun in the air, it interchanged between the man and the appearance of the figure the children said they had seen—the one who had appeared to Kinsey on the other side of the ring, whom he had seen burn and blister half of a tree in a show of extraordinary horror.

The coin spun quicker, the face kept flickering, melting into one gruesome, ghastly expression. As a child, Kinsey had once seen a documentary on a bombed-out waxworks. It had left him disturbed enough to shy away from playing with toy figurines and plastic models; the melted features of the lifeless figures gave him nightmares for weeks. It was the same disgusting scene that unfolded before him now as he sat in the middle of nature. Confronted by the menace of man's ability to mimic the abhorrent and the sacred, he couldn't help himself and watched in horror-filled fascination as the image settled somewhere between the two faces, neither man nor monster.

Whatever was left of Marbon at that moment, Kinsey was unsure, but he was certain he would be protected by the ring encircling him. He had faith that he could sit still and not be shot at. But such dreams were fancy illusions, and even in the greatest of faiths, illusions must shatter.

Whatever passed for Marbon was struck by great physical pain as he crossed the divide, but he was still able to penetrate it by stepping over the ring. Kinsey shuffled back a few inches, shocked that his belief had suddenly deserted him. Marbon spoke, but it was with a very different, hollow voice.

"Kinnnnseeeeeyyyy… Feelingggg ill?"

Kinsey struggled to his feet, his legs giving way twice before he was upright. Another sound came from the river—a screech, the maddening, high-pitched wail of a banshee caught in a trap. This time, it was enough to pause the momentum of the Marbon creature. Kinsey played for time, caught in his own trap, not wanting to leave the circle which on two occasions had diminished the pain in his head, but also finding he was now standing between two entities he could not explain, and the monster before him was just as scary as whatever was coming up from the river. Seeing as running back out of the woods to the safety of the farm was completely out of the question, he decided that the only way he could deal with the situation was to confront Marbon with questions.

"Who is Shea? You tell me that she knows me—tell me how?" He stood firm, refusing to be seen as being as a coward, even in the presence of one whose face reminded him of the moments where Indiana Jones warns his companion that something was coming out of the Ark, where his nemesis and fellow archaeologist Belloq melts in the face of the angels. Kinsey didn't have a companion to whisper and wait for the heavenly winds to stop bellowing and screaming around them, but he did have a man in front of him who looked as if he'd been under the knife of a disreputable plastic surgeon.

"Shea, you know Sheaaaa." Marbon's face contorted once more, the lips quivering and turning downwards. A thick tongue licked at the stubble surrounding the mouth as if it were dribbling in anticipation of a meal. That thought disturbed Kinsey even more. Being eaten by his assailant was a turn he had not considered when he'd contemplated ways his life might end. He tried a different approach, taking a step forward.

"All right, so I know her. She gave me everything I asked for, and you know why. She said I was a better man—even for an Englishman, I looked as though I was better in bed." He took another step forward, driving the point home, even though he wasn't sure if it was doing any good. Hurt the ego of the man and the beast might reveal itself.

Marbon didn't say anything, but his lips quivered and then blew out, the teeth showing their descent into luminescence, the face becoming transparent. The hybrid creature snarled and convulsed as if it were uncomfortable, two bodies in the same space, fighting for time, combatting for the words with a foreign tongue connecting them.

Marbon took a step, and Kinsey matched it, unsure what the creature outside the circle looked like. Perhaps it was the same as Marbon, all arrogance and secrets. Kinsey hoped the true form of the creature could be observed—that the glow of mist hanging at the edge of the circle would alert them to the monster, and they would see what the children—what he had seen.

Kinsey looked around him, almost spinning on his toes, swiftly taking in a thought. The mist wasn't inside the circle. Only the monster had found a way past the spell or incantation that had made it possible for Kinsey to feel like his old self. Depending on which teacher you listened to at school, he was either too clever for his own good or he was reckless, prone to finding himself in trouble. He supposed it was better to have a ghost of chance of standing out, whichever path he took, and if he was able to somehow remove the rifle from the beast, he at least stood a chance. He speculated that the man could be hurt—that the mist and the spirit driving him would not be able to save him.

It took less than ten seconds for him to think this through, but as with everything in life, time waits for no one, and as he made his move, he was stopped in his tracks by a vision he glimpsed out the corner of his eye. The drenched body of a young girl stood erect and staring at him with wildness and wrath etched all over her face.

Chapter Thirty-Three

THE GIRL HAD been walking for a half an hour, head down, slightly cocked to one side as if she was listening to a conversation that Rebecca and her comrades would never be privy too. She kept up a good pace as well, and at one point, Rebecca noted that had they not been in the car following her, they might have struggled to keep up.

In that time, whenever another vehicle drove past her, it would misfire, and the headlights would dim. Rebecca and her two companions kept their distance, letting the girl walk a couple of hundred yards ahead whilst still in the town. This tactic was harder to keep up once they hit the country roads that led like threaded veins out of the town, and they had to get closer lest the girl took a shortcut across a field.

Eventually, she did just that, at the turning point where a person could choose to head on towards Buckingham, through the neat and respectable villages that separated the two counties of Buckinghamshire and Oxfordshire or towards the river and the two farms.

"She's heading to the river," Silvanus confirmed under his breath. "Look—the Whittles' farmhouse. There are lights on, but she isn't heading there. If she follows that line, she will come out opposite the circle."

Against her better judgement, Silvanus's daughter followed her father's instructions and parked the car as close to the woods as she could. She got out, paused to take a small, stump-like cigar out of her skirt pocket and lit it up in front of her father. The air, which had already turned blue, took on the impression of lit cornflowers as the first gasps of smoke were blown out in retribution.

Rebecca had seen that type of display before. She had done it herself a hundred times when her father or mother had told her to take the bins out, asked her to stop at home so they could go out for a meal, when her grades had not been good enough, when she dropped out of the Girl Guides—always too much hassle to silently comply. She was glad to see that independent, rebellious streak in another, and for the record, Silvanus treated his daughter like she was trash, and Rebecca told him so.

Silvanus looked at her through narrowed eyes and said, "My daughter is the only one who can drive that vehicle. We need help, not manners and sulking petitions of why it is her responsibility to bring whatever is plaguing the town to its knees. She disagreed. I make the decision that is best for us. Now, can we catch up with that girl before she reaches the river?"

Like Silvanus's daughter, Rebecca wanted to have a cigarette and blow smoke up the old man's nose, but instead, she climbed over the low stone wall and shrugged off her exasperation at the old man's ways. Until they saw the girl standing motionless on the riverbank, not a word was said between them, and for his part, Silvanus seemed to enjoy the period of quiet.

It was Rebecca who broke the silence, more out of questioning what was happening rather than wanting to get in to a deep, profound conversation about the old man's ethics and life choices.

"Whatever's happening, why aren't more people being affected?"

Silvanus kept his eyes firmly on the girl but took care to acknowledge the query from his companion.

"I've been thinking, and I believe I understand. There are two forces at work here—one driven by poison, the other by memory. Something has brought them into the world, and as yet, neither has been strong enough to truly wield their power. Before we were moved on, my family had managed to keep such spirits at bay, and to my shame, Rebecca, I thought we had beaten the mist that came off the river.

"But why now?" Rebecca pointed at the girl, whose head shifted from side to side as if she were having an animated exchange with a best friend. "Like her, she's obviously not in her right mind."

"The poison is not yet ripe enough. It has been working away at the system for years and is now at a point where it can change the way people think and act. It's attacking the more malleable brains of society—the young, the teenagers who are already going through turmoil. They see planes fly overhead, and they know that the pilots are on their way to bomb people. Hundreds of ordinary folk will die, and they get emotional. These entities feed on such moments, not because they want to, but because it is all they are offered."

The old man's eyes widened, and he grabbed Rebecca's hand to steady himself.

"It is not just the young who are being affected by this. A woman I have known for years through her causes, who once stood her ground so we might live in these woods—she broke a policeman's jaw this morning. Does that sound like the behaviour of a contented and unaffected individual? I followed your Mr. Kinsey home a couple of nights ago. He has been ill for quite some time, and sure, he has an underlying problem, but he too senses it. The man who died, the army fellow—I think he was murdered by these otherworldly forces, and then there is the facility at Wendlefields. I don't know what exactly is going on in there, but my own eyes tell me that all is not well, that here in this place and down on the land formerly owned by that scoundrel Yobe, there is a bomb waiting to…"

Silvanus's voice trailed off as the young girl they had been following slipped quietly into the water.

"She must be mad," Rebecca said. "The water will be freezing."

Silvanus nodded. "How far to the wooden bridge, the part where the river narrows? About half a mile, would you say?

Rebecca calculated the distance quickly. "Nearer to a mile." She pointed to the lights in the distance. "That's the estate where the boy was found in his shed. It's about a mile away, and the bridge is just before that, at the bottom of Kerr Field."

"Well, we'd better get a move on, unless you want to catch your death by swimming the river, and I wouldn't recommend it."

Rebecca grew frightened. It all suddenly became real to her. She had no choice, as Silvanus had said to her, but to act with as much courage as she could muster.

"What's on the other side of the river? You said something about a circle. What's it for? she asked, but before the old man could answer, a voice shattered the illusion of peace with a loud, terrifying and enraged declaration of fury. She thought she recognised the accent; she certainly recognised the name being shouted.

Silvanus, despite his age, began to run as if he himself was possessed, shouting back his answer as Rebecca ran after him.

"For protection, and I hope Kinsey finds it."

Chapter Thirty-Four

PORTIA YOBE STOPPED her car where the voice had told her she should wait. Her husband's mistress would be along soon, and then she could finally have it out with her. All those times he claimed he had to nip out for meetings with investors, health and safety matters, production schedules—anything but face up to the way he made her feel—as if she repulsed him. Now she could confront the woman responsible, the one who whispered sweet nothings into her husband's ears.

She also recognised that her own behaviour at times may have forced Adam to look elsewhere, and who better to do it with than someone he claimed to hate so much? It all made perfect sense now; for months, she had brooded on who the woman was. He'd been so careful, she'd never caught him drooling over any other woman, he never let his guard down around her. Such was the man. However, tonight she had the proof she had sought. Strange though, the 'friend' who had called didn't give her name, but Portia knew who had delivered sweet illumination; she had thanked her anonymous benefactor and put down the telephone.

Who needs a gun when I can confront her with something equally as good! She remembered thinking that as she got into her car and drove to the rendezvous point.

Self-righteous Sam McCarthy: she should have guessed. A man doesn't talk about a woman to the point of obsession without reason. Oh, he told Portia the journalist was ruining his name around the town, running a hate campaign, but it was a smokescreen to lead her away from the truth that he and McCarthy were fucking on a daily basis.

When did it start? After the baby died or before? Does it matter? Portia supposed not. He'd buried the baby whilst she was in hospital and then got on with his life. The baby had died, the doctors told her, because she had conceived too late in life. She had argued there must have been another reason, perhaps environmental, maybe dietary, until she was blue in the face. They could try again. But she had been talked out of it—by her husband, by the doctors—*"Learn to live with your grief and move on. You're not helping yourself by all this continued torture."* So she let it go, and in doing so, withdrew into herself as grief slowly eroded the woman she was, young, free-spirited and drawn to the ethereal essence of life, until all that remained was a bitter, twisted creature who slept through the day and listened as her own demons chiselled away at her confidence at night.

Several cars had passed, but none of them were the one she was looking for. Hidden in darkness at the side of the road, she watched a teenage girl stride briskly towards her, then suddenly veer off and climb over a wall. The girl looked straight at her, but Portia didn't care whether she had been seen or not; she only cared about The Other Woman.

Another car, old and battered, unlike the others that had passed—all of which, oddly, seemed to be having trouble with their lights—ground to a halt, and three people got out and argued briefly before one of them got back in, turned the car around and headed back to Perchester. The two that remained followed the girl over the wall and disappeared out of sight.

Portia didn't recognise the girl or any of the three people, not that it mattered. She barely recognised anyone in the town anymore. They had all stopped coming after the baby died in her. They were embarrassed, ashamed, her grief was too much for them or they simply had better things to do.

Not once had she considered it might be because they didn't what to say nor realised how much she had changed since her stay in hospital. She had been living in a bewildering fog, a peasouper of emotions that left her continually exhausted. Now she had been given a helping hand to find her way out and into the clear air.

Another car approached, and like the others it seemed to lose a vestige of power suddenly, the wheels swerving and the lights dimming. This time, the car's owner was not so fortunate and skidded the full width of the carriageway, slamming into an oak tree on the other side of the road.

This must be her. Portia smiled to herself. The caller had said the woman would be delivered to her. Walking back to her own car, she opened the boot and took out a large, heavy tyre wrench, thrilling at the cool weight of it in her hand and the strength of purpose it gave her.

***

Sam McCarthy's car stereo started playing up as she left the town, a burst of static cutting through a Queen track the over-enthusiastic disc jockey seemed to favour in his current playlist. Silence followed, and with one eye on the road, McCarthy fiddled with the radio's settings until she settled on a news discussion. Relaxing once more, she drove on, past the final house which the town claimed as its own and out onto the country lanes.

As she went past fields and dark, looming barns, the radio signal slipped once more, this time producing a sound that made static seem pleasurable. If she hadn't known better, she'd have said a banshee had homed in her, shrieking as it descended. McCarthy covered one ear and kept driving, waiting for the signal to pick up again, but the noise was unbearable. She reached for the radio's power switch, but it wouldn't turn off. She tried the volume dial to no effect. In her driver's side mirror, she caught sight of another car coming up behind her. It was still a little way off but seemed to be speeding along. The headlights lights flashed a couple of times, and the car slowed down. McCarthy shifted her gaze to the road ahead and then up to the rear-view mirror...

Seconds later, she wondered if she'd crashed before or after the radio returned with its unsettling mix of news broadcast and heartbeat, not that there was a thing she could do about it, lying half out the door, her head on the tarmac, the seat belt slicing between her breasts as a face, alabaster white but for the droplets of blood running from its sunken eyes down to its grinning, partly open mouth full of decaying teeth, river reeds tangled in its bedraggled dark hair...

Before or after the event, it wasn't the radio that caused McCarthy to lose control and skid headlong into a tree. It was a large index finger coming out of the gloom of the back seat and placing itself over that grinning mouth, the two lips coming together in a quiet *shhhhhhh*...

She had a feeling she'd briefly lost consciousness, but it couldn't have been for long. She remembered the other car that was close by. Had they seen the accident? Would they have reported it? She listened hard for the sound of sirens but heard instead someone approaching—women's shoes, unmistakable by the clicks of the thin heels.

"Please help me. I'm stuck, I can't release the seat belt—there's a knife in my glove compartment. You just have to reach in and pass it to me. Please?" Begging didn't come naturally to McCarthy. She had not begged her husband not to leave when he found out about her and Kinsey; she hadn't begged Rebecca to stay with her rather than go with her dad; they were the two most important people in her life, and yet here she was, trapped and frightened, begging for a stranger's help.

The sound of footsteps ceased, but she saw no one. At the point where she almost convinced herself she had imagined it, a face appeared next to hers, the features contorted by anger, an arm raised and a glint of metal—a tyre wrench in the woman's hand.

***

202

Adam Yobe recognised Sam McCarthy's car even in the dark. He had seen it often enough—the shape of it, the make and model. Unless someone from out of town had decided to drive through Perchester's countryside tonight, it was a sure bet that the car in front of him belonged to the one person he would have loved to ram off the road if he could have got away with it.

Yobe scrunched up his nose as his own car lost power underneath the railway bridge and again on the unlit lane. He took his foot off the gas and slowed down; he didn't like taking chances when driving. Up ahead, McCarthy's tail lights flared and then darted sharp left. As if cued, the moon emerged from behind a cloud, lighting up the scene perfectly, and he watched— partly out of morbid interest but surprisingly also part concern— McCarthy's car slam into a tree and tip slightly as it juddered a few feet up the grass embankment.

Yobe hit the brakes and pulled over. However much he hated the woman, he wouldn't leave her to suffer. He was about to open his car door when he spotted a figure appear on the other side of the road. In disbelief, he leaned closer to the windscreen. *Portia...What the hell...?* He'd left her sleeping at home. He'd only stopped for fuel, so she had to have come out straight after him to be here now.

Leaving the door ajar in case he needed to make a quick getaway, he got out of the car and moved stealthily towards the scene, his eyes firmly fixed on his wife, who held a tyre wrench in her hand, allowing it to flirt with the idea of scraping the grass and mud when she reached the verge. She hesitated, which caused him to waver in his own actions. His mind was racing. He still couldn't understand what she was doing here—what had possessed her to drive out to this spot in the middle of the night? She moved off again, this time with purpose, and stopped next to the driver's side of McCarthy's car.

Yobe quickened his steps. McCarthy was begging Portia not to hurt her, and then Portia's arm fell, and he felt the sickening blow as the tyre wrench came down on the journalist's head. Running now, Yobe rounded the car and managed somehow to catch his wife's arm as it began its second descent. The wrench hit the glass in the open door, shattering it on impact.

"What the hell, Portia?" he yelled. All his self-control and restraint fled in an instant, leaving him emotionally naked, vulnerable.

"Doing what I should done a long time ago," Portia spat. "Showing your mistress exactly what happens when you mess with another woman's husband!" Spittle foam at the sides of her mouth, specks of blood dotting her cheeks, her eyes barren, drained but on fire, Yobe could almost feel the heat emanating from them as his wife's ire searched for another soul to infect with its blistering zeal.

She struggled in his grip, her weight shifting from side to side as if shaking off a tight-fitting dress. When that didn't work, she tried to bite down on his hand, scraping his knuckles. He yanked his hand away and swore.

"McCarthy? She's not my mistress! I can't abide the woman! And anyway, I don't have a mistress, you loon. I can't handle more than one of you crazy women." His answer was cruel but honest. Sure, he fancied the professor's wife; most men did, even a few of the women in the town—in fact, anyone who had seen her beauty and poise and felt entranced by her sophistication and ruby lips. But he hadn't made a play for her. Why would he? His best days, if he ever had any, were far behind him.

"Don't you lie—don't you *fucking lie to me*, Adam Yobe! The person who rang after you left told me everything. Not that I hadn't guessed, not that it wasn't obvious. Meetings my eye. What was it? The baby? Was I getting you down, not pleasing you in bed? Or is it that you're just a weak man, believing that because you have money, a woman would sleep with you?" Portia Yobe screamed, her accusations stinging her husband's pride.

He loosened his grip slightly, feeling the pain of her wrath in his heart. She took the chance to stamp a heel down hard on his foot.

It was fortunate they were on grass and not the road, as she lost her footing, only saved from serious harm by her husband's quick reactions and the car door frame, which caught her breast sharply. Yobe steadied her and turned her around, releasing her in horror. Where had been a figurative fire of fury in her eyes, there was now an inferno, an inextinguishable, out-of-control conflagration.

Yobe stood petrified as the searing hot flames danced in his wife's eye sockets, a deep burning red calling out for him to join in the madness. She scratched at his face with her long nails, drawing blood and leaving welts like long pulsating worms squirming underneath the surface.

Out of self-preservation and shock, he couldn't stop himself. His fist struck her in the face, and he watched, sickened by his own actions, as her body shuddered and crumpled to the ground. The air was deathly quiet, and Yobe suddenly became aware that he was not breathing. He looked down at his wife and then to McCarthy. Checking both women, he was relieved to find both had a pulse, whilst knowing that if he didn't call for an ambulance soon. McCarthy would not survive Portia's brutal attack.

He thought fast, such was his way. Picking his wife from the ground, he carried her back to his car and, remembering her violence, placed her in the boot, making sure the lock was securely fastened. That done, he ran across the road and pushed Portia's car further into the trees; he'd come and retrieve it once he got to the farm. Dennis, if he was still there, would have to give him a hand.

Returning to his car, he about to drive off when he heard a scream in the distance. At first, he thought McCarthy had come to, but the scream was piercing, inhuman, agony to his ears. He put his hands over them to block out the noise, recalling old tales of a banshee driving the uneducated folk of a village crazy with its penetrating shriek. It sounded like Death warning them that finally their sins had found them out and he was coming for them all.

Letting go of his head, Yobe wound up the window, which had no effect on the loudness or the depth of the scream, but he thought he might be able to outrun it. He turned the radio to its maximum volume, not realising that he was also drowning out the noises coming from the boot of his wife waking.

Chapter Thirty-Five

SIDNEY MUTTON STARED at his wife and Dr. Moran. He had been called to the facility by Laurence Sears, who stood by, looking grave and worn, as Moran told a story Mutton found difficult to believe. Finally, he allowed his pent-up anger to explode.

"What the hell were you playing at, Hattie? Dr. Moran? When you showed me the first case, you presented it as an unknown profile, and I told you I didn't want it hampering what we do here at the facility." He jabbed a finger at Moran. "I blame you for this. What was it? Money? Power? A shot at fame and glory in *The Lancet*? It sure as hell wasn't for the betterment of humanity, was it?"

Moran returned his boss's hard stare for a second, then relented. He'd spent the past hour trying to clean up the mess on Cox's face, by which time the policeman had escaped into the night. He had sent the caretaker after Taylor, believing he couldn't have got far with the pain he'd be in, but he was long gone, a walking ghost who could climb out of smashed windows.

Hattie Mutton spoke up in Moran's defence. "He knew nothing of this particular episode, Sidney. It's all on me, and quite frankly, you should be grateful. My experiments have proved that the adult mind can take the serum. I have invested in you for so long—let's not forget that when I met you, you had nothing, not a scrap of money to your name. I put you on the map with this facility, your own work into curing addiction psychosis is only possible because of the connections I built from the ground up."

A woman had died in the course of the experiment. The police were no doubt about to kick the door down and arrest them all—the only saving grace being that Hattie and Moran had thought to get the Frampton women out of the building. Of course, as the inspector had pointed when he greeted the professor at the entrance to the side road skirting the property, Frampton's daughter would need constant evaluation and check-ups; there was no guarantee she'd survive, and that would be more blood on Mutton's hands.

He held those hands in partial surrender. He accepted his wife's argument in part. As a child who had been brought to Britain to stay with relatives in the wake of Kristallnacht, he knew full well the power of research. He had diligently worked his way through university and made his mother proud when finally he saw her again, six months before she died of a drug overdose, alone, consumed by nightmares and still bearing the gift the Nazi regime had bestowed upon her. She had risked her life so he could do something good—something that might save others from the agony she had endured—and he found in this moment, surrounded by the people in whom he had placed his trust, that the experiments always continue and evil never truly went away.

Moran raised his head once more, sensing an opportunity to save face. "What we have to do now is make sure we're all in agreement. Yes, the activist woman is dead. We can't cover that up, but we can tell the press the boy is alive. The toxins in his body have been removed, and we can show the police, the press, the whole damn community if we have to, that this place is clean."

"Clean?" Mutton repeated incredulously. "I have never felt so dirty in all my life! What has happened here is intolerable. Do you think the inspector is here out of ongoing concern for the drug problem becoming an epidemic? How do we explain away a dissolving body? We'll be lucky to find a single square foot untouched by this."

"The policeman was still suffering the after-effects of his injury," Moran persisted. "Who knows what he saw? The woman, Serena Cox, she was off her head, and she has a history of violence—something our inspector friend here can back up. After that, we're the only ones who know what Hattie...Mrs. Mutton I mean, and I were up to. And whilst I agree, sorry Hattie, that we went too far, there's nothing else to worry about. It didn't start here—we just found a way to utilise it for other means. The press and the police, with the exception of our friend here, know nothing. We can start again when the furore dies down. You have to admit, Sidney, research into renewing the brain's pathways is a good thing. So what if we have to use...alternative ways of finding a cure?"

Sidney Mutton turned away from his wife and two staff members and looked to the inspector for any sign of dissent or argument. He was complicit in this but had no doubt fooled himself into thinking it was acceptable for the sake of the local population. Published data showed drug abuse was down, and drug-related crime was being erased. Criminal justice and medicine working in harmony—get them off the streets, keep them in the facility for as long as it took, get them clean.

Inspector Sears bobbed his head. Only the professor saw it, just as the policeman intended.

"Hattie, this is not over. I want a full, detailed account of your plan, and if anyone else has died because of your gross negligence, trust me, I will hand you to the authorities myself, even it costs me everything. Inspector Sears, please arrange an autopsy for Ms. Cox. Nurse Hasser, check on the other patients, make sure they're comfortable. Dr. Moran..." Mutton eyed his once-trusted colleague, disappointed and devastated, but showing it would be a sign of weakness. "You will come with me. We're going to prepare a statement."

"What am I to do?" Hattie asked.

"You, my dear, are to go home. The inspector will drive you. You're in no fit state to do anything useful. I shall return once Moran and I have finished the statement. Then tomorrow, you and I are going to see the Frampton girl and offer her free consultations for life. The same with the boy, no matter the cost."

Hattie Moran murmured under her breath, but the professor ignored it.

"We have invited evil into our lives, and evil has a way of punishing those who thought they were doing good. I learned that as a young boy in Munich."

Inspector Sears helped Hattie to her feet and turned on his radio. Immediately, a woman's voice came through calling for him.

"This is Sears, over."

"Inspector, thank God! I've been trying to get hold of you."

"Who is this, and what is the problem?"

"WPC Laybourne, sir. There's been…an incident at the station. Two officers dead, one man seriously injured."

The inspector looked at Mutton. "Evil strikes, Sidney."

"Sir, are you there, over?"

"I'm on my way, Laybourne. Hold tight." Sears signed off. "I think this takes precedence over taking your wife home. Sorry, Sidney."

The professor nodded in agreement. "What happened here is only the tip of the iceberg. There is an evil abroad in this town, something perhaps we aided. Go, Inspector. Report back as soon as you can. Take the side road. There's still a gathering of reporters at the front gate."

Sears smiled, a watery, grave upturn on his face, and turned smartly on his heels.

"Well then, my dear," Mutton said to his wife, still leaning on Moran for support. "It looks like you'll have to stay and help Nurse Hasser. I suggest you behave. She doesn't have time for games—she'll eat you alive."

Chapter Thirty-Six

DANIOR SILET, DAUGHTER *of Silvanus*. That was how she had always introduced herself when asked, although she had no record of her birth, no way of knowing if the name she used was the one her father had gone by when he was a young man, or indeed if her mother's name was really Hester. Nobody spoke about her mother; no matter how hard she tried to nudge them into sharing something, they clammed up and changed the subject.

As she had grown older, the less it became an issue. She had learned that she was different, in both name and purpose, and tonight, even though her father had once again disrespected her by sending her on this foolish errand, she had proved her worth to those who travelled the roads and set up sanctuary for the restless spirits that inhabited them—some would say 'haunted'—or guided the living into committing acts of malevolence, conduits for their revenge.

The girl they had followed, there was a rage in her that drove her forward, but she was different. In her soul, two destructive forces were at work, one ancient, the other frightened, lashing out, wanting to tear the world apart so it could finally rest. Danior wasn't sure which terrified her the most, but together, unless contained, they would see this town burn.

Danior was not a master of what she saw. The last one who had the complete control of light had been dead since her father was a little boy, and she was unsure of how old he actually was. Several years ago, he'd told her he was approaching sixty. However, the oldest remaining member of the group, one who didn't shy away from revealing her age, had let slip that the pair of them had grown up together during summer fayres, and she was remembered the dark days of the First World War and the need to keep still, to be quiet as they hid in the old forgotten forests of Europe.

As Danior drove back into the town, taking in the houses with TVs and lights blazing and the lack of interaction between the people, she wondered how long it would take them to notice a change. Would they be so complacent about their house rules with a kitchen knife rammed through their heart? Evil had a habit of spreading: the bigger the community, the larger the lie that it could be contained, a mere aberration.

She wondered too if she would be taken seriously at the police station. Her clothes, ragged by the day's standards, had 'gypsy' written all over them, and whilst she was comfortable in her way of life, she had long since learned that others found ways to look down on her. It amused rather than concerned her, and if all went to plan, by midnight, she would be sitting in front of the fire and making jokes at townsfolk's expense.

How long before the contagion spread out of control? To her and her father's knowledge, the beast had been walking amongst the people of the town for a while, but it had not been strong enough to take lives until now. She shuddered as she remembered the first time she had seen the figure of the man, the wispy, mist-like entity losing its shape and being blown by the wind as the trees and the circle kept her and the others safe. It was old, born of the river and the trees, but it was darker, a malicious energy that welcomed carnage and fed on fear and lust, on the sins of someone's past.

Her father had told her of a young girl who had drowned just upriver, a small, young thing, and Danior had tried to imagine what that felt like, the emotional turmoil of knowing you would die. To feel your heart straining and your lungs bursting, and then finally the slow mercy of release, eyes open but sight failing as the last breath you had savoured finally diminished. When she concentrated, she could feel the girl panicking as her young mind wrestled to comprehend why someone had pushed her underwater, felt terror surge through her body and bones as she tried in vain to free herself, to scream out for her parents, someone, anyone to help her. The effort was too much for Danior; it had left her emotionally drained, the helplessness for her magnified, amplified to the point of exhaustion.

It was for that reason she couldn't bear to be around too many people. Whereas her father felt equally at ease in the company of one or a thousand, she had to keep as much distance as possible, and whilst she would have loved to have had some of those chips Silvanus had taunted her with earlier, to be around the group of men, their raging thoughts, the drunken lies tumbling out of their mouths as they sought to ridicule and impress, it would have sent her over the edge, just like before. Just like in the circle, when she felt the mind of evil.

Up ahead, she saw the roundabout where she could deviate from her designated route and drive off, leave her father handle the situation. Or she could carry on, do her father's bidding, remain in the circle and be safe. She wasn't sure why she was considering running away or how long the thought had been in her mind, but when she saw who was in the car that passed her, she realised the thought had been seeded by another. Something had tried to pull her out of the circle.

She thought she recognised the woman in the car from a confrontation once in the woods, but the woman had been on her family's side, reporting on the injustice. Back then, nobody knew they had only set up camp to destroy, or at least contain, the evil that resided there. The spot had once been the outer walls of a monastery, long since fallen to rack and ruin, barely anything left except for a few large stones and a couple of tunnels that led out of the woods, on towards the manor house, the other winding up the hill to the larger of the two farms.

In the back seat of the woman's car was a figure like moving ice. It reflected the back of the woman's seat and radiated a presence of the unknown. Danior was somewhat relieved that neither the woman nor whatever was hitching a lift had noticed her.

That relief was short-lived, however, as a second car careered around the roundabout. This driver she recognised instantly as Yobe, the owner of the larger farm, who had started the petition against the camp. She remembered him pushing her father, jabbing at her father's chest, his face grotesque as he demanded the travellers be removed. He didn't see her any more than he saw the figure in the passenger seat, a defined representation of the mist that had tried to form outside of the circle. It grinned at her, its sunken cheeks almost ripping open under the strain, and as the car drew level with hers, the ice-white figure raised a finger to its mouth.

Danior's car engine cut out as Yobe sped off into the distance, and it took several attempts to bring it back to life. She breathed heavily, the menace given off by the figure riding shotgun. Her resolve now fixed, she put her foot down, at pains to admit it, but her father had been right to send her on this errand. If she had stayed, she would have been vulnerable to attack, and the creature, whatever it was, would have got inside her head.

"Who killed you, little one?" she spoke softly to the memory of the drowned girl as she slowed outside the police station. "I want to help you." She said the words knowing they wouldn't be heard; better the comfort of her own voice than the fearsome trespasser in her mind.

On the police station steps stood a young policewoman in conversation with a taller male officer. Two ambulances, initially hidden by the bank of trees, came into view as Danior got out of the car and walked towards the pair, who were now staring at her. Sorrow struck at her heart: the woman's face, seemingly strong and in command, betrayed her grief, and the distress was overwhelming, seeping out of every pore. Some great calamity had happened here.

Danior held out her hand to show she meant no harm. The male officer continued to stare at her in hostility, but there was something else, something hidden.

"I'm sorry, Miss, but the station is closed until further notice. Any matter, I'm sure, can be directed to the Oxford City Police."

"It's about what's going on in this town—the strange occurrences, the sightings. We've seen the girl who you had in custody, and we think we know what's going on…" The image filled Danior's mind, as powerful as when it had first come. She looked directly at whom she supposed was the superior officer and said, "We know about the ghost apples."

215

Chapter Thirty-Seven

WITH A HEAVY heart, Dennis waved off the truck driver. He hated this part of the job, and as the driver left the farmyard, it was always with trepidation that Dennis walked towards the large iron shed which housed the animals at night, close bound, no room to move, just cramped and sweaty, fit for nothing except eating and shitting.

Yobe had already sent home the young farmhand. Marcus was a good lad, easily led but a damned hard worker, the only problem being that he couldn't stand to see the animals in such conditions, and whilst his parents were in so much debt that he could be trusted not to give the game away, he flatly refused to go inside the building. Put him in an open field and he was content; ask him to feed the cows and pigs at night and he turned as white as a sheet.

Had it not been for Dennis's constant reminder that they wouldn't find another farmhand as cheap or hard-working as Marcus, Yobe would've got rid of him months ago. There was always someone yanking Yobe's chain—if not Marcus, then that reporter he despised so much. Every couple of days, he would curse her name and throw across the yard. All it took was a piece he took exception to in the local rag.

Tonight, though, he hadn't mentioned her once or given Marcus hell for being useless. He kept looking across to his car and occasionally, when the wind was right, Dennis thought he heard a banging coming from the boot. He knew better than to ask; like Marcus, he needed the job.

"How long ago since the lad left on his bike?" Yobe asked out of the blue.

Puzzled, Dennis looked at his watch. "Thirty minutes—should be nearly home by now."

"I suppose he will have kept to the road, rather than cutting across Halstish Field."

"He never cuts across the field. It's boggy at the best of times."

Yobe nodded, seeming reassured by the news. "Okay, so he should have got to the bank about fifteen minutes ago."

Dennis frowned. He'd never known the boss to show any concern for Marcus's welfare, so this sudden line of questioning made him suspicious.

Yobe opened the small door that led to the feeding area, and the sound of distressed animals hit the night air. The cacophony of noise always made Dennis ill at ease; tonight, however, there was a lot more than cows bellowing and pigs squealing to make him suddenly nervous.

Yobe poked his head around the door, a grim smile stretching his mouth. "You coming or what? I want to be out of here by two at the latest."

Dennis raised his hand in acknowledgement, and when Yobe disappeared from view, he looked across to the car. Above the sound of the animals, he had heard a woman's voice screaming and the banging of metal. Someone was trying to punch their way out of the boot.

Chapter Thirty-Eight

KINSEY STOOD BETWEEN two phantasmagorias, each shifting in their facial perspective, both of them terrifying. He had placed his trust in the circle made of wood and flowers, though he flinched when the one in Marbon's skin screamed, a horrible howl that shook the air and rippled the ground beneath Kinsey's feet. He had been prepared to rush the creature and attack with whatever strength remained in his body; but for the appearance of the wet girl, he would have done so gladly.

The creature raging in Marbon's body finally noticed the girl and screamed again. From inside the make-do shell, Kinsey screamed in return, "What do you want from me? I don't know why you're here! I don't understand why I can see you." He pointed at the girl. "I get why he's here—some figment of my bitter disease. I hate the man and want to expose his evil, but you...I don't know who or what you are."

He bravely took a step towards the girl, then another, and then finally, with trembling hands but sure of foot, he walked to within a yard of the girl and stopped. He stared at her face, the complexity of emotions shifting like windswept sands. As it shifted, trying to adapt to two emotional states, Kinsey's eyes focused on something deeper than the girl's body.

"I see you," he said quietly. From behind him, the Marbon creature screamed and began to inch round the circle.

"You're the girl who was taken away by the police earlier, but you're different this time. You're not being controlled by whatever was in the windmill—whatever made you kill that boy—

and that's because it's now fully in control of my Irish friend, isn't it?" He didn't doubt that the 'contagion' had spread to such an extent that the creature could inhabit two souls at once, but whatever had taken over the girl was something else.

She blinked and smiled—a smile of someone too young to be in harm's way. Her eyes darted to Kinsey's right, and he followed her line of sight. When he looked back at her, she'd moved, eerily skipping out of reach of the Marbon creature's grasping hands. Kinsey rolled out of the way as a hand came close to penetrating the natural barrier. The creature snarled, the sickly yellow of its eyes glowing as if it were filled with malignant pus, a gurgling geyser ready to explode.

Kinsey scrambled back another couple of feet but kept his eyes on the creature until it stopped in its tracks and sniffed the air, catching the scent of something else. For a moment, it seemed confused, and Marbon's face became more apparent, which wasn't an improvement, however it proved to Kinsey that the two were still separate beings, that the creature could still leave its vessel spent and useless if it so wished.

"Marbon, listen to me. I know we've had our differences, and quite frankly, I think there is something terribly evil about you regardless of what this creature is, but you are human. Fight it, push it out, you can..." The rest of words failed him, strangled in their delivery as the creature's face returned, sickly yellow all over and cold, so cold, Kinsey felt the dank, callous aloofness crawling off its skin. The mist grew thicker, entrails slithering through the grass, trying to penetrate the soil, to find a way underneath the circle. Each time it came back, tingling at the outer edges, and then dived again, the result was the same. It could not breach the protective boundary.

A surge of courage fell upon Kinsey. He stood and moved closer to the yellow-faced creature, staring down that shifting face of callow sinew and ruthless, inhuman knot and line.

"That isn't just Marbon in there, is it? It's you—the boy who nearly robbed me of my sight and drowned that girl by the windmills. By what unholy act have you risen from the grave dug for you by Theresa Whittle?"

Kinsey moved to within a foot of the entity. All that separated them was the circle, and now he was close enough to see its neck. "Your wife left a lasting impression—a good deep wound, that. I wonder, did you die quickly? Or was it slow and painful? Did you scream out and beg for forgiveness?"

Kinsey stood his ground as the creature roared in his face. A film fanatic, he couldn't but help think of the moment in *Alien* when the crew of the Nostromo come face-to-face with the creature, but this was not the monster that had made Kinsey shudder in the cinema on a wet Wednesday afternoon. It was a person no longer in control, guided and abused from within.

The creature screamed again, but this time, Kinsey noticed the pain behind it. Marbon was screaming as well, tortured by the memory of the boy who murdered a young girl in the river, left Kinsey for dead and more than likely mentally and physically abused his wife, who had taken his life and then tried to take her own.

Kinsey smiled, mocking the creature. He needed to surprise it if he stood any chance of separating Marbon from it. Something told him the girl was waiting for him to do it—that the drowned girl might be able to subdue one but not both combined.

"Tell me something, either of you," he addressed the bile-hued face of Marbon and the dead man. "How did this happen? Where did you come from?"

The creature's eyes lit up and shifted in the direction of the farm on the hill, then rolled back, past Kinsey's line of sight, beyond the figure of the silent girl. Kinsey turned to see what the creature was looking at, but all he could see were the remains of a ruined building, the place where the travellers had fought to stay when the police rushed them as the sun went down over the Oxfordshire countryside.

"Why show me the ruined building?"

"Meat."

"What do you mean meat?"

The creature slavered and licked its lips. "Meat, juices, brains, guts, blood, entrails…all seeps down through the cracks in the earth. The soil is rich with it, corroded by its essence. It comes out through the old monastery and skirts this precious circle before finally finding its way into the water through an old pipe underground. I have crawled through the soil, through this dirt and dust for years. I am not what you think I am. I am a manifestation of what you fear, what you have forgotten, and I took the soul of the man who killed a little girl for pleasure. I am returned to form to bring the town to rubble. I will have you all."

Kinsey was shocked by the normalness of its speech, a human-like scheming, lecherous, driven and consumed by lust.

The girl had settled into one form. The teenager from the windmill was no doubt still in there somewhere, but she was surrounded by the figure of a young child, her hair in pigtails, her summer dress blooming with detail, her face sad. Kinsey wanted to cry for her. He'd tried once before to find justice, bring her peace, and he'd failed—not from taking a beating, but by his own sense of pride and his belief that he could bring a criminal to book, be a hero. It was his arrogance that had caused this child further suffering, and he hated himself for it.

He turned his attention back to the creature. As he stepped forward to confront it, he noticed it shimmer as it once again sniffed the air and snarled. Whatever it could smell, the girl could too, and she smiled. Kinsey saw the advantage and was about to make his move, when a young woman shouted, "Kinsey, don't step out of the circle!"

The creature screamed and moved in the direction of the voice. Kinsey stepped one foot outside of the ring and howled in pain. With whatever strength he still possessed, he grabbed the creature and pulled him inside the ring. His hand was like ice as he delved beneath the veneer of man and monster, his fingers numb as he jerked Marbon free, and as they both tumbled to the ground, the full extent of Marbon's time trapped beneath the surface of whirling mist and yellow pus eyes became evident. His body was ravaged, depleted of substance, a barely functioning human being. He was dying.

Kinsey had no such luxury. His eyes were bleeding, and the pain in his head had come back with a vengeance. He heard the creature scream in pain, and then it disappeared, Kinsey's ice-cold fingers the only proof it had been there. Sensing Rebecca close by and another person running not far behind her, he felt a strange presence place a hand on his forehead, and at last he felt peace.

Chapter Thirty-Nine

IT HAD BEEN a fun day at the fair—the first time she had been allowed to go and see what her two cousins had already experienced and spent the entire of last summer talking about. Her parents were together at last, joined at the hip and enjoying life after three years of enforced separation. She had missed her dad terribly; any young girl would, but the war had not only sent him away before she was born, something had happened after the fighting that kept him from being sent home until very recently.

Sally felt as if she'd known her dad long before she saw him in the flesh. Her mother told her stories of how handsome he was, and how much he wished he could be part of their lives, but he wasn't allowed to come home, not yet. She often asked her mum where he was, what was he doing; she saw other men and their families out together at the market on a Saturday morning or walking home as evening darkness fell over the Oxfordshire town. Her mother always answered in the same unembellished manner: "Away, my sweet, but one day, you watch—he'll walk through that door and our problems will finally end."

Her mother went away for a few days every month, kissing Sally on the forehead and fussing about her hair not being tidy before she boarded the large steam train that threatened to engulf Sally in smoke and memories, and for a while, she would be sad, never truly knowing if her mum was coming back. The sadness never lasted long; her aunt, a jolly woman a few years older than her mother and with a broader smile, took care of her when her mum went away. She would buy her sweets at the shop on the corner and let her sleep with her cousins till her mum

223

came back again, as she always did, somehow happier, more at ease for a couple of weeks before starting her slide towards what her aunt said was 'melancholy'. Sally didn't understand the word, and it was too big for her to say properly—whenever she tried, it sounded like some sort of chocolate bar—but she knew what it was like to live with her mum during those times.

If she had been older, she might have better appreciated her mum's state of mind. As it was, she could only hold her hand and be good and wish her daddy would hurry up and come home.

Then one day, not long after Easter Sunday, a man walked through the door and did exactly what her mum had promised. He called out in a large, friendly voice, and she rushed down the stairs, throwing herself off the second to last step and into his big, warm arms. As he held her tightly, her mother came rushing in from the back yard, several pairs of stockings still in her hands and a peg in her mouth and cried out his name so loudly Sally thought the whole town must have heard. She hoped so.

For a while, Sally's life was as normal as could be. Her father was home, her mother was happy, people who Sally didn't know came by, and their house with its small kitchen and dusty yard was filled with laughter and promises. Sally didn't understand, but she liked the attention, revelling in this new phase in her life and the sweets and comics that were handed to her. It seemed that the family's hardship was over—even her male cousin, too aloof to notice her before, became her friend.

A family picnic was arranged, suggested by her aunt.

"We can make a day of it, go up to the fair by the three windmills. That's always fun. Young Sally would like to go, wouldn't you, darling? You've never seen the fair before."

Sally was overjoyed. Her two girl cousins had been to the fair three times and came back with tales of candy floss and goldfish, clowns and rides, of music being played, so much to see and do, and they promised her a share of their pocket money if she had none herself.

Sally looked up at her dad, half expecting him to say she was too young, but he smiled, then burst out laughing and nodded his agreement, and she and her cousins danced around in delight as her big cousin watched on, smiling. He had been looking after her the last couple of months, sharing his sweets, allowing her to sit on his knee when there wasn't room on the chairs, but there was something different in his eyes now—the same look her mum had before her dad came home

The following Saturday, the entire family got on the special bus that went out towards the farm where the fair was held. Sally had never been past the road where the train station loomed over the town, and from there, she couldn't take her eyes off the random houses dotted along the way, the markings of what her dad told her was a set of new houses: "Homes for the likes of us, with a garden instead of a yard. I have seen the plans, my little love. It's going to be a wonderful future for us." He squeezed her hand tightly and kissed her mum.

They went past the outskirts of an old wood, and her dad started to tell a story of goblins and fairies and how the wood was haunted by a brave monk who had battled a demon king and won but at the expense of his monastery. Sally's mum admonished him for scaring their young daughter, but Sally was enthralled and wanted to hear more. Her father gave her a sly wink, an unspoken promise he would continue the story when her mum wasn't around to hear.

"I know how the story ends, Sally," her big cousin told her after they had been at the fair for a couple of hours. He had been quiet all day, and whilst his sisters had squealed with joy at everything they had to show Sally, he had just watched, silently following the three girls' movement around the various stalls, pretending to listen to the polite, sometimes merry conversation between his aunt and uncle and his own mother.

His sisters had gone back to the picnic area, not far from the river that glistened in the summer haze, their day filled to the brim with glee and stories to tell their friends when they went back to school in a couple of weeks' time.

"Do you want to know how your dad's story ends, and what he missed out because he didn't want to scare you?"

Sally nodded, excitement building in her young bones.

Her cousin told the story with more detail than her dad had dared go into, and when he was finished, Sally was thrilled, but she made a promise to herself that she wouldn't tell her dad the ending; she wanted him to believe she had not heard it before.

"Your dad's a coward. He didn't fight in the war, not like my dad did. I don't have a dad anymore. His body is somewhere in the water, lost to the sea around France. Your dad comes home from prison, and all of a sudden, the town thinks he's a hero. He stuck to his principles and fought only the cold and wet of a cell—his punishment? Picking potatoes at dawn."

Sally looked at her cousin and began to cry. Why would he say such a thing? Her daddy wasn't a coward, her mummy had told her so. So had her aunt.

"She was lying to make you smile. To make you feel special and wanted. *You* shouldn't have been born. You were conceived on one of your mum's visits to your dad's billet." Her cousin's face blazed with anger, and Sally began to feel afraid.

"You see that building up there on the hill? That's a slaughterhouse for the unwanted animals—all the baby cows and pigs destroyed because they are only fit for eating. Would you like to be eaten, little Sally? Would you like to be devoured and have your carcass thrown away into a pit?"

Sally stood fixed to the spot. Tears streamed down her face as she looked up the hill and saw the building looming over the fields below. She imagined the screams of the dying and the playful noise of children enjoying a freedom denied by so many years of war. The sounds merged together, laughter mingling the last bellows of a cow dying in agony. The noise was unbearable, frightening, and she began to wail.

"I'm going to tell on you! My daddy is a hero, and he'll smack your backside for telling tales!" She angrily spoke out, finding a piece of bravery in her tiny soul.

Her cousin, unconcerned by the threat, laughed at her. "Your dear daddy won't do a thing. He'll be too ashamed to even look me in the eye, let alone smack me. A Conscientious Objector who went to jail—a coward who had to look after the brain dead in a hospital and refused to kill the enemy. Your mum is more of a man than he is—at least she found work in the factory making shells. At least she supported my Dad when he volunteered. She mourned after D-Day when the telegram came. What did your dad do? Picked potatoes, wrote letters of condemnation, looked after the feeble and the excuses."

Sally stamped her foot, finally losing her patience. She turned as if to leave but only found her cousin's hand smothering her mouth, a tight grip making it difficult to breathe. He whispered words of warning into her ear and then took her behind the furthest windmill, out of sight from the folk at the fair and the happy families bathing in the sunshine.

She struggled and somehow managed to bite down on the inside of his hand, hard enough that he lessened his grip on her for a second.

"Ever wonder why your dear daddy took so long to come from the war? I mean, it's been over for so long. It was because he didn't want you!"

"You liar! You big fat liar! I hate you!"

"Witch, small tiny, insignificant witch. Have you heard what they did to witches in the old days? They drowned them—you'd like that, wouldn't you?"

Without a second thought, he dragged her to the river at a spot where no one could see them. "All too busy playing happy families," he growled at his terrified cousin. He walked down the slope into the river and steadied himself against the bank. Then, with a violent splash, he dropped Sally into the water and put his foot on her body, pushing her under.

Sally couldn't swim. Her mum hadn't seen the point in teaching her, and whilst her dad had said he would take her every week once his new job started, so far, he hadn't been able to.

The struggle was brief, and she fought valiantly, but to no avail. Her cousin's strength overwhelmed her, and she breathed in one last time, hoping to hold her breath forever.

It was the last she knew. She didn't see her cousin calmly walk away from the river and find a group of girls to talk to, making them laugh with his John Wayne impression—lines he had learned from the old town cinema before it closed down. She didn't know that her mum and dad spent an hour looking for her amongst all the rides, nor that one small gypsy girl had watched from behind the windmill and would have nightmares about that day for the rest of her life. All she knew was the wet and the cold despite the beautiful sunshine that slowly darkened around her.

***

Kinsey opened his eyes and saw the young girl before him.

"You can see her as well, Rebecca?"

Rebecca could only nod. Her mouth opened, but no words came out. Only the old man spoke—Kinsey didn't know who he was or where he'd come from, but tears poured from the old man's eyes and were caught on his unshaven cheek, sitting there like a drop of dew in the early morning grass.

A weak groan turned their attention to where Marbon had landed after being pulled into the ring. Some of his colour had returned, but his body had been ravaged by the entity, which had been in control for so long, Marbon looked like he'd lost about four stone. He'd become dinner.

Rebecca gasped as the girl in front of them began to fade, smiling and vindicated. Slowly, the face of the young teenage girl who had been possessed by Sally Witherton reappeared as, with one last mouthed thank-you, the young girl simply evaporated away.

Kinsey moved to stand, and Rebecca tried her best to hold him down. "You're not well, Uncle Simon. Your head—I think a piece of skull is penetrating your brain."

Kinsey sighed softly. "I think you may be right. The girl has eased it—don't ask me how. I just know I'm conscious and this needs to end. Help me tie up these two. I don't think they're going to be of much more help."

Chapter Forty

IN THE OFFICE on the first floor, Inspector Laurence Sears dialled a number he suddenly found distasteful. The whole edifice was falling apart, and he couldn't stem the inevitable storm, the flood that was going to take them all.

Downstairs, ambulances had taken away the dead police officers, now stripped to the bare bones. Sears was thankful the desk sergeant was safe, and his spoken testimony—broken, often completely bizarre—tallied with what had been captured on the grainy CCTV. The image showed the two officers attack the sergeant, one with a knife he must have taken from the evidence locker, and it was only by physical strength that the sergeant had got away with his life, albeit that he had taken both of theirs as he fought back bravely. What disturbed the inspector most as he watched the playback in his darkened office was the ghostly image, only there for a few seconds, of an immaterial man, insubstantial and threadbare, standing naked in amongst the carnage and smiling directly into the eye of the camera.

The paused screen flickered, and whilst the phone rang out, Sears found himself thinking that such a thing would not truly catch on as an aid to police investigations. It was too grainy by far. A voice at the other end stopped this train of thought.

"Mutton here."

"Sidney, it's Laurence. The situation we discussed—it's graver than we thought. I suggest you remove all obstacles to being seen as clean and do it immediately. Can we trust the nurse?

Sidney Mutton spoke with confidence but didn't answer the question directly.

"Ah, yes, well, I see. Thank you for the update. Yes, we can arrange that, certainly. Well, thank you for telling me about Mr. Taylor. It's good to know he's been found. You'll deal with it from that end? Excellent. Yes, see you later, Inspector."

The phone line went dead, and Laurence Sears mused on who was in the room with the professor. Their association went back further than the others in the group realised, and he knew that if the instruction came, the facility would suffer.

He turned his chair round to face the window; from here, he could see the last ambulance take the desk sergeant away. Too many good people had been killed in the line of duty, and if he wasn't careful, there would be more. How best to handle this tonight? How could they come out on top? The girl had b interested and frightened him in equal measure, the way she looked at him—the way her eyes sparkled in the darkness yet remained as deep as coal—she was an enigma who had plucked a thought directly out of his mind. *Ghost apples.* That was exactly how he had described the boy who had melted away. What else had she seen? What would she tell if she had the chance?

On the screen behind him, the picture changed. The policemen stayed static, but the naked figure, the one whose very being seemed to shimmer in time with the rolling black-and-white image, moved, just slightly, then taking another larger, bolder step, stood right in the centre of the screen, blotting out the men under the inspector's command. The man, this incandescent being, stared deep into the camera and placed its knotted finger over its rubber-stretched face, each rotation of the pause line moving it on a frame until the finger covered the lips. Then, frame by frame, it moved the finger away and roared, its gaping mouth a black hole of fear.

A knock at the door brought the inspector round from his deep thoughts.

"Sir, are we going? The woman downstairs, Danior— she believes we may be too late if we don't leave now."

231

The inspector turned to face the only officer left in the building, "I want you to stay here, Laybourne. Lock the doors as soon as we're gone. I think myself and the gypsy girl can handle this."

Andrea Laybourne started to argue; she thought his decision was wrong. With kindness in his eyes, he placated his only WPC, held up his hands and told her in a fatherly tone that he was dreadfully worried about her. He had already lost officers, good men; he was not about to lose his brightest hope.

The policewoman could only try to disagree. The television programmes were full of female officers, leading lights in their profession who had changed the way policing was seen, but not here, not yet in this town, where the force was still full of men. She had to bide her time and play the rotten game.

"Yes, sir."

Inspector Sears smiled at her and put on his coat. As he rounded his oak desk, he patted the monitor he had been watching. "I know you will be all right, Laybourne. I have every faith in you. Stay inside, keep on the radio."

***

Danior didn't like this. A wave of bad feeling was pressing on her chest. She had watched a taxi turn up for the solicitor, who grumbled about lost time and promised he'd still be billing the inspector. As she helped him into the taxi, passing over the man's leather briefcase once he was settled in on the back seat, the taxi driver asked him where he wanted to go and on receiving his instruction said, "No trains out of there tonight, guvnor. Kids on the line, so the word is. And with no police back-up, they had to suspend the service."

The solicitor gave Danior a hard stare of contempt as if it was her fault. She half expected him to ask for her name and address so he knew where to send the bill. He turned his attention back to the driver. "Aylesbury, then—in fact, you may as well go direct to Wendover. I have the cash." Returning his stare to Danior, he said, "Tell the inspector I shall be reimbursed for the journey. Whenever you're ready, driver."

Danior watched them leave, the gravel spraying as the car turned onto the main road back out of town. Danior gave the now departed solicitor her own smile of contempt and muttered, "Good luck with that."

From behind, she heard the voices of the inspector and the policewoman.

"My car's the Skoda over there. May not look much, but it's never let me down."

Danior grinned back at him. "That's nice, but we're going in my car, and I'm driving." Her forceful nature threw the inspector, and Andrea Laybourne did her utmost to suppress a giggle.

Spluttering, the inspector tried to regain his composure. "We would get there quicker in mine…" His voice trailed off as Danior strode to her car and open the door.

"Hurry up. We don't have all night." She tapped on her wrist.

Flustered, the inspector did as Danior said, calling back to his subordinate, "Shut the door, be safe, stay on the radio." He then walked to the woman's car and meekly got inside.

***

Andrea Laybourne saw Danior smile at her, and a thought seemed to pass between them—*that's how you keep them on their toes, Andrea.* She waved them goodbye and walked back inside the police station. By the front desk, there was still pools of blood on the floor.

Bugger this for a game of soldiers. She picked up the telephone and dialled her home number.

"Dad? I'm on my own at the station. Will you and Nat come down and stay with me until someone else gets here?"

Her father agreed immediately. She ended the call and dialled out again, this time the number for Oxford City Police.

Her call was answered by a gruff inspector who sound disgruntled but listened as she explained who she was and the situation as far as she knew it. It might not have been the right thing to do, but she felt it was the most sensible thing in the circumstances. The inspector at Oxford was horrified that she'd been left alone in charge of a building and with no back-up. He told her to hang tight; he and several other officers would drive over as soon as they could.

Feeling a little more secure, Andrea passed the time thinking back over the day's events. She wasn't scared, not in the normal sense, but there was something evil watching her, watching the town, toying with it. Kids and police officers were dead; Bill Taylor was missing. Earlier, when she'd knocked on the inspector's door, she'd have sworn she heard him talking to the man at the facility—words that meant no sense, but having grown up around boys and their secrets, she knew by his tone that something else was going to happen that night, and she had to be ready for it.

She noticed the small, bloodied knife the desk sergeant had used to defend himself from the savage attack by two officers Andrea had been proud to call friends and colleagues. She picked it up and held it close to her side; *anything that dares to come near, I'm having its guts turned into garters.*

Upstairs in an ornate office, surrounded by the many pictures of the inspector—being presented with a medal for gallantry, meeting the Queen during her Silver Jubilee, the inaugural cocktail evening with Sidney Mutton and so on—a black-and-white monitor, still on pause, showed a figure with a snarl on its face looking down the eye of the camera as it filmed a fight between three men.

Chapter Forty-One

SIDNEY MUTTON PUT down the phone and apologised for the interruption. He smiled and with a deep sigh placed his hands in his lap.

"Anything wrong, Sidney?" Moran asked, recognising the look upon his boss's face. He'd always struck Moran as a worrier. That so-called detachment and professional exterior was a man reliving the days of Nazi rule in his home country, the fear that had engulfed him every day as a Jewish boy, the agony and unease that forced its way into his and his family's lives as they saw the disquiet grow, the tension build, until finally Kristallnacht took any lingering hope away.

Mutton rarely spoke of that time, but when the mood was upon him, when he questioned the sanity of what they were trying to do at the facility, he saw faces from the past of those who had argued for the extermination of such worthless sacks of skin—the disabled, the feeble, the drug users, the poets, the coloureds, the intellectuals who had delivered Germany on a plate to the British, the French and the Americans, Jews, all who were not wanted in this newfound land of righteous people.

Once, Moran had caught him weeping. He thought it was because Hattie was cheating on him again—there was always someone, just never the professor or Moran—but when he asked if he was all right later on that day, Mutton told him a story of a young girl whose parents had fought with a sister and an uncle about her sickly disposition, her immune system left weak by an attack of several childhood diseases in a short time. It was before the horror and terror that came to pass during Kristallnacht, so the parents continued on, caring for their daughter, pleased when she wanted to go outside and play in the sunshine with her brother, concerned when she became listless.

"What happened to her, the little girl?" Moran had asked.

"After Kristallnacht, I was sent to England, so I lost touch with the family, but I received news that in the end, and under much pressure and talk amongst neighbours, the authorities came and took her away. The mother was distraught. She herself was Jewish, and whilst the father was, in the terms of the law, a thoroughbred German, the daughter had to be taken to a place of rehabilitation. Knowing what was going to happen, her father took her for one last visit to her grandparents' graves before he slit her throat and then his own."

"And the mother?"

"I only saw *my* mother again long after the war had ended. Somehow, she survived the concentration camp, but she was never the same woman."

It was a conversation Moran had never forgotten and one he found himself thinking about as he watched the professor unfold his hands and open a desk drawer. Smiling at Moran, he pressed a button on the intercom. "Hasser, I'm sending Moran to your position. He will assist my wife in making sure the patients in the old block are safe. I need you to come here and make good with the tanks." He let go of the button and explained to Moran what he needed.

"Nurse Hasser, I'm sure you'll agree, is stronger than you or my wife. That was Sears on the phone. He was calling from the police station. When he got there, there was a crowd of reporters waiting for him. It seems that this fine institution has been found out. Now, I don't blame you, Moran. This is down to my wife, and I need you to keep her busy, engage with her, but don't bring up what has transpired. I was going to get her out of the country, but the policeman she was going to operate on has told all. But if she was *never* here, we still have the upper hand."

Moran sat up, startled by the quick turn of events. He drummed his fingers rapidly against the arm of the chair.

"What exactly do you want me to do, Sidney?"

"Take the dead woman to the furthest section of the new building, get my wife to help you. Make sure the boy in the coma is in this building and then return to the new build, where you will open the gas tanks. Nurse Hasser will move the tank from here and switch the pump. Of course, there must be no loose ends. My wife's actions and connections with the airbase have put us in a perilous position. When the tank valve is open, flick a switch from the outside, and part of problem will be solved— did you know what she was doing? I certainly didn't. There is no paper trail, so all that remains is to deal with our friend, the inspector. He only knows what we know. Don't look so worried, Moran, we will rebuild."

Moran understood he was being offered a way out of his involvement with Hattie Mutton, and he jumped at the chance. The last few days had become too much for him. He once considered himself a good man, a moral man, a man to whom the Hippocratic Oath was sacrosanct, and now, in the space of a few days, his world had not only crumbled; he had been instrumental in helping it happen.

He nodded and then, with sadness in his voice, said, "Whatever you think is right, Professor Mutton."

Nurse Hasser walked into the room without knocking. She never knocked, and the impudence bugged Moran, but Mutton paid it no mind.

"Ah, excellent. Nurse Hasser. Dr. Moran is just leaving."

Moran heard his cue but suddenly felt the weight of the world upon him. His back ached and his temples throbbed from the stress of the task he had to fulfil—making sure Hattie Moran didn't live to tell her side of the story—and as he trudged out of the room, his feet dragging on the cold, sterile floor, he caught Hasser's gaze. *Bloody bitch, she's enjoying this.*

***

Hasser watched Moran walk the length of the corridor and turn off towards the new build—the section where he had found Hattie only a short time before all this began to crumble.

Confident he would not return to spy upon their meeting, Hasser shut the door and waited for the professor to speak.

***

As Moran walked the corridors, he recounted the names of those he could remember whom the facility had helped…

The woman who had been found in the lock-up garage, drugged up to the eyeballs, her baby stuck with needles ready to plunged poison into his tiny system—he touched her door as he went past, thankful they had been able to treat her, even though she would never truly recover.

The lad who begun to hear voices as a ten-year-old, and believed the word of God was coming from his computer.

The old man who had begun to imagine himself as a prophet of disaster, found cutting out newspaper columns of airplane crashes and mass shootings, claiming he could control the events. He'd given Moran the creeps, to the extent that he was glad when the old man finally died.

…So many good things, and then along came Hattie Mutton, and in a short time, it had all gone to hell.

Moran made sure all the sprinklers were turned on as he walked, until he came to the new annexe. He saw the boy in his bed at the other end of the corridor and shut the doors behind him, closing off all but one of the rooms before he switched on the sprinkler in there and opened a window, making sure he would fit through it, then returned to the corridor where Hattie Mutton was waiting for him.

They carefully disconnected the boy from the drips and monitors and then carried him to the end of the corridor, no words passing between them as they took the limp but alive body to a room by the large metal doors which separated the two parts of the facility.

It was only as they walked back to the room to collect Serena Cox's body that Hattie spoke.

"For what's it's worth, I'm sorry." Her hand touched his briefly, and in that moment, Moran felt the happiest he had ever been.

Just the simple touch of a woman whom he admired was enough to send him completely over the edge. He smiled, so lost in the daydream he didn't hear the doors behind him open.

Neither of the pair saw Nurse Hasser quietly make her way to the room in which they had placed the boy and carry him to the old part of the facility.

It was a flash of light that caused them both to stop walking, the roar of fire which triggered the sudden realisation that the professor had meant to eradicate them both.

Moran looked back up the hall to the exit and saw the doors were firmly closed. "I left a window open, just up there on the right. We can still get out. Run, Hattie!"

Moran grabbed her hand, the sexual fantasy replaced by preservation, no tingling of nerves, just a pulse racing to escape death. As they got close to the room with the unlocked window, a ball of fire bellowed out as if forged from the very heart of the dragon. Moran felt like his face was peeling away, his skin on the brink of blistering under the strain of the fire that was about to consume them. *Damn Sidney Mutton.*

"The sprinklers—why aren't they working?" Hattie cried out.

Moran didn't answer. If he was going to die, let the woman he had imagined in a thousand fantasies believe he was as innocent as she wanted him to be.

Moran tried several doors close by, all locked as planned. He threw himself against one, and it budged slightly. He did it again, putting all his weight into the action, and it shifted but not by much. He looked to the professor's wife for support, but her legs had gone from under her, and as the fire crept along the walls and across the ceiling, black smoke closing in from both ends of the corridor, she gave up.

"Come on, Hattie! Help me with this door."

She looked up at Moran, tears streaming down her face as her hair caught alight. Moran knew she was lost to him and the world, but he wasn't giving up that easily. Despite the smoke clogging his lungs, pulling him under, he managed to run at the door and cheered as the lock gave way and the door swung open. He took one last look at Hattie Mutton and closed his eyes. Her mouth was closed, refusing to scream, as her face melted, her eyelids seared, and her marble-white skin turned to charcoal.

The ceiling above his head gave way, the remains of plaster and plastic from the strip lights exploding in a shower of flames, and as his lungs succumbed to the smoke and his body to the inferno, he cursed his employer's name again.

***

In another part of the building, a solitary finger dialled 999. When the connection was made, the operator spoke efficiently and without drama.

"Fire service, please. Wendlefields Drug Rehabilitation Centre, near Perchester. Come quick—I fear for my patients, and I cannot find my wife."

"Please, sir, don't panic. Help is on the way. Just get out of the building if you can."

Sidney Mutton assured her that he would and put down the phone. He looked at Nurse Hasser's face—did he detect a flash of pleasure? So what if he did. He knew what she was capable of, and that she was absolutely loyal to him.

"Are the patients ready?"

"All accounted for, Professor. All except Ms. Cox and, of course, Mrs. Mutton and Dr. Moran, who must have gone back in to find the poor woman."

"And what of Brill? Is he still looking for the police officer? I fear he is long gone. Best to alert Brill to come home."

Hasser nodded in compliance as Sidney Mutton eased himself from his chair and beckoned for her to vacate the room.

"We will not forget their sacrifice, should they have perished in this awful fire. When we reopen, I suggest we name a couple of wings after them, or perhaps two rooms, side by side. It's what they would have wanted."

Chapter Forty-Two

A S THE PAIR ran towards the main road, through brambles and past trees that groaned in the wind, Kinsey asked Rebecca through heavy breaths about the old man they had left behind to care for Marbon and the girl who had saved his life.

"I only met him tonight, but it feels like I've known him forever. I bought him some chips. His name is Silvanus. I didn't catch his daughter's name."

In the back of Kinsey's mind, a memory stirred, small, opaque, obscure, like the name. He had heard that name before, but he couldn't think where.

Rebecca asked him a question, but the wind rattled the trees around his ears, and he had to ask her to repeat it.

"Are you dying, Simon? I think there's something terribly wrong in your head, but..."

"But what?"

"The girl. She did something to you. I don't think Silvanus saw, but I certainly did. Her face was not the girl we tied up, it was someone younger, just a child. She put her hands on your head and showed you something, didn't she? But I think she also took something away. Did she make you better?"

Kinsey stopped running. He had not run so far since he left school, as the stitch in his side reminded him, but Rebecca had kept herself fit. Kinsey stared at the woman she had become and once more regretted his involvement with her family. Her father was a good man. Where was he now? Back in Hong Kong?

Did she see him at all? He wanted to ask but was afraid of reopening a wound which might still be under repair.

"I don't know what the girl did," he said, "but I don't think she has healed me. It wasn't that kind of faith I felt. I think she gave me respite—a chance to undo all the evil that's been brewing in the town the last few days. She showed me her life, cut short by the man who did this to me. He killed her and tried to use Marbon to kill me. She also gave me a glimpse of where the creature was heading—to the farm on the hill."

He puffed out his cheeks and they set off once more, though this time not at such a frenetic pace. He looked at Rebecca by his side; the regret gnawed at his stomach.

"When this is over, can we—your mum, you and me—talk properly? I need to apologise to you both."

Rebecca smiled. "Let's get to the farm before we decide on the next step. Do you have a plan, by the way?

***

Silvanus sat in the middle of the circle. The air was clear, and for the first time in days, there was no mist or dense fog to be seen. He watched the two people under his care, the man and the teenage girl convened before him, like a council of three, but there could be only one judge, one member of the jury, and he was ready to listen. He closed his eyes and thought of his daughter, a child herself when the shadow fell on this stretch of water—a child who had seen the darkness, and he had told her to forget what she had witnessed, suppressing the truth from others, making sure she was not involved in any way. He had told himself that he had done it out of fatherly concern, to protect his beautiful girl. All lies.

It came late to him in life that he was as much to blame for this monster. It might have been a small morsel, a few crumbs baked in denial and allowed to stew on its own, but he was as much to blame as anyone. Would his conscience have been pricked if he hadn't read about the woman who dropped dead of a heart attack on the fields between the woods and Sterhan Close? Would he have felt dread if he hadn't remembered that those fields and the new housing estate had once been flood plains for the river? Would he have understood the gravity of the situation if he had not been able to pay the easily bribed and bored young man in charge of the mortuary in the hospital to see the horror in the dead woman's eyes? If blame were divided out, his share would be larger than most.

He wanted to know what these two vessels knew, what had driven them to be possessed in such a way—one by a child murderer, the other by the child herself. He closed his eyes and began to speak. Had Rebecca and Simon Kinsey still been within the circle, they would have been convinced that he was speaking in tongues or invoking some sort of magic. The truth was somewhere in between—his own haze, his own type of shimmer.

The trees outside the circle protested. The abandonment of old ways had fractured the land, and he could feel the earth within the circle judging him, considering his actions, and he was afraid.

The girl and the man resisted at first, both still weary from their ordeal, and he was desperately sorry for the girl in particular, who had been touched not just by the image of Sally Witherton but by that of the man as well. She began to weep uncontrollably as the memory of what she had done to her schoolfriend—the ritual of an entity born of bad blood and revived by the strains of slaughter, of the unholy practices of humankind who, in search of greater profit, unaware that the price they were paying was driven not by the pound or the dollar, but by what it did to people's souls.

Silvanus opened his eyes and stared into the teenager's. Her soul was haunted by her actions, and her mind wanted to forget. He could not allow her to see such visions again, her heart had been damaged, her soul corrupted, but not because of who she loved, not because she was a teenager who had at times slid off the rails, but because an infection had got into her system.

"Sleep now, child," Silvanus commanded softly.

Lorraine closed her eyes and gently slumped to one side, her breath becoming shallow, her death, so the coroner would ascertain, would be attributed to exposure. Privately, Silvanus would tell the detective from Oxford that he thought she may have died from the strain of her actions, the reality of the destruction too much for her teenage brain.

Silvanus shed tears for the girl, for the sanctity of the circle. He hoped Rebecca and Kinsey would get to the farm and finish the job before the power surrounding him began to fade. He stared at Marbon, who was looking down in bewilderment at the figure of the girl by his side, her eyes closed in peace, all sins removed, at least in the next world, and whilst her name would appear in newspapers and be the source of discussion for years to come, she was absolved of any crime.

Marbon lifted his head, his face unblemished by tears, his body and mind restored to him, and he began to rage, thunderous words sneaking through the cracks in the circle. He stared with contempt at the traveller, his hatred no longer tethered by the unholy and unearthly.

"What did you do to her, travelling man? You've killed her. Oh, they will make mincemeat of you."

"She is at peace now. She showed me her life—will you show me yours? The beast was attracted to you for a reason, just as the young child it killed was attracted to her."

Marbon licked his lips, slowly, cruelly. "I'm going to kill you, old man. And when I'm done with you, I'm going to find that reporter and make him tell me about his connections, then I'm going to rip his throat out."

Silvanus smiled grimly. "I see that the beast didn't have to work hard on you. You are a quite the deceiver. The devil must have got to your soul a long time ago." Silvanus closed his eyes, and Marbon struggled to untie himself, but each time he moved, his wrists were pierced by the thorns of the roses that adorned the wire.

"Your fascination with death goes back a long way, Mr. Marbon. You really should have listened to your parents when they told you not to go and play in the bottom field."

"Stop that, stop that. Get out my head, you old goat," Marbon snarled.

"Such brutality! Although you did try to get them to abort the bombing in Birmingham, I should consider that when passing judgement. But, Mr. Marbon, just because you think you did a couple of good things in your life, it doesn't mean they were down to kindness or a will for the greater good. Yes, you found the girl in the woods, but your soul tells me it was driven by the urge to do something unspeakable to her. You lusted after the girl. You found her an easy target, didn't you Mr. Marbon? Just be nice to her, take an interest in her life, tip her well…"

Silvanus opened his eyes and stared into the burning embers of the devil. "You disgust me, Mr. Marbon. Almost as much as I am disappointed in myself for not having seen you before."

Silvanus began to feel the circle's strength fade and knew he didn't have time. The sentence needed to be registered. He stood and looked down with pity at the girl.

"You are wicked, Mr. Marbon. This girl, she was innocent, corrupted only by the evil that must be stopped. Your malevolence deserves to rot, to find itself screaming in agony every day. The mind is a perfect prison, I find. However, I don't have time to move you far from here, and I cannot do it on my own. Therefore, Mr. Marbon, and only because you tried to stop a bomb which killed so many innocents, motivated by the horror you saw in that dreadful factory, I am inclined to show some mercy. You wanted to be the hero, a hero you shall be, but not for long."

Marbon's eyes blazed as the old man showed him his fate, the police finding his body a few yards away from the girl's, their conclusion that he had tried to save her from drowning. For a couple of days, he would be lauded in the press, garner words of endearment from all those who knew him. Then, as with all things, a journalist would reveal his true nature, and a person with connections to the IRA would come forth and tell all about the girl he left to die, his association with numerous, previously unsolved murders, and his part in the farm on the hill, which had been party to the disease.

The fire in Marbon's eyes slowly dwindled, a final puff of smoke left his mouth, and Silvanus collapsed to his knees. Struggling back to his feet, he rolled the dying man toward the river. Half in, half out, his head dropped into the icy cold in forever damned slumber. Returning to the girl, he removed her gently from the circle, and placed her body just out of reach of Marbon, to make it look as if he had tried to save her but had failed and, in his exhaustion, also drowned.

Silvanus had one last job to do before he made his way to the farm, his own contribution to what he hoped Kinsey or Rebecca would realise they had to do. He walked over to the pipe out of which all the fumes and poison were pouring, and he began the arduous process of blocking it up.

Chapter Forty-Three

DANIOR PARKED THE car by the side of the road a short distance behind the accident and watched as the inspector released his seat belt and opened the door. A young boy approached them, his face frantic, uncertain of how to talk to a man in uniform.

"'Ello, can you 'elp me?" He pointed to the car crash behind him, "She is still alive but in a bad way."

The inspector peered at the car, recognition swamping his emotions, and he urged the boy out of the way before sprinting to McCarthy's car, nearly losing his footing on the wet ground.

Danior turned off the engine and walked on the verge, the sodden ground squelching up around her boots.

The boy joined her, concern written across his young face. "I don't where this water's come from. It hasn't been raining. And if you go further up the road, see where the two weeping willows are, it's dry as a bone. I got to within a couple 'undred yards and the road is covered. You can't even see the car's skid marks now its underwater. I didn't know what to do. I live too far away, and we don't 'ave a phone at 'ome. I was going to cycle back to the farm, but then I saw your car 'eadlights and thought you might be able to 'elp."

Danior placed a hand on the boy's shoulder and gave him a well-done smile. The boy was obviously distraught; best to keep him onside if she could.

"You work at the farm—the Whittle place?

"No, mam. I work at the one on the hill. I look after the cows and the sheep on the far side. The bosses, well, I don't like going actually to the barns. I feel sick when I go near them—the noise those creatures make upsets me. Mr. Yobe is forever trying to get me to work in there, even threatening me with the sack. Some of the workers tell him to leave me alone." He paused for breath, his words rushing out as if fired by a catapult stretched beyond its capability.

"It's McCarthy, the journalist," the inspector shouted. "She must have hit the patch of water and aquaplaned. She's alive, but her pulse is weak. Taken a huge bash to the head."

"Do we move her? I can get her back in the car and take her to hospital." Danior looked over the inspector's bowed head at the woman hanging out of the driver's door, only her seat belt preventing her from tumbling to the sodden ground.

"She needs an ambulance. I think if we try to move her, she will certainly die." The inspector took his radio out of his pocket and got hold of Laybourne. He gave his position and told her what had happened to McCarthy, asking her to send an ambulance.

"I will do my best, sir, but it might be difficult. There's a fire at Wendlefields, and all hell has broken loose."

Danior watched him lower his eyes, picking up the guilt that swept over his body. "She won't last that long. I'll stay with her. The boy will keep me company. I think you need to get to the farm. After all, if hell is breaking loose, don't you want to be fighting off the hounds rather than just watching it burn?"

"How do I get up there? It's not exactly an easy walk!"

The boy raised his hand, and Danior realised he must have come from a good home, but one where they had been exploited, where they had been terrorised into toeing the line.

"There is a car over there, in the bushes. I have checked. The keys are still in the ignition, but I can't drive. Not old enough. My dad can drive a tractor, but 'e doesn't get much work these days. I could cycle and bring my mum out—we wouldn't be too long. She can sit on my saddle and she can drive you up there, sir."

Whilst Danior found the boy's nervousness and quickness of voice refreshing, it plainly irked the inspector. He patted the young lad condescendingly on the head and took another look at the journalist. Danior wondered if the news of the fire at the facility had anything to with his lapse of concentration or if there was something blocking his vision because the wound on her head was not the result of an accident.

He gave both Danior and the boy instructions, and she replied for them both, not wanting to keep him from moving on by listening to the nervous lad complete another paragraph of explanation. Soon after, the inspector drove off in the abandoned car.

Danior acted quickly. She told the boy to go around to the other side of the journalist's car and ease himself in, taking care not to tip it any further. He did as he was told and then awaited instructions.

"Okay, I have her full weight. Gently release her seat belt."

It took a couple of goes for him to press down hard enough, but eventually he managed it. Danior grunted with the shift in weight but held the woman safely in her arms. The boy eased himself out of the car and walked through the rising water, a good inch higher now than when he had arrived.

"Help me move her to my car, then you and I are going to take her to hospital. That ambulance won't get here in time. Now do as I say and no questions, all right?" Danior found she had to be forceful. The woman's breathing was erratic, and there was no time to lose. The boy seemed to understand, and between them, they managed to get her safely to the car. McCarthy's car was now up to three inches in water; Danior hoped that whatever her father was doing, he was doing it as quickly as he could.

Chapter Forty-Four

I T'S ALL IN *the timing*. Had Kinsey and Rebecca been able to run faster, they might have reached the farm on the hill at the same time as Inspector Laurence Sears pulled up inside the yard where, not half an hour before, two men in jackets and with barrels of feed ready to be distributed to the livestock, had waved off the driver and his truck before he headed back towards the nearby American army base. If Kinsey hadn't had to keep stopping to catch his breath and make his young running companion wonder if his heart or lungs were going to give out before his head imploded…

As it was, the decorated army veteran turned successful and rapidly promoted policeman, arrived at Calisdale Farm alone, the sense of foreboding not helped by the car's headlights beginning to flicker and then finally giving out, much like the engine a minute later, as he pulled up alongside Adam Yobe's vehicle.

Sears stared at the now-dark dashboard in confusion and tried to turn the engine over once more, then again, and a third time, but he couldn't even coax a metallic, stubborn groan out of it. He looked around: aside from a small orange light above what looked like the entrance to the metal barn, there seemed to be no power at all on the farm.

He opened the car door slowly, careful not alert the shadows of his presence, and slid gently out of the borrowed car. He had wondered whose it—there had been no visual clues in the glove box, no paperwork to indicate the owner's name, and whilst he admired the handling of the car, even compared to his own, he couldn't practically drive one of these machines around.

Walking to the ridge, he stepped up onto a small stile and looked down the hill. There, far below, were two flashlights, slowly sweeping across the fields and occasionally catching the silhouettes of two policemen shuffling about in an effort to keep warm. Sear tried to contact them, to make them aware he was on the scene and to keep alert should he require their assistance, but the only sound he heard was static, as if the air was being flayed of its precious skin. He pulled his ear away from the noise and turned off the communicator.

For a brief second, all was quiet; all remained as it should in the darkness. Then, from behind him, close to where he had parked the stranger's car, a cacophony of commotion filled the night air. Sears almost toppled over the stile, such was his alarm at the shrieking and the hammering on metal. Composing himself, he jumped down and walked cautiously towards the sound. A flash of memory came to mind, the first time he had walked into an asylum to survey some of the issues that had arisen in the Nigerian Civil War. The screams of the mad who had been locked away had haunted him gravely for years afterwards, and he never forgot the torment in the eyes of those who'd seen the disease of war—children, women, mothers, all on the verge of starvation. That was what the British had claimed was collateral damage and worth the preserve of cheap oil for their own industry and pleasure.

It was that experience which led him eventually to meeting Professor Sidney Mutton, and as they talked over the drugs epidemic and the problems with psychosis, he related the story of the asylum to the imposing figure of a man, delighted in the interest he took in the idea of helping those individuals who needed to be kept in a facility that genuinely cared for their well-being.

Sears had located the source of the noise. Somebody was in the boot of Yobe's car, a woman screaming more than blue murder, and it was positively frightening, explosively delivered expletives, muffled only by the thin metal that separated the owner of the voice from the outside world. Sears tried to release the boot catch, but it was as if it had been welded shut, as Pandora's Box should have been before humanity's curiosity got out of hand.

"Hold on, please stop screaming. I am here to help you." he calmly whispered, his head almost touching the metal. A loud thump indicated the message had been received.

He scanned the yard for anything that might help release the catch. He didn't want to break a but he would if he needed to and hang the consequences of his actions when Yobe found out. He knew the man by reputation and by his association with other less-than-ideal people in the town, and whilst he could be quite fierce, it was his ability to spread discourse and gossip that stopped Sears from immediately vandalising the car without considering the alternatives.

In the corner, underneath the orange light, was a small scythe, which looked as though it would fit in his hand and give him the leverage needed to spring open the lock. It was the only plan he had.

As he bent over to pick up the odd remnant of old farming, he heard a grinding noise coming from within the barn—sounds of distress, not human, a churning, crushing sound that grated against his ears and made his stomach turn. Above him, the orange light flickered maddeningly, and from out of nowhere, the headlamps on the car he had driven suddenly turned on full-beam, bathing him in the spotlight glare of a prisoner of war cutting through the wire.

The lights went off quickly, but it was enough to send a chill up the inspector's spine. He stood up carefully, unsure if he was being watched, played with, tormented. He'd had the same unsettling thoughts at the station, the urge to strangle the young policewoman, and as he'd sat in the car with the gypsy girl, he'd wanted to grab the steering wheel and push her out, speed up and reverse over her body—fleeting glimpses of his world if he allowed himself to fall. He had felt something—an aura, as the gypsy girl would have no doubt insisted on calling it—as he'd driven the stranger's car, and he'd checked the rear-view mirror a few times. There was no one behind him, but out of the corner of his eye, he thought he saw the wisps of malevolence trying to find form, the whisper of evil attempting to pull itself back together.

He shook off the feelings as paranoia brought on by lack of sleep and his own part in the fire at Wendlefields, which by now was probably blazing away, and if he were to stand on the barn roof, he would be able to see the inferno burning a hole into the Oxfordshire night sky.

Metal against metal, the valiant fight of armoured knights grappling with each other until one was vanquished—that was the image that came to mind as he struggled to release the catch, and just as he thought he would have to give in, break the window, possibly alerting anyone whose sights he had thus far avoided, the car boot sprang open. Inside was the still body of a woman, her eyes open but unblinking. He was too late; she had probably run out of air; he had taken too long—his imagination ran so violently along in the dark that he had forgotten the principles he had vowed to uphold. Anger and regret surged through his mind, grappling with each other for precedence. He had been losing the fight since this all started. He'd wanted to do something constructive, to have his name linked with eradicating the evil of the times, but instead here he was, too late to have save an innocent woman's life.

He closed his eyes and found for the first time since he joined the army that he was saying a silent prayer for those who had perished in his glorious attempt at immortality.

He never saw the woman's hand move, and wouldn't have believed that someone, let alone a woman, could have swung the four-way wheel wrench with such force, and whilst it no longer mattered when his mind was slowly losing its ability to function, he was glad he had his eyes closed and didn't see the look on the woman's face as she pulled the protruding metal from his throat and brought it back down on his skull.

Chapter Forty-Five

REBECCA WASN'T SURE what Simon Kinsey was running on, but as they finally came to a halt at the edge of the yard of Calisdale Farm and Kinsey doubled over, dry-heaving, the young woman was sure it would be the death of him. She placed a comforting hand on his back and as she bent to see if he was all right, she couldn't help but notice a dark smell, like bile that had festered in a sewer for a few weeks. She wrinkled her nose but said nothing; it was not the time to tell the man who, in the last few hours, she had begun to care about after years of hating him.

What had changed, she could only surmise as he spat out the remains of the froth from his mouth, was that she saw what her mother had seen in him and not what she had believed when she was growing up. Fun Uncle Simon, cool Uncle Simon, who spent a lot of time with her mum. Then beastly Simon who tried so hard to be another dad to her when her actual father could no longer tolerate the lies and—worse—try-to-be-a-friend Simon. It was so easy to hate him when he kept on apologising to her mum and tried valiantly to get her dad to hit him, to provoke a fight one Sunday afternoon, repeating loudly, "Take a swing. Please hit me. I will not fight back. Punch me, you bastard, *fight for her.*"

Finally, Kinsey stood up, blew hard out of his mouth and smiled at her. "If we get out of this tonight, the beer is gone and I will train to do the London Marathon by 1990, I promise."

"What time is it?"

Kinsey looked at his wrist, but his watch had broken, the glass smashed and the hands both pointing south. "Well, unless

255

it took us five hours to run here, I would say my watch is buggered. The last time I looked was about an hour ago, before I sat in the circle, and it was around twelve, I think. You know what—the last twenty-four hours have been a relentless tidal wave. I don't think I care anymore."

Then it hit Rebecca, his verbal punch landing square in the part of the brain that dealt with realisations and understandings, of the empathy for another. He didn't care; he really didn't. He was exhausted. He had been drinking himself almost to death for years—since the affair with her mum—and sleeping so few hours his imagination was probably the only thing keeping him going. But by focusing so hard on atoning for his sins, he had allowed himself to fall ill, and who was there to care? His brain was exploding, and he wanted it to stop, even it meant pulling the trigger himself.

Rebecca changed the subject, not liking where the train of thought was taking her. "Don't suppose you've got a smoke on you?" She pulled a lighter from her pocket.

Kinsey raised an eyebrow. "Does your mother know you smoke?"

"Does she know *you* do?"

Despite himself, Kinsey laughed. "Touché, Miss McCarthy."

Rebecca shrugged and absent-mindedly spun the flint wheel on the lighter as she looked around the yard. "Such a big place, but I can't hear anything. Are you sure the answers are here?"

Kinsey was staring directly ahead, puzzlement taking form on his face. "All I can tell you is what the girl showed me, but even she didn't go into details. Didn't that Silvanus chap tell you anything more?"

Rebecca shook her head, but she may as well have kept quiet for Kinsey was paying her no attention. He had started to edge forward, his eyes, already accustomed to the darkness, focused on what looked like a black bag of rubbish left to rot beside two cars on the cold stone. Rebecca moved with him and saw it was a man's body, his legs folded under him as he if had landed on his haunches, decided it was a comfortable position and stayed put. There was also something sticking out of his head.

Kinsey reached the body and told her to stay where she was, not to come closer, which was like an open invitation to her, not disobedience but strong will, determination—qualities she'd inherited from her mother.

"What is *that*?

"A wheel brace. Whoever did this to our inspector obviously took the application too far. If it were not for his uniform and his build, I don't think I would have recognised him at all."

Kinsey stood up and turned away from the broken man, blinded, brain dead and with his trousers pulled down to his knees, his testicles and penis having been removed. This time Kinsey was actually sick in the open boot of the car, which might have earned a rebuke from a crime scene officer for contaminating the evidence, but he didn't have the energy to find a discreet corner.

When he was done, he sought out his companion, smiling proudly when he saw her noting down the particulars of the policeman's demise, the grisly scene not fazing her at all. She caught his eye and became self-conscious.

"I'm sorry, I just thought…"

"No, it's all right. I'm pleased to see you taking such care. Perhaps it's time we had another pair of eyes in the firm." Despite all that had happened, the pain and suffering, he began to laugh.

His laughter was cut short as a clatter of noise from the other side of the yard alerted them to the presence of another. A door opened wide, and suddenly the most horrific noises filled the air. The screams of children could not have produced such a terrifying crescendo. A man stepped out from the bright light, his body covered in cuts, his coat ripped and torn, coming to ghoulish life as a slight breeze made the pieces that were hanging by threads flap wildly, a gruesome pageant waved onwards by the ecstatic cheering of crowds and their bunting.

The sight of the dead policeman may not have done much to upset Rebecca, but the wailing of the man, coupled with the noises coming from the building, made her fall backwards and scramble on her bottom until she was virtually at Kinsey's feet. The man let out a howl, a deep, ravaged complaint of pain. The orange light above his head framed the blood pouring from his cheeks and the side of his neck. He seemed to be trying to shout, but all that came out was a muted gargling sound and a gush of blood. He put his hand up to his neck, a pathetic attempt to stop the flow, and stuttered out a few words.

Kinsey watched the man being pulled back in, his arm as flimsy as marzipan stretched beyond its integrity, the brute strength of the oppressor snatching him out of sight. The door slammed shut, blocking the horrendous noise, and Kinsey felt a chill run down his spine as he registered the man's words.

"Please forgive us."

Kinsey was all for rushing inside the building, but it took several minutes for Rebecca to compose herself. Breathing heavily, she remained at Kinsey's feet, though she was no longer staring into the distance; she was looking at the police inspector's body.

"Kinsey, who…or what removed his erm…his bits? I can't see any other weapon, but surely that—what did you call it? A wheel brace? That couldn't have been used to remove those?"

***

Kinsey looked around the yard, but there was nothing—no sharp implement which could have removed someone's testicles. Now he felt fear. Whatever was in that building, whatever had been controlling Marbon earlier, may no longer have a gun, but it was able to hold something else, something much sharper and older than a rifle and more intimate than a shotgun.

258

Chapter Forty-Six

WITH APPREHENSION BUILDING in their bodies, as nerves that had held with courage slowly ebbed away, Kinsey and Rebecca opened the door to the building and were greeted with the screams of slaughter. Kinsey had never given it much thought before; he may have been a boy of the country, a man surrounded by fields and nature, but he had never once considered the animal that grazed on the grass, that ate from the trough. He'd claimed he liked animals and believed in their humane treatment, but with shame, he realised he didn't have a clue beyond his own preconceptions.

"We can't wait for help, Rebecca. We must do this, even if we are alone." Kinsey talked directly into her ear, and even then, he wasn't sure if she had understood his true meaning, but she took his hand, and without another word, they stepped into hell.

Inside the building, the scene was breath-taking, not in a beautiful, scenic way but one of horror. Even from the door, the pair could see the animals inside tightly crammed pens, their troughs overflowing with what looked like rancid, rotten flesh, pigs squealing in unison, twelve, thirteen, fourteen to a pen, the floors buried under their effluence. Kinsey noticed a pen close by and gasped in open-mouthed, rising disgust. In amongst the mud and shit, a half-eaten carcass of a pig lay, it head removed from its body, severed at the top of its spine, being kicked around like a football by others fighting for space. A cow appeared next to Rebecca, fear and confusion in its eyes, its back legs wobbling as if it were punch drunk.

Kinsey was glad he had been sick outside, not that he was concerned about adding to the filth on the floor so much as he was about one of the animals breaking out of its prison to feast upon this new diet of human waste. He looked at Rebecca; the pity, the sorrow of it all had turned her face a sickly shade of white.

Above him, in the centre of the building, was a platform, a stage from which tubes and thin runways ran down into the troughs that fed the animals. In the middle of the platform was a hook, and attached to that hook was the squirming body of Adam Yobe. His shoulder had been torn and was half hanging off, and his face had been hit repeatedly. For the bruises to be so vivid from a distance, the violence must have been ferocious. On the platform beside him was a woman whom Kinsey remembered meeting, not long after she had lost her baby—skittish fragile, incomplete—and here she was torturing the man to whom she was married.

Under her breath, and almost out of Kinsey's earshot, Rebecca muttered that the foul stench was making her gag. Kinsey hadn't noticed it until that moment, mesmerised by the scene, the freak show they had walked into. If there was a hell, after this, it would hold no fear.

On the floor, some twenty feet away, was the chopped-up remains of the man they had seen crashing out of the door just a few minutes before, his body cut hurriedly but with precision and placed in a trough that fed a particularly mad-looking cow. Kinsey couldn't see the man's head; he only recognised him by the clothes that he had been wearing. He hoped it had been quick because it surely couldn't have been painless. Leaning against the bottom rail of the tight pen was a scythe, and Kinsey finally understood how the inspector had lost his genitals.

The noise from the animals became frantic, fearsome, disturbing to the point that it was like an aural bludgeoning, and Kinsey's ears thrummed painfully. He noticed Rebecca covering hers with her hands and that she was screaming. Then without warning, the noise stopped. Even Rebecca became mute, leaving an almost subsonic white noise that seemed to emanate from everything around him.

Portia Yobe began to talk, but this wasn't the voice of a woman; this, Kinsey realised, was the true nature of the beast, one who had been slowly worming its way into the local population, starting with those whose imaginations were strongest, their minds were not yet formed to the point of disbelief. How easy it was to destroy from within! As she spoke, she placed a hand on the farmer's side, and Kinsey shook, unable to disguise his reaction to seeing the man's body grow cold and turn to ice. Kinsey knew what was going to happen; he'd seen the end result with the girl at the windmill, and there was not a thing he could do to stop it.

"Mr. Simon Kinsey, Miss Rebecca McCarthy—how very good of you to join me. You had me at a disadvantage in that other body. His rage was insubstantial. This form, however, this woman's fury...it's delicious, unhinged, indignant. Coursing through her veins, pumping hate through her mind, through her heart—it's almost as enjoyable as the passion that used to run through my body until that bitch put a knife through my neck."

A pig grunted, which started the whole barn off once more. Kinsey wasn't sure how much Rebecca could take, but he felt as if he had already lost his mind, surrounded by so much insanity and cruelty.

"What was Yobe up to?

Portia's face looked down at him, human questioning wrapped around a monster's soul. "Does it matter? The suffering is enough. But as you asked...I believe he found a way to make the most of the diseased remains of dear Uncle Sam's boys. All that bad blood and waste, it had to go somewhere. Why not make a profit out of it? Why not use it as feed? After all, what do the pigs care as long as they are fed?"

A solitary pig oinked somewhere in the building, as if seconding the motion at a public debate. Portia Yobe looked across to where the noise came from and smiled, acknowledging the vote in favour.

The smell was becoming unbearable. More than sickly, it was the smell of disease and death haunting Kinsey's nose. He gripped Rebecca's hand, his fingers edging the top of the lighter that Rebecca was still holding. He would have killed for a cigarette right then.

He shouted out once more, his voice echoing in the silence. "Why can't Yobe tell me? Let him confess so at least his conscience will be clear when I write this up."

"You will not live to do such a deed, Mr. Kinsey. But why not let the great man talk of how he brought me back to life, how his operation reawakened the evil? What was it you said earlier, Miss McCarthy? Something about evil and good men? Well, I am no longer a man. I am in this body now. I control this woman, and pity all in this town who will feel my wrath! You got off lightly, Simon. What I did to you—that will be nothing when I start to kill again!" Portia Yobe laughed heartlessly and then added, "But, sure, why not, let's hear the great Adam Yobe talk."

She took her hand off his body, his frame by now covered in a silvery white sheen and turning almost blue. She reached behind him, setting off the whirring, grinding of the machine lifting the hook.

"Oops! Almost forgot!" Portia reached down and picked up a bucket. Her eyes never once leaving Kinsey's, as if conjuring a bunch of plastic flowers from a top hat, she produced with a flourish a man's genitals. The animals below began their noise again, though the mood had changed. To Kinsey, it felt like a roar of approval from the crowd, the big top's audience applauding wildly at the magician's trick. She placed the genitals in her husband's mouth and kissed his cheek.

Yobe's body left the platform, and he tried to scream but choked on the amputated member. Kinsey watched the woman, keeping his eyes firmly on her, not wanting to look at the man anymore, his stomach turning, and as the build-up of methane and the sweat of the tightly confined animals tore his senses apart, he knew what he had to do. He unclenched Rebecca's hand and took the lighter from her.

Portia Yobe released the button that controlled the machine and pressed the lever next to it. The hook opened, and Adam Yobe fell into the pens below. Still Kinsey kept his eyes on Portia. Adam Yobe was a dead man anyway; Kinsey had known that as soon as the ice formed around his body—was it any consolation that he had not turned to mush, that he had not become a ghost apple? His body shattered on impact, the echo of the fall and the mad frenzy of the pigs below too much for Rebecca, who slumped against Kinsey and let out a sob of despair.

Up on the platform, Portia Yobe took a bow and then threw the bucket into the air in celebration.

"Now, what to do with you. Your choice—cow food or do you want to become part of a liquid diet?"

The animals bayed at the words, and Portia beamed like Nero, taking in her glorious victory. Kinsey seized his chance; he grabbed Rebecca and ran for the door.

"Running won't help you!" Portia screeched. "But please do. It adds so much flavour to the experience—just like that little girl tried to do before I pushed her head underwater, before I slowly took her life from her."

Crashing through the door, Kinsey was surprised to see Silvanus waiting outside in Portia's car and revving the engine. There was no time for pleasantries, no time for explanations, he shoved Rebecca onto the back seat and ripped a sleeve off his shirt.

"Some petrol?" Silvanus offered up a cannister to the reporter, who took it without question and dipped his shirt into it, then reopened the door and threw the rag inside. Taking one last look at the face of Portia Yobe, he flicked the flint wheel and threw the lighter on the rag, which immediately caught alight. Portia Yobe paid no attention, the entity in her feasting on the last remaining part of her humanity and crowing over its future.

Kinsey slammed the door and dived into the car. "Drive, drive!"

***

The explosion was heard across the fields, as far as Oxford and Banbury. The fire could be seen raging into the sky for several days, and at its height, firefighters from three counties were involved in trying to contain it. Some said the black cloud above the farmland was darker than anything they had ever seen, and villages and towns close by were given warnings about the air quality, urged to stay indoors as much as possible.

This meant nothing to Kinsey as he was interviewed by several detectives over the next twenty-four hours. If not for the surgeon intervening and declaring that he needed an operation immediately, the barrage of questions might never have ended. They needed someone to blame, and Kinsey held the key to determining who that person should be. He would have told them to ask the strange old man, but Silvanus and his daughter had disappeared into the night, asking only that Rebecca McCarthy and Simon Kinsey forget they ever saw them.

The Final Editorial

THANK YOU, LOCAL reader, for allowing me into your homes the two months whilst your editor and award-winning journalist, Samantha McCarthy and Simon Kinsey, have been convalescing and recovering from the injuries sustained during what has been the most unusual story they have covered. For my own part, I can only say that what I have been able to write on their behalf does not do these two journalists the credit they so richly deserve.

You will be pleased to know that Officer Bill Taylor is on the mend and will be returning to his duties very soon. He will also receive a commendation for his bravery in the face of danger.

Some will be forever scarred by their experiences, and we can only hope that time heals their pain, as it will this beautiful town of which it has been my pleasure to curate its news for the last four weeks. I know you are saddened by the loss of your outstanding police inspector who, alongside Simon Kinsey and Rebecca McCarthy, was able to bring to light the abhorrent practices of animal misuse at Calisdale Farm. Ms. McCarthy has re-joined her father in Hong Kong and is, I am told, looking forward to meeting her relatives as she tours the lands of her ancestors.

Simon Kinsey paid vocal tribute to the fallen officer from his hospital bed, where the winning Oxford United captain visited him, along with several other players of the successful Wembley side:

"It is to my deep regret that the dedicated upholder of the law didn't survive to see the effect his actions had on the case. Without the bravery of Inspector Laurence Sears, Perchester could have been swapped with the raw animal product we found and destroyed."

Away from the incident at Calisdale Farm, this paper notes the continued clearing of the partially burned-out Wendlefields facility. Professor Sidney Mutton wasn't available for comment as the bodies of his wife and loyal colleague Dr. Moran were finally uncovered, both of whom unselfishly acted to aid our noted local campaigner Serena Cox, who sadly also perished in the fire.

Every other patient was saved, and most are now back in the comfort of the facility's care.

I want to thank you again, dear local reader, but I also wish to leave you with an exclusive. For many years now, Samantha McCarthy has worked tirelessly for you. She has been a stalwart of the community and deserves her place in our hearts. It is my great personal pleasure to confirm that she has agreed to join me at Fleet Street in a managerial role, which, I am sure you will agree, she has earned. It is not goodbye, though, to this wonderful traditional local newspaper. After all, it is you, members of the local community, who have held this paper in high esteem, and from Monday, Simon Kinsey will be take over as editor. A more capable pair of hands I know we could not find. He has told me he wishes to continue in the same fashion, albeit with less excitement, and that he intends to take on a couple of apprentice reporters to give back to the community, one being the talented Cheryl Frampton, who many of you will have had the pleasure of having been your paper girl for a few years.

There is little more for me to say, except to remind you that you can follow my story in the *Gazette* of the town's fallen hero and the inquest into the activities of Cyril Marbon.

It has been my honour to serve the news to you, and remember – keep local news, real.

Andrew Fillus

***

Such bollocks, Andrew Fillus thought to himself as he tore off the sheet of paper from the typewriter. Such a fine web of lies to keep the devastating truth from the locals. He meant every word about having enjoyed his time amongst the people of the town, but they hadn't taken to him. They missed their champion. How they would have gnashed their teeth and wrung their hands had he not returned after the cover-up.

Samantha McCarthy had been easy: her daughter's life was in danger, and she wanted to make sure Rebecca was safe. Where better than the enlightened city on the edge of Asia? She had signed the Official Secrets Act without hesitation, grasping the chance to leave the town and its memories behind.

Bill Taylor was trickier to contain. Suitable words were made in his ear, his life spared on the condition he spoke only of scrambling out of a window after the fire had taken hold, but he would be forever scrutinised and held to keep his silence.

Simon Kinsey had also proved a difficult splinter to ease out, but the chance to finally put history right and see Sally Witherton's killer publicly named—an assured bestseller—would hopefully hasten his recovery time and improve his prognosis.

All lies, the fire. Andrew Fillus could have wept at the story that had passed through their hands. The professor could not be contacted, but his work, so sources said, was too important to abandon. He would be quietly moved aside, and a new doctor would take charge. *Best of luck*, thought the newsman bitterly.

He'd wanted to write another editorial entirely; to expose the truth, warn the people of the terrible things Simon Kinsey had witnessed, the warning issued to Rebecca by the strange gypsy traveller, the lost lives of the Liverpool youngsters, the farmer and her brother relocated with new identities, the many dead police officers, and the brutal, savage death of a local boy. All would have been explained and held to account instead of existing only as myths and whispers passed from one generation to the next.

Of course, most of it could readily be passed off as mass hysteria brought on by contaminated food, but what of the detail? The terrifying form who first killed a soldier—a soldier who, it seemed, had been part of the chain delivering rotten carcasses to Calisdale Farm.

Lies sell papers. Sometimes we need to be comforted; other times, we need to be stirred into a state of obnoxious self-delusion; there is no middle ground. That was the truth with which Andrew Fillus wanted to sign off his time at the helm. Instead, he rose from the desk, walked over to the door and switched off the lights. Outside, mist rose off the stream that led to the river. It clung to the pavements, dank and obscure.

The truth can remain hidden, after all. What does it matter?

The End

Acknowledgements

I have suffered with nightmares all my life. I think it was part of the reason why I didn't want to place my soul into attempting to write a horror, and until a university friend of mine, the wonderful Chris Brook, asked why this was so at the book launch of my first novel, *The Death of Poetry*, it was the only answer I could give. My imagination, I'd always insisted, was too fluid without putting it through the mental stress of actually sitting down and writing something I enjoyed from others but might open a window to which I could never again close.

It is to my dear uncle, Tony Hards, that I owe my love of reading horror. He found out in the last days of 1983 I had been reading George Orwell's *Nineteen Eighty-Four*. He asked me if I had read any James Herbert or Stephen King, and up to that point, I hadn't. He implored me to go to Woolworths on Bicester's Sheep Street the next day and find some, to choose one or two books that I thought might interest me. I could not help but be drawn to *The Rats*, mainly because of the horror instilled in me as the rats make their appearance in *Nineteen Eighty-Four*, and *The Survivor*. It wasn't until later on that year when *Domain* was released that I realised just how powerful horror was and how it has remained in my life. It is in the ordinary that horror leaves its mark after all.

A few years back, there was an evening held in honour inside the entrance hall of the Williamson Tunnels in Liverpool. The occasion: a kind of wake for James Herbert, who had been due to appear there to talk about the genre but who had unfortunately passed on some weeks before the event. It was there, talking to others perhaps for the first time about his impact on me, that I understood how much he meant to others.

It is to my uncle that I dedicate this book, for without him, it perhaps might never have been written. However, I want to say a huge thank-you to many others, notably Chris Brook for the question that stoked the fire of curiosity within me. I owe a debt of thanks to those who took time out of their lives to read this story and give me valued feedback and their encouragement when I felt the world was turning darker. My dear friend and fellow Marillion fan Felicity Pryke; my old Bicester School pal Justin Brown; the exceptional musician and avid booker reader Mark Luker; the two men who encouraged me from the beginning of my writing adventure: Mr. Tony Higginson and fellow author Bob Stone; another University of Liverpool friend and indeed many times confident, Maria Freel, who deserves so much credit for continually phoning me when she knew the pressure was getting to me; and to my cousin, Bryan Beck, the man who gave me Megadeth and Metallica and to whom I value my life.

I also owe a debt of gratitude to Helen Duke. Her friendship when I badly needed a pal to just sit and listen at the very depth of depression is something I won't forget.

For the tremendous backing of Debbie McGowan and all at Beaten Track Publishing, I cannot thank you enough, it is a rare gift to find someone who will understand your reasons for not wanting to deal with those consumed by a different type of darkness: rampant self-interest. I love you for this and always will.

Most of all, I want to thank my wife, Judith, for her continued and valued support; without her allowing me the freedom to live inside my own head, nothing would make sense.

I will head back to my hermit cell now. Thank you for allowing me a moment to breathe in the light; the darkness calls again.

Ian D. Hall, 2019

About the Author

Having been found on a 'Co-op' shelf in Stirchley, Birmingham by a Cornish woman and a man of dubious footballing taste, Ian grew up in neighbouring Selly Park and Bicester in Oxfordshire. After travelling far and wide, he now considers Liverpool to be his home.

Ian was educated at Moor Green School, Bicester Senior School, and the University of Liverpool, where he gained a 2:1 (BA Hons) in English Literature.

He now reviews and publishes daily on the music, theatre and culture within Merseyside.

Please visit www.liverpoolsoundandvision.co.uk

By the Author

Beaten Track Publishing

For more titles from Beaten Track Publishing,
please visit our website:

https://www.beatentrackpublishing.com

Thanks for reading!